Eden Bradley has been writing since she could hold a pen

The Seduction of Valentine Day

EDEN BRADLEY

BLACK
LACE

1 3 5 7 9 10 8 6 4 2

First published in the United States of America in 2009 as
A 21st Century Courtesan by Bantam Dell, A Division of Random House, Inc.
Published in the UK in 2014 by Black Lace, an imprint of Ebury Publishing
A Random House Group Company

Copyright © Eden Bradley, 2009
Extract from *The Darker Side of Pleasure* © Eden Bradley, 2007

The Random House Group Limited Reg. No. 954009

Addresses for companies within the Random House Group can be found at:
www.randomhouse.co.uk

A CIP catalogue record for this book is
available from the British Library

The Random House Group Limited supports the Forest Stewardship
Council® (FSC®), the leading international forest certification organisation.
Our books carrying the FSC label are printed on FSC® certified paper.
FSC is the only forest certification scheme supported by the
leading environmental organisations, including Greenpeace.
Our paper procurement policy can be found at:
www.randomhouse.co.uk/environment

Printed and bound by Clays Ltd, St Ives plc

ISBN 9780352347213

To buy books by your favourite authors and register for offers visit
www.randomhouse.co.uk
www.blacklace.co.uk

To my father:
I love you, Dad.

Acknowledgments

This book would never have come together without the help of my dear friends, R. G. Alexander, Crystal Jordan, and especially Lilly Feisty, and as always, my fabulous and loyal critique partner, Gemma Halliday. You all know what you did for this book, and what you mean to me. I couldn't ask for a more creative, dynamic, and supportive bunch of people in my life. I am eternally grateful.

I also must acknowledge my editor, Shauna Summers, for her guidance, and for allowing me to take some unusual risks with this story, for trusting me that much. Thank you!

The Seduction of Valentine Day

Chapter One

THE COSTLY SCENTS OF the finest imported champagne and custom-blended cologne fill my nostrils as I straddle his prone figure on the big bed. I love these beds at the Beverly Wilshire—plush and lovely, with soft Egyptian cotton sheets. Only the best for Enzo Alighieri. Including me.

"Fuck me now, my Valentine," he says, his elegant, Italian-accented voice rough with desire. "You know just how to do it, *mi tesoro.*"

"Ah, Enzo . . ." I sigh in pleasure as I lower myself onto his erect cock.

I have always loved Enzo's cock. The skin is a deep gold, as it is all over his body, which is still fine and beautiful, no matter his age. He is strong, well muscled. And he has the stamina of a twenty-year-old. Which is the only way he manages to please his wife, his mistress, and me. And he does please me.

I squeeze the walls of my sex around his cock and he moans a little. Pleasure is swarming my system already and I smile down at him, moving my hips, grinding onto him.

"Touch me, Enzo."

He reaches up and takes my breasts in his hands, plumping them, kneading them, playing my hardened nipples between his fingers.

"Oh, yes . . ."

I reach back and slip my hand between his thighs, caressing his balls. He loves this. He loves my every touch, to hear my panting breath, to watch me come. Oh, yes, I know exactly what he loves, what he needs. It's my job to know. And I am nothing if not a perfectionist.

He pumps up into my body, shafts of pleasure filling me, spreading, making me shiver. One of his hands has snaked down and is teasing my clit, tugging, rubbing, pinching. He knows how to make me come. After all, we've been together nearly a decade, Enzo and I. My mentor, my friend. My client.

Why is that the most important part? But I don't want to question it as his thrusting hips take on a more urgent rhythm. His breath is a panting gasp now, and I feel him tense beneath me.

"Ah, just another moment, Enzo. Give it to me . . . I know you can do it."

"You will be the death of me, Valentine," he says, his voice rough.

But he does it, pistoning into me, his clever fingers never leaving my throbbing clit, my swollen nipple, until I'm coming in a flood of heat onto his thick, lovely cock.

"Oh, yes . . ."

I throw my head back, let it wash over me. And he tenses beneath me, cries out, his hands going to my hips, his fingers digging into my flesh.

And I catch that scent I adore, the scent of arousal, the

scent of come, beneath his expensive cologne. And underlying it all, the scent of money.

—

I LEARNED ABOUT SOMETHING called suspension of disbelief a number of years ago in one of my English lit classes. This is when a writer must make the reader buy into the unusual long enough to be drawn in and believe in the world the writer has created.

It's something like that with my line of work. Our clients must suspend their disbelief long enough to believe the girl likes it. My particular "talent," if you want to call it that—my particular perversion, really—is that they don't have to do that with me. The truth is, I love it.

This is my dirty little secret. Because this is supposed to be taboo among the professionals of my world. Call girls. Prostitutes. Hookers. It doesn't matter what you call us. The fact is, I get paid for sex. And it's the only kind of sex I can get off on.

Who knew a nice Jewish girl from the Valley could end up here? Well, half Jewish, anyway, my father being a lapsed Catholic. And maybe I've never been all that nice.

I grew up in Van Nuys. Van Nuys is possibly the most generic, boring place on earth. Middle class, cardboard-box houses that all look the same, block after block. The entire area looks as though a dull film has settled over it.

My family was at the lower end of the middle class. Not that we were poor. We always had a roof over our heads, food on the table. My father, a construction foreman, worked a lot, but he spent his money anywhere but at home. My mother never did much other than drink. Strange that he wasn't the drinker. Jews don't tend to be drinkers. Not that it ever stopped my mother. But my life has been a combination of the utterly dull and the most perverse, in every way, on every level. Classic hard life story, I know, but that's my story. Or it was. Too fucking bad.

I make a lot of money. Enough to keep me very comfortable in my Hollywood Hills home. Enough to pay for the expensive clothes I buy at Barney's and Kitson, my weekly facials and massage at the spa. Enough to pay for the breezy little Mercedes I drive, if it hadn't been a gift from a happy client. This is why I do it.

Actually, that's a lie. It's what I tell myself when I'm not in the mood for the kind of deep, soul-searching honesty that keeps me up at night. How I justify it in the most basic, simple terms.

The truth, or part of it, anyway, is that I began in this business because I needed to distance myself from what I was before. From that lower-middle-class Jewish girl from the Valley whose mother was always passed out on the couch, surrounded by a sticky puddle of whatever she was drinking on the floor, the overflowing ashtrays. Repulsive. I won't even allow my clients to smoke around me. If they don't like it, they can find another girl. I'm at a point in my career where I can make a few demands of my own, and I do.

I am someone else entirely now.

I look different. I *am* different. No one from my old life would even recognize me. And truly, I wouldn't care if they did. My life before this is almost in another dimension, in my mind. I like it that way.

I don't look like the average girl from the Valley. My one gift from my mother is a fine-featured, beautiful face. I don't mean to be vain; I am beautiful. People who pretend not to know these things are full of crap. I have long legs, a great body, hard and tight, even this close to thirty. My brown hair, highlighted in gold and caramel, hangs in layers almost to my waist. Most men prefer long hair on a woman, so I rarely cut it. My eyes are green, without the colored contacts the other girls wear. High cheekbones, a full, lush mouth. My ass is superb. I've been told so often enough. But what really gets them is that I love what I do. I love sex. I don't care who I'm doing it with. I just like to fuck. I like to suck cock. I love the anonymity of these men not knowing who I really am. I get off on it.

But there's one catch. I have to get paid.

I have never had an orgasm with a man unless he's paying to have sex with me. My first trick was like an epiphany. The moment he handed that wad of cash over into my greedy little hand, my body started to heat up, my legs began to shake, and I was coming almost as soon as he touched me. That's when it became magic for me.

Which brings me to Italian film producer Enzo Alighieri.

He was one of my first clients. Enzo found me at this cheap call girl outfit where I got my start. And he knew right away I was different from the other girls there. He told me I was too beautiful, in his lovely Italian accent. I adored him on the spot. Not the way a normal woman might adore a lover. It was never that complicated. I liked him the moment he walked into the room. So sophisticated. Elegant. And he's sexy. He really is, even at nearly seventy now. He has that commanding air about him; I'm sure everyone else in his life kowtows to him. Everyone but me. He lets me get away with anything.

I understand perfectly well that I'm nothing more than a sort of pet to him. A project. And a priceless piece of ass. He often tells me so. But it was Enzo who took me under his wing, got me out of that dump of a whorehouse in Hollywood, and made me go to school.

Yes, school. Because if you're going to be what amounts to a modern-day American geisha, a 21st-century courtesan, you must be well educated, just as the geishas are. Just as the old Venetian courtesans were.

In addition to having studied history, literature, business, and political science, I now know how to play golf and tennis, although not too well. Men prefer to win, don't they? I read the *Wall Street Journal* and *Forbes*. I've studied massage therapy, I know wine. I've learned to speak German, a little French and Italian, and even a few words of Japanese and Arabic, both of which are a necessity in my line of work.

The Middle Eastern rich have tons of money. More than the usual wealthy do, and they aren't at all shy about spending it on whatever brings them pleasure. I admire that in a person. They're the ones who fly the girls to Miami for a week, to Europe, even. Give us entire wardrobes of designer clothes. They like to have a lot of girls at once. I don't mind. We all get paid, regardless, and it makes the workload a little easier. And the food is always superb. Unfortunately, I'm thinner than most of them like, so I don't get those dates the way some of my friends do. But once a man is with me, he'll always come back for more.

They can always tell, my clients. Even the most selfish, the most dense. They know right away that I'm into it, that my orgasms are the real thing. And these men are the sexual sophisticates of the world. They've had first-class ass in every corner of the planet: the pros in Amsterdam, Paris, Berlin.

I know I sound crude when I talk about these things, but this is a crude world. I'm not bitter, I swear it. I see the beauty in the world, too. I've spent far too much time around the rich and privileged to be blind to beauty, not to appreciate it. I love the ballet, could watch it for hours. I could wander every museum on earth and never get enough. My current obsession is art history, and I've been taking classes off and on for the last few years, soaking it all up. This is something I do purely for me. I may be a classless kid from the Valley, but I've learned about the rest of the world, seen enough to develop a real appetite for the finer things in life. And for me, art has become a necessity.

There is the gritty side to my lifestyle, of course. Even the girls at the top of this food chain can get into trouble. There was Trina, a gorgeous girl, new to the business, who was kidnapped and taken to some godforsaken place in Southeast Asia and never heard from again. These things happen, and when they do, when we working girls hear about it, it scares us, even if we pretend it doesn't. This job, as luxurious as it is, is not entirely without risk. But we keep doing it anyway, don't we? Some sick part of me gets off a little on the cheap thrill, I'll admit to that.

I don't like fast cars, in particular, and you'll never catch me climbing a mountain. My thrills are all of a sexual nature. Which makes me the perfect woman for this job. I am embedded in this life for the long haul. It suits me to a T. It makes having a "real" relationship entirely impossible. But the circumstances of my life since childhood have made that impossible anyway, so I've never minded. What other sort of life would I have? What would I even want? No, I'm perfectly fine right where I am.

THE SUN IS BEGINNING to lower in the sky as the cab exits the freeway and turns onto Grand Avenue. I love this time of day: the pale light turning the sky an ethereal shade of gold, like an iridescent film over the deepening blue. It's even lovelier now, in the fall, when that bit of moisture in the air, that first hint of the coming cooler weather, adds a pearly glow to everything. But it's difficult to really enjoy it; it's after seven and I'm running late. I hate being late, especially to meet a client. It's unprofessional. But the traffic was horrible, as usual in Los Angeles.

We pull up in front of the Dorothy Chandler Pavilion and I pay the driver. My cell phone goes off as I step out into the warm evening.

"This is Val."

"Val, it's Bennett. I'm not going to be able to make it tonight. A problem at the office."

"Oh, I'm so sorry. Shall we meet later?"

"No, no. This is going to keep me busy all night. But you shouldn't waste the tickets. It's opening night."

"I do love *La Traviata*."

This opera is the story of a prostitute. Why wouldn't I love it? And I've become a huge opera fan, thanks to Enzo's expert guidance.

"Enjoy it, then. I'll call you to reschedule in the next week or two."

"I hope you will, Bennett. I'm so sorry you have to work tonight and miss this."

"You can tell me all about it when I see you. Ah, there's my other line, I have to go."

I flip my phone shut, turn it off, and get my ticket at the will-call window, feeling a lovely sense of freedom at having the night off. Being able to enjoy the opera without having to be "on."

Of course, this also means no sex for me tonight. But for once, spending the evening on my own sounds even better. I realize I've been craving some time away from work lately.

Strange for me. But I have been doing this most of my adult life. I suppose it shouldn't come as a surprise. When was the last time I even took a small vacation—three years? Four?

Inside, the theater is cool, lovely in its stark modernity. The lights are bright, making me blink. I really would love a cocktail, but nearly everyone is seated already; I'd hate to be locked out of the first act.

An usher, all gangly legs and leering eyes, shows me to my seat. Not that I mind. A woman in my position can't afford to be offended by male attention. And I wore this champagne bias-cut silk dress to show off my lean curves, my pale skin. I don't have much in the way of cleavage, but the boy eyes the low neckline, anyway. My nipples have gone hard from the air-conditioning, so perhaps there's something to look at after all.

I slide in, murmuring apologies to those already seated as I go. The seats are fabulous: third-row center. I settle in, leaning down to set my small bag at my feet.

And that's when I catch a scent in the air, something masculine, sophisticated. I sit up and turn my head to see who is sitting next to me. I'm trained to be attuned to men. I can't help it.

He smiles. A gorgeous smile. His face is beautiful. That fact is what I notice first, and it's a few moments before I see that his features are a bit irregular. But still beautiful, in the most masculine way possible.

He has dark brown hair with a few natural highlights, cut very short, a little spiky on top. Warm hazel eyes, a full mouth, a strong, clean jaw. Broad shoulders in his designer suit. Nice. And he's young, maybe thirty-five. Too young for my tastes. So why is my body heating up? Why do I want to touch his mouth, just put my fingertips to his lips?

Stop it.

I make an effort to smile back, then turn away, looking at my program. But I'm not really seeing it, the faces of the cast members, the synopsis a blur. I can't stop noticing him out of the corner of my eye.

He seems entirely relaxed, something you don't often find in a man of his age. This makes him all the more intriguing. And there is a strange sense of anticipation, of tension. It's almost as though I can feel the heat of his body next to me. And I am hyperaware of that scent. Crisp and dark at the same time, like the woods with a faint wash of citrus.

I roll my program up in my hands, my fingers tightening around the glossy paper as I look around the auditorium. Why can't I calm down?

Finally, he turns to me and asks, "Are you waiting for someone?"

"No. My friend had to cancel."

"Ah, mine did, too. Well, my mother, not my friend."

"Oh." I don't know what else to say. I can always talk to men. It's my job to talk to men. Among other things. What on earth is wrong with me?

"I'm sorry, I didn't mean to intrude," he says, mistaking my tied tongue for offense.

"Oh, no, it's fine. I'm sorry, I was . . . distracted. It's lovely that you come to the opera with your mother."

"She loves the opera. I've learned to enjoy it, although it's taken years. But I like *La Traviata*. I like the tragedy of it."

"Most operas are tragic," I say.

"Yes, but no one does tragedy like the Italians."

I smile. "True. Unless it's the French."

We sit quietly for a moment, and that's when I notice he's looking right at me. I don't mean that in any sort of romantic terms. But I'm used to men seeing me as an object. That doesn't offend me. It's a requirement of my occupation. But when a man really looks at me, sees *me,* I notice.

This man is obviously far too nice a guy to be talking to a woman like me. Not that my clients aren't good people. But this nice man thinks he's flirting with a nice woman. If he only knew.

But that doesn't mean I can't enjoy it, does it? Just an evening of innocent flirtation. It's fun being a bit of a tease now and then, something I rarely get to do. When you get paid for sex, everyone knows up front what you're there for, even when a client simply wants me to be arm candy at an event. Of course, even those evenings usually end in sex. It's far too easy for the guy. I'm right there, paid in full. Why wouldn't he want to have sex with me? Or a quick blow job in the car, at the very least. I am every bit as good at being a companion as I am at sex. But it's nice to play at it for a little while. To simply be myself, to savor this sort of attention.

The house lights dim, go dark, and the orchestra begins. I let the music wash over me, trying to ignore this man seated only inches away. This man who I have no business flirting with.

The opera is wonderful, the woman singing the part of Violetta is beautiful and incredibly talented, a lovely, pure soprano. But I'm unable to become lost in the story. I am much too aware of his scent, his presence. I swear I can feel the heat emanating from him like an invitation.

I glance over at him, looking for a moment too long, and he turns and smiles at me.

I look away, flustered now. Embarrassed.

When was the last time a man managed to fluster me?

I force myself to focus on the music, on the costumes. It

really is a wonderful production, the sets colorful, dynamic, the costumes gorgeous. And the singing is superb.

Hours later, or so it seems, the lights come up. Intermission. God, I need a drink. I rise quickly and make my way to the lobby bar.

It's crowded, as it always is during the intermission. Voices, laughter, mingled with the clink of ice in glasses, the flash of jewelry. I look around, scanning the crowd. I realize that I'm looking for *him*.

I realize that I have turned into some sort of foolish schoolgirl. I shake my head in disgust.

A voice just over my shoulder. *His* voice.

"It's impossible to elbow your way to the front at these things, isn't it? Let me order a drink for you."

"Oh, no, that's not necessary."

His gaze catches mine. I can see flecks of green and gold in his eyes in the bright lights of the lobby. He's taller than I'd thought.

"I'd like to buy you a drink."

I feel momentarily stunned. Whatever is wrong with me? "Well. Alright. I'd appreciate it. A Tanqueray and tonic."

"Don't go anywhere," he says, giving me a wink.

I watch as he makes his way to the bar, shifting into the crowd. Utterly confident. Polite. Graceful.

There is a certain kind of man who moves that way. Men of power. Men who are entirely assured of themselves. A small shiver runs through me.

He returns in only a few minutes, handing me the drink and a paper napkin. I notice he's drinking scotch on the rocks. I can smell it, a nice blend.

"Thank you. I'm Valentine Day, by the way," I tell him, giving him my full name. My clients know me only as Val. Only

Enzo gets to call me Valentine. Only Enzo knows my last name. But my name is *mine*. I have to draw the line somewhere.

He takes my hand in his. "I'm Joshua Spencer."

A current flashes up my arm, shafting deep into my body. Heat. Desire. I pull my hand back, trying not to do it too quickly, trying not to appear rude.

"So," I ask, pausing to sip my drink, covering my discomfort, "what do you do besides taking your mother to the opera?"

"Professionally? As in 'what do you do'?"

He's grinning, but there's nothing mocking in it; he's just being nice.

"Professionally, personally. Whatever you'd like to tell me."

"My job is fairly boring. I'm in real estate development. A family business."

"I don't think that's boring at all."

He shrugs. He has the broad shoulders of an athlete. Nice. "It doesn't make for exciting discussion unless you're also in real estate. Are you?"

I can see he's teasing me, but I like it. "No. I'm definitely not in real estate."

"Ah, good. Because I really hate to talk about work."

"Tell me something else, then."

"Something else?" He pauses. "I play hockey twice a week. I'm on a team. I run sometimes in the mornings. I don't have time for much else. The occasional play. Or the opera with my mother. Or without my mother, as the case may be." He flashes a boyish grin. "And I love art. I like to go to the Getty at least once every couple of months. I'll see whatever's there."

"I love the Getty."

He steps closer, his voice lowering, as though we're having

a private conversation. Perhaps we are. Another shiver runs up my spine, long and slow and warm. Exactly as I imagine his touch would be.

He says, "Let me guess. You like the Impressionists. Paintings from the more romantic eras."

"I do like the Impressionists, especially those who came into the game a little later. But I'll admit what I really love are the Neoclassicists. Leighton, Alma-Tadema, Collier. Waterhouse, of course."

"Ah, but still romantic." He gestures with his drink, then takes a sip. I watch the muscles in his throat work as he swallows.

I smile. "Yes, I suppose they are. But I'm afraid my taste in art isn't very sophisticated. I like it to be pretty."

"A feminine trait. Not necessarily a bad one."

He moves in a step closer, a few inches, really. But I feel as though we are in our own bubble, apart from the crowd around us.

"What about you? I'd guess you like something completely masculine, the more modern artists. Pollack? de Kooning?"

"Actually, I prefer the surrealists. Hockney. Dalí."

I nod my head. I love a man who knows art; it really makes me swoon. Or maybe it's just him?

"So, what do you do for work, Valentine?"

I freeze for a moment. I have a few standard answers I use in order to sidestep this question. But suddenly my mind is a blank. The lies won't leave my mouth. I lift my drink, take a long swallow, letting the gin go to work, loosening my insides. I still have no idea what to say.

The house lights flash.

"Time to go back in," he says. "Let me get rid of these glasses."

He takes mine, holding it between his fingers along with his, brings them to the rapidly emptying bar while I stand there, feeling a bit lost. Then he's back at my side, his hand going to the small of my back as he guides me through the theater doors.

His palm is warm through the thin silk of my dress. And my sex is going so damp from this nearly innocent touch, I'm almost afraid to sit down. To try to hold still for another hour or more, next to him in the dark.

I manage to do it. But the entire time I am more aware than ever of his tall, muscular body next to mine. I don't dare to look at him. I don't have to. I can feel him. And I'm soaked the entire time.

Torture.

When the show is over we stand and I feel awkward again. Do I simply leave and say good-bye?

"Did you drive?" he asks.

"I took a cab."

"Let me find one for you."

His hand at my waist again as we walk out of the theater. I can hardly stand for him to touch me. To touch me but not *touch* me.

At the curb he waves a taxi down.

"I won't be so rude as to ask for your address, so you'll have to tell the driver where you're going. But I hope you'll call me."

He pulls a business card from his pocket and slips it into my hand, grasping it with his fingers for a moment. He's looking into my eyes, and even in the dark I swear I can see a dim green and gold glow in his. He is too beautiful, this man.

I want him to kiss me. I want to pull him into the cab with me. I want to take him home and fuck him. But I do none of this.

"Thank you for the drink. And for the conversation."

He gives my fingers a final squeeze. "It was my pleasure. Call me, Valentine."

I smile, nod, and he hands me into the cab. He shuts the door, and I give one last shiver.

The cab pulls into the night, and we are immediately stuck in traffic. I don't dare look behind me to see if he is standing there.

Joshua.

I clear my throat, smooth a hand over my hair. His card is in the other hand. I should tear it up. Toss it out the window. But instead I slip it into my bag. I can throw it away later. That's exactly what I should do. Anything else would be ridiculous. Unrealistic. And life has taught me to be realistic. I am the poster child for accepting reality, no matter how ugly. It's this beautiful, nice man who's thrown me off balance.

I know what I should do. But I close my purse, my fingers tightening on the metal clasp, as though I am still holding the card in my hand. As though I really can call him tomorrow, go on a date. One in which I don't get paid.

I'm not the sort of woman who can afford to indulge in this kind of fantasy. I will toss the card the moment I get home.

Won't I?

Chapter Two

I let myself into my house, the heavy wood door swinging shut behind me. The moment my feet hit the small rug in the entry hall I step out of my gold stiletto heels, curling my toes, enjoying the warm flow of blood. I love the way my legs look in a good stiletto, but they hurt like hell.

I flip on lights as I make my way down the short hall and into the living room, flopping onto the long dark-brown leather sofa and lying back against the Indian and Moroccan pillows piled there.

I love this house. It's a big Spanish style with an open floor plan that makes me feel like I can breathe. So different from the oppressive environment I grew up in. But I don't want to think about that now. No, now I just want to enjoy my house.

I've been decorating for the last four years, ever since I bought the place. It's my favorite thing to do. Besides sex. I love picking out individual pieces. Exotic imports are my favorite; I have a lot of heavy, carved pieces from India, Spain, Southeast Asia. My artwork is a mix of those same ethnic cultures and a few pieces from Japan. I love the stark esthetics of modern Japanese art; it's soothing. And all the dark, rich colors put together feel homey to me. I adore the exotic fabrics of these countries: the embroidery and damask, the dark, earthy tones mixed with bolder accents. And then there's my collection of orchids.

I know, I hardly seem the type. But there's something special about orchids. They seem so fragile, but they're stronger than they look. I can't help but admire that. And they look like the darkest, loveliest part of a woman. I'm not the first person to make the comparison.

A small collection of orchids sit on the window seat built into the wall of windows facing west, into the hillside, so they don't get too much sun. I have a particular fondness for the white varieties, but I have some in shades of purple, from pale lilac to deep amethyst.

But enough about my flowers, my house. What I really want to think about is Joshua Spencer. I eye my satin bag, sitting on the table in the entry hall. My fingers itch to take that card out. To feel the papery smoothness between my fingers. To dream of the impossible.

Because being with a man like him, being with any man when it's not a business arrangement, is entirely out of the question. These things do not happen to girls in my industry. And I've been in it far too long to delude myself.

Almost ten years. Has it really been that long? I was barely twenty when Enzo found me, and thirty is on the horizon. I suppose I should retire someday. But not yet. No, retiring now would mean giving up the only sexual satisfaction I can attain. Why would I even consider doing that?

Because maybe then I could have a normal life, a small

voice tells me. But no, not me. I will never be normal, whatever that is.

I'm brooding now. I hate when I get like this.

I get up and pad across the cool floors into the kitchen. Pale red granite on the counters, brass pots shining on hooks over the sink, a few more of my precious orchids on the windowsill. It's a great kitchen. Too bad I work so often at night; I love to cook. I love to experiment with Thai dishes, delicate French sauces. But right now all I want is another drink.

I pull the gin out, a glass, some mixer. The ice cubes hit the side of the glass, the sound seeming to echo in my quiet house. I don't mind. I like the peace. I mix the drink, take a long sip, then another.

I don't like myself when I drink. It makes me feel pathetic. But I need it tonight. All these broody thoughts. All because of *him*.

I am suddenly questioning myself. Just because I want a man. But it's more than mere want. No, it's not wanting in the usual way. It's this ridiculous yearning, craving, that won't let me go. My body is stirred with desire.

I take another gulp of the gin. No use in giving in to this kind of desire. Not even here by myself. It never works.

Damn it.

Throwing back the rest of the drink, I feel the alcohol buzz into my system, and head toward the bedroom.

Just get to bed. Forget about him.

I unzip my dress and wriggle out of it, hang it in the closet. Naked, I reach into my nightstand drawer and pull out a gummi bear from a plastic bag I keep there. Silly, I know, but this has been my bedtime comfort since I was a kid. I pop it into my mouth as I crawl into the big carved four-poster bed from Indonesia, beneath the heavy silk duvet cover done in shades of pale blue and deep chocolate brown. Soothing colors. But as I lay there in the dark, I don't feel soothed. Even the gin hasn't done its job. And I'm not enough of a drinker to get up and have some more. Not after growing up with my mother.

Shit, I really do *not* want to think about her right now. No, better to think about Joshua Spencer. About what I can't have. Makes it all the more tempting, doesn't it?

He's tempting enough all on his own. Those eyes, like amber flecked with malachite and silver. He has long, dark lashes. Lashes any girl would love to have. It's the one thing about his face which looks completely innocent. The rest is all rugged bone structure, and that lush mouth that looks too purely sexual to be at all pure.

Just thinking about him is making me hot all over, my nipples going taut, my sex damp. I squeeze my legs together beneath the weight of the covers. It doesn't help.

What would his skin taste like beneath my tongue? What would his cock look like, feel like in my hand? In my mouth?

I take in a deep breath and imagine his scent on the air. And I'm absolutely drenched now, the naked lips of my sex swollen and needy when I brush my fingertips over them.

I really do need another drink.

Instead, I roll over and reach into the drawer of my night-stand, pull out the big, phallic vibrator my friends Regan and Rosalyn gave me for my last birthday. I rarely use it. It's of very little use to me. But I need something, need it badly enough to try.

I lie back on my pillows, switch it on, and lower it between my thighs. And in my mind is Joshua Spencer's face.

I can feel the buzz of the vibrator as I touch it to my aching clit, and there is that lovely, momentary shock of pleasure. But as soon as I feel it, it's gone.

No.

Think of him. Joshua.

Imagine what he'd look like without his shirt on: strong pecs, arms heavily muscled from playing hockey. Washboard abs.

I lick my lips, try the vibrator again. And once more, that one delicious moment before it dissipates.

Concentrate.

His pants have to come next, revealing strong thighs. And in between them, his beautifully erect cock. Yes, now my mouth is watering. Smooth golden skin, the purple head glistening with pre-come. And I take him into my mouth, the swollen head hitting the back of my throat, the scent of him, of desire, filling my mind.

I run the vibrator over my clitoris once more, savor the thrill of sensation, the image of Joshua's cock going down my throat, sucking him, hearing him moan. But that's not where I need him most.

Moving the big vibrator farther down, I part my thighs as if for a lover. I'm so damn wet I don't need any lube. As wet as though there was a pile of cash on the night table, waiting for me. Oh, yes, my pussy gives a hard squeeze at the thought.

Joshua.

Yes, think of Joshua . . .

Think of him entering me, his cock slipping inside as I spread a little wider to take the tip of the vibrating shaft into me. A shiver of sensation, the low thrumming buzz of the pink, plastic machine. I angle to hit my G-spot, and another shock of pleasure shafts deep into my system.

Oh, yes . . .

Joshua . . .

His face, his fine hands. I'd looked at them at the opera. He has big hands, beautiful skin, yet a real man's hands. Strong looking.

Oh, yes, touch me . . . fuck me.

I plunge the plastic shaft deeper, and the vibration is really starting to get to me. I pump my hips, thrust it deeper, using the heel of my hand to press onto my hard clit.

And soon I sense that first raw edge. Pleasure ripples through me in long, undulating waves. Almost there.

Joshua . . .

Oh, yes, his cock driving into me, his mouth on mine. He tastes like good scotch: that smooth, that silky. His tongue in my mouth, his cock deep inside me, and I'm nearly coming now . . . *ah, yes . . .*

My hips arch into the vibrator, my sex clenches . . . and then, nothing.

No!

I bury the vibrator deeper, angle it harder, and my climax starts again, that heaviness weighing down on my belly, simmering, spreading. But once more it tapers off, disappears.

Fuck!

I almost want to cry. But I take a deep breath, picture his face again.

His mouth is one of the hottest things I've ever seen. Yes, imagine that mouth between my thighs, licking my damp slit, sucking on my clit, hard and steady, just the way I like it. And his big hands gripping my hips, holding me down.

Yes . . .

Warm and wet and sucking . . .

My body is shaking so damn hard with the need to come,

I can barely hold the vibrator. I grip harder, thrust it in and out, moving my hips in time. There is sweat on the back of my neck, between my breasts, between my thighs. If he were here with me, he'd be slippery with my sweat, his face buried in my soaking wet mound, loving my shaved pussy.

A long surge of pleasure running through me. My elusive orgasm builds once more, higher and higher. I squeeze my eyes shut tight, see his face, his tongue in my mouth and in my pussy at the same time, his cock plunging into me, his hands on my breasts, squeezing my nipples.

Oh, yes!

I reach for that peak, pleasure shivering through me, and poise on the edge.

Joshua!

I tremble, begin to come.

Ah, yes . . .

And it's gone, as if it never existed. And I am defeated once more.

God damn it!

I really do want to cry now. But I knew this is how it would end. It always does. I am always left panting and weak with unmet need.

Too bad I can't pick up the phone, call one of my clients. But we never, ever do that.

I want to throw the vibrator across the room. But I set it on the night table and throw the covers back instead, get out of bed and walk naked to the kitchen. I'm having that damn drink.

I pour the gin and take it back to bed with me, sitting up against the pillows, my body still shivering with need that will not be met tonight. And along with it, that sense of revulsion

I have on those rare occasions when I allow myself to drink like this: to comfort myself, to *use* the alcohol. But I'm drinking it anyway.

The moonlight is coming through the heavy paned windows, washing the room in silver. Everything looks surreal in the moonlight. Everything feels surreal to me: the aching desire in my body, the memory of the opera tonight. It's almost as though none of it ever happened. Maybe it didn't. I almost want to get up again and look for his card in my purse.

But it may as well have never happened, for all the good it'll do me. Because I cannot become involved with this man. Impossible. Fucking impossible. This is the condition of my life, and I have to accept it. I *have* accepted it.

God damn it.

THE SUN WAKES ME. I squint into the light, roll over, and pull my pillow over my head. I swear my sex is still quivering with need. So hard I have to squeeze my thighs together, trying to make it go away. No use.

I dreamed of him last night. I don't remember much, just a dark writhing of naked flesh, his face, his mouth. My fingers reaching out to touch it, those lush lips, then him taking my fingers into his mouth, that exquisite moist heat.

God.

I really need to stop.

I need to work, is what I need to do.

I roll out of bed and check my messages. One from Deirdre, letting me know Louis wants to see me. Apparently he tried to reach me last night, but my cell was off while I was at the opera. My regulars can usually reach me directly, but they know what to do if I'm not available enough for them: call Deirdre and have her get me, or find them another girl.

Deirdre is my madam, I suppose you would call her, although we who work for her call her The Broker. She's a cold woman, but she does her job incredibly well. She is elegant, sophisticated, has connections in the highest circles. She's more than fair to us. We make plenty of money for her; she should be. And she's not the type to resent the private gifts our clients give us: jewelry, designer clothes, even extra cash. She knows that her clients are satisfied when her girls are happy.

So, it's to be Louis today. I'm happy about that. I adore Louis. He's one of my favorites. He's sweet to me, and the most sensual of lovers. The fact that he's blind probably has something to do with that.

I don't pity him, which is why he asks for me, again and again. He's a strong man, a smart man; there's nothing to pity if you look beyond his inability to see. And he's ridiculously rich. His gifts to me are always extravagant. In fact, the car I currently drive was from Louis after a particularly long weekend of debauchery at his weekend house in Palm Springs. But today I need him more for the sex than anything else.

My body is buzzing again, alive, ready. In the shower I run my hands over my slick skin, between my thighs, and shiver with anticipation.

Yes, think about Louis, my client. Don't think of Joshua Spencer.

But of course he is all I can think of.

I'm to see Louis at lunch today, so I don't have much time. I put my makeup on, even though he can't see it. I always look my best. I would never consider leaving the house if I didn't. A woman in my position can't afford to risk that.

I dress in a soft knit wrap dress because it feels lovely and it'll be fun for him to take off. And beneath it, a lacy bra and G-string. Louis loves me in a G-string. He likes to go down on me, to fuck me without having to take it off.

I slip into a pair of heeled sandals and grab my purse and my keys. Outside it's warm and sunny, the air filled with the tangy scent of the eucalyptus trees that grow all over these canyons. I love living in the Hollywood Hills. There is an utter sense of privacy here, yet I can feel the hum of energy from the city below. Maybe it's all in my head. But I love it. It is the exact opposite of the deathly dull environment I was raised in. And as much as I hate to think about my past, I like to revel in the sensation of that utter contrast.

My slick little black Mercedes coupe is in the driveway, and I slide in behind the wheel. It starts with its customary purr. Taking in a long breath, I inhale the new leather scent, mixed now with the scent of the trees outside.

I hit the button which opens the gates to my property and back out of the drive, shifting as I swing down the road. It's a short drive to Beverly Hills and I'm early, but I want to stop and pick up a loaf of Louis's favorite bread at this little Italian bakery in my neighborhood.

I'm there in only moments. The bakery smells like heaven, and I realize I'm hungry. I hope a lunch date means lunch today, along with the sex. I should have eaten a little something before I left the house. I'm not thinking today. I can blame it on my slight hangover, but I know that's not what it's about.

I really need to get Joshua out of my head before I get into bed with Louis.

You see, this is one reason why a relationship doesn't work for a woman in my position. It makes us lose focus.

The guy behind the bakery counter asks what I want. He's

one of those pretty gay boys, all smooth skin and wide, glossy eyes. He's flirting with me, anyway, which is one reason why I adore gay men. My body heats up a little in response; I can feel my nipples going hard just watching his mouth move as he asks me what I want.

God, I'm in bad shape. My dear Louis is going to get the fuck of his life.

I get my bread and leave, make the short drive to Louis's house. Although calling it a house is a bit absurd. This place is a mansion, of the classic Beverly Hills variety. A large colonial, with soaring white columns, a large, circular drive with a fountain in the middle, the water splashing, gleaming in the sun.

Louis's valet, Thomas, answers the door. His face is expressionless, as always. He knows exactly who and what I am. If he has an opinion about it, it never shows on his stony features. He leads me to the back terrace overlooking the garden and the pool. The table is gorgeously set with china and crystal, a lovely centerpiece filled with enormous Casablanca lilies. Their perfume would be a bit overwhelming if we weren't outside.

Louis's gardens are beautiful, and it's a shame he can't enjoy the view. But he's had his gardeners plant fragrant roses, rosemary, tuberose, everything that smells good, so that the air is always perfumed.

He is already seated at the table, but ever the gentleman, he rises as I step outside, a moment before the first click of my heels on the patio.

"Louis, how lovely! I didn't expect to see you today. I'm so glad you called."

"I'm glad you were available. I had a cancellation and hoped you would make time for me."

He reaches out and I put my hand in his. That first tingle, just from the warmth of his touch. I truly like Louis. He's a wonderful man, a longtime client, so gentle, so kind. Far too alone.

"Sit down, Val, and eat with me. Are you hungry?"

"Yes, I'm starving. I brought some of that Italian bread you like." I hand it to his valet, who will take it into the kitchen and have it sliced for us.

"I thought I smelled it. You're an angel, Val."

He settles back into his chair gracefully, as he does everything. He is a large man, a bit bulky, yet still elegant in his demeanor. He's not particularly attractive, but that doesn't matter to me. He has an average face, his eyes covered with dark glasses. Good teeth, thinning brown hair. But it's his hands I love. They are the most sensitive hands, as though he can almost see with them. They really are his eyes, I suppose. His touch is entirely unique. Incredibly knowing, tender.

I give a long shiver of need.

Lunch is served, a nicely done salad with grilled salmon, a little white wine. I don't bother to ask about the vintage; Louis is a gourmand and I know it will be superb. It is.

As we eat we chat about his business, how tired he is of it, how he'll retire soon. Louis has been threatening to retire as long as I've known him. But he won't do it until he must, I'm sure. He needs to feel needed, useful. That's part of my job.

I reach out and touch his hand.

"Have you had time to digest, Louis?"

He smiles, turns toward me. "I ate lightly on purpose, Val. Just enough to fuel me."

"Then take me inside and fuck me. Please?"

"Such dirty talk, Val."

But his smile broadens, and I really can hardly wait. I'm throbbing all over simply anticipating it.

He stands and I take his hand, and he leads me into the house. His bedroom is on the first floor, a large room with an enormous bed in the center. One of those grand affairs you'd expect to find in a mansion, with four ornately carved posts soaring toward the vaulted ceiling. Everything is done in creamy shades on silk and velvet, the lovely textures that make his world come alive. Beautiful against the dark wood.

He sits on the end of the bed and I go to him, pull his hands to my face. He spends a moment exploring my features, as he always does.

"I'll have an extra gift for you today, Val, for coming on such short notice."

"Oh, I intend to," I joke, making him smile once more.

His fingers dip between my lips, and I pull them into my mouth, sucking on them. My dream from last night flashes through my head: Joshua Spencer's wet mouth wrapped around my own fingers, pulling, sucking. Ah . . .

I am soaked already.

"That's so good, Val," Louis tells me, his voice gone quiet. "But I want my cock there."

"So do I," I tell him, dropping to my knees and opening his trousers to release his hard flesh.

Louis's cock is a nice size, perhaps a bit larger than average. Only half hard now, but I'll take care of that quickly enough.

I lower my head and blow on it. I know he loves that, the feel of my warm breath on his flesh. His cock stirs, and I smile to myself. There is such a sense of power in what we can do to a man. They truly are powerless at times like this. I could ask him for anything. But all I want is his touch today, his cock. And of course, the knowledge that I will be paid for my services. But today it could be a dollar.

I lean closer and breathe him in. He is all clean soap and a hint of aftershave. His skin is sweet as I take the head into my mouth. I linger there, curling my tongue around his hardening flesh, teasing him. I hear him moan above me.

"Ah, that's it, Val." A gentle hand goes into my hair, and he runs his fingers through it. "So soft," he murmurs. "Your hair, your mouth . . ."

I pull him in deeper and begin to suck, curling my hand under his balls, fondling them gently.

"You're going to make me come too soon, Val. You know how much I love that."

I pull back for a moment to ask him, "Do you want me to stop? Or do you want to come in my mouth, Louis?"

"If you keep talking to me like that, I'm going to come all over your face, you minx." He chuckles.

He's really a good boy. A little bit of dirtiness goes a long way with him.

"Tell me how you want it, Louis."

"I want you to suck me for another minute or two, then I want to lick you. I want to feel you come. And then I want to screw you, come inside you."

Yes, a good boy. He never says "fuck."

"You're the boss, Louis. Your wish is my command."

I bend over him once more and really go to work, sucking hard, sliding his shaft in and out of my mouth, taking him deep into my throat, until he's moaning, squirming. Until I know he's nearly coming. I stop.

"Ah," he groans. "Perfect. Now I need to touch you, Val."

I stand up, and find I'm a bit shaky on my feet. And when

he runs his hands over my body, goose bumps rise all over my skin. He smiles a little when he feels the soft texture of the dress. Untying it, he slides it from my body, his hands somehow never leaving my flesh. He explores me slowly, his fingers running over the lace of my bra, making my nipples harden into two stiff peaks. Then he moves lower, brushing the small lacy triangle between my thighs. I let out a sigh.

"Eager today, Val?"

"I'm so ready for you, Louis. Touch me and see."

He does, a gentle glide of fingers beneath my G-string and over my aching slit.

"Very nice," he says, his voice rough with lust, making me smile.

His hands move back up my body, to my breasts, and he squeezes gently. Unfastening the clasp in the front, he slides the bra from my shoulders, and I feel gloriously free, almost as though the air itself is caressing my skin.

But in moments it is Louis's clever hands, soft on my flesh. His touch is so gentle, and from another man I might find this frustrating, but with Louis it is always lovely. That slip and slide of his fingers over my skin, circling my nipples until they hurt. God, they hurt.

"Suck on them, Louis," I plead with him.

He does just that, leaning in and taking one hard nub of flesh into his mouth. Ah, warm and wet and sweet, that sweep of his tongue. And I'm shivering, pleasure pouring through my system.

He moves his mouth down my body, circles my waist with his soft hands, pulling me around and laying me down on the bed so that my legs hang over the edge. He goes down on his knees, and I tremble all over, waiting for his mouth between my thighs. A moment later he parts my legs wider, teases at the edge of the lacy G-string with his fingers, then pulls it aside. Using his tongue, he teases the very tip of my hardened clit, and I'm shivering, clenching already.

"Yes, Louis. Lick me."

His tongue flicks against my clit again, then moves lower, licking at my swollen pussy lips.

"Inside, Louis. Please."

I arch my hips, and he obliges, his soft, warm tongue dipping inside me. Pleasure seeps into me like water, like the heat of his wet mouth.

His hands are on my thighs, making little circles on my skin. I love when he does this; it's a dual sensation, as though I am being touched everywhere, making my skin hot, sensitive. It's a lovely sort of distraction from what he's doing to my pussy, so that I won't come too quickly.

His fingers trace a long line down the insides of my legs, to my ankles. His fingertips skim the bones there, tickling a little, as his tongue laps at my clit, gently, featherlike, until I can hardly stand it.

"Make me come, Louis. Make me come in your mouth. You know I love that. You know you love that."

He moans, his tone as gentle as everything else about him. And he licks me in a slow, steady rhythm, his fingers now teasing at the lips of my sex, adding to the sensation, layer upon layer. Pleasure swarms my system, and as the first wave of climax shivers over my skin, Joshua's face appears before me. And I let him be there, let it be *him* licking me gently to orgasm as the waves come crashing down on me. Pleasure courses through me, sharp, sharper, with Joshua's beautiful face in my mind, Joshua and the knowledge that it's Louis between my thighs. My paying client.

I'm coming harder and harder, can't seem to stop. I'm

shaking with the power of it, and Louis is moaning now along with me.

Finally it's over. He lifts his head.

"That was spectacular," he says, his voice low.

"Yes it was," I agree. I don't have to tell him why. "You're going to fuck me now, aren't you, Louis?"

"You are a very dirty girl, Val," he says, chuckling. "But yes, I am."

I sit up and help him out of his clothes, taking a few moments to run my hand over his skin, making sure to keep that sensory contact with him while I grab a condom from my purse on the floor by my feet.

When he's naked I pull him down on the bed and climb on top of him, slip the condom over his cock, then hold myself over his body, tucking the head inside me with my fingers. I leave just the head there for a moment, savoring that first sensation of fullness, needing more. I need to come again. Once wasn't nearly enough, not today.

Louis's hands are on me once more, cruising over my skin, making me shiver. His fingers tease my nipples, and I lean into him, almost wishing for once that he would tug on them, pinch them. But that's not Louis. And I'm here for his pleasure. My own is secondary.

I press down onto his cock, a little at a time. He groans, thrusts gently up into me.

"Yes, that's good, Val, so good."

I'd love to really ride him hard, to fuck him like I would Enzo. I'll do it with Louis sometimes, but I know he likes these long, slow fucks the most. I force myself to keep it slow, to tease him, to tease myself. My body is full of need, my sex pulsing once more. And his fingers brushing my nipples are driving me mad; they're so damn hard. Joshua's face in my mind again, his mouth coming down to cover my nipples, pulling them in, sucking deep inside his mouth.

Oh, yes!

I tilt my hips, pressing a little harder on Louis's cock, a little faster. I can't handle slow anymore.

"Ah, you're a wild one today, Val," Louis says, but there's no admonishment in his voice.

"I need it today," I tell him truthfully, my words coming out between sharp, gasping breaths.

I move faster, grinding my mound into him. He's panting now, his hands on my breasts a little rougher than usual.

"Oh, yes, Louis. Touch me, yes . . ."

He pumps up into me, his fingers brushing my nipples, and that's all it takes. I come, hard, pleasure gripping my body in long spasms. I'm moaning, gasping. And Louis tenses beneath me, groans aloud, his hips jerking.

My climax is short and sharp, the sensation stabbing into me. When I stop shivering I look down at Louis. But all I can see behind my orgasm-glazed eyes is Joshua's face.

Chapter Three

AT HOME ALONE AND I don't have a date set up for tonight. You'd think my afternoon with Louis would have been enough, but no. I need more. I need to come again. Again and again. I need to know that it is these men making me come, my clients, my lovers who pay for sex.

I need to know that Joshua Spencer has absolutely nothing to do with it.

I have never, ever fantasized about another man while with a client. I don't have to. And I feel as if I've betrayed Louis.

Ridiculous, I know. He is not my lover. He certainly has no delusions of faithfulness. He sees other girls besides me. Of course he does. He has enough money to do whatever he wants, and we working girls cannot have any sense of possession over our clients. And I don't. But he felt my change in mood as soon as I rolled off him; he told me later. I'd gone to the bathroom and brought a hot towel to him, slipped the condom from his softening cock, cleaned him up as I always do. He knew from my touch, somehow. I tried to tell him I was just tired. But I can't risk this happening again. My trademark, what I'm known for, what my entire career rests on, is that I'm the girl who is *right there,* in the moment, getting off on whatever I'm doing with my clients.

What the hell is wrong with you, Valentine?

It's him. Joshua. But is that really all it is?

I hate when I get philosophical. Better for a woman like me not to ask herself too many questions.

My mind flashes back to my very first trick. The client was your average guy. Not attractive. Not unattractive. Didn't matter. What mattered was that thrill coursing through my body, simply knowing he was paying to have sex with me. I was thrilled and just guilty enough to make it even better.

He wasn't a very good fuck, but I came and came. I flooded the bed. I made him come twice. I could tell he was surprised. In shock. But he came back to see me once a week after that, every payday, for months. Until Enzo took me out of that place.

I'm getting warm all over, remembering. Either I need to get up from the sofa and make myself a cup of tea, try to calm down, or I need to slip my hand between my thighs and try to get myself off. But I know how that will end. I'm disappointed enough in myself already. I get up to go put the kettle on but pull the bottle of Tanqueray out instead. The kitchen floor is cold on my bare feet, making my toes curl, but I don't care. I need to cool down. Need to do something.

I pour a shot of the gin over ice, add a little tonic water. I lift the glass to my lips and pause, a small shudder of self-loathing rippling over my skin. Turning to the booze again. Two days in a row. But fuck it, I deserve it now and then—to feel a little sorry for myself. I'm careful enough never to let it get out of control. No, control is my thing, my modus operandi.

I'm feeling a little out of control right now.

That's when I remember my pretty silk evening bag is still on the console table in the hall. And in the bag is his card.

Don't do it, Valentine.

But I'm moving toward the hall, my half-forgotten gin and tonic in my hand. I eye the pale gold bag as though it were a poison apple. Dangerous. Tempting. I take a breath, take a sip of my drink, letting the alcohol burn down my throat. A drink for courage.

When have I ever needed that? I've always been brave. An adventurer.

The scent of the gin in my glass hits my nostrils, and I have one of those vague, unpleasant flashes I get sometimes, of my ugly, lonely childhood, the bars my mother would sometimes drag me into looking for my absent father. Dad and his famous disappearing acts.

I hated those bars. It was always far too late for a kid my age to be out; she'd drag me, half asleep, from my bed. But it was there I first saw them, the women in their makeup and high-heeled shoes, beautiful to me in their false glamour. These were the women who got the attention from the men. The men were absolutely fawning over them. It was years before I understood that many of them were working girls. And even then it was as glamorous to me, as exotic, as it was dirty. But when I was really young, those places scared the hell out of me. My mother scared the hell out of me, with her sour breath and her tears.

Fuck.

Alright, maybe I haven't always been brave. But I don't think about those times anymore. I try not to, anyway.

What the hell has gotten into me?

I step forward, put my hand out, let it hover. I feel ridiculous.

Yet my heart is pounding in my chest, the same way it does when you're on a roller coaster, and about to fly down that first long drop into the empty air. I am that breathless.

Setting my drink down on the long, narrow table, I take the bag in my hand, twist the jeweled clasp open. His card sits in the red satin interior, nestled like a pearl in an oyster between a tube of lipstick and a small enameled compact.

My fingertips flutter against the paper for a moment before pulling it from the bag. I swear I can almost hear the slide of it against the fabric. I turn it over in my hand and look at it.

A simple business card: heavy linen paper, very fine quality. His name in raised black ink. An e-mail address. A telephone number.

I swallow hard, my throat parched, tight. Then I remember my drink, pick it up and take a sip. Yes, better. I carry my glass and the card back to the sofa, sit down, turn the small rectangle of paper over and over. Each time I see his name my pulse races. I feel like I am twelve years old. I want to call him so badly it hurts, my chest pulling as though someone has tied it in a knot.

He has tied me in a knot.

Don't do it.

Do it.

I reach for the phone on a side table. It feels heavy in my hand, as though I am acutely aware of every single thing around me on some cellular level. The fading orange sunlight coming through the windows. The scent of the gin in my glass, sweeter to me now than it was a few moments ago. The rhythm of my own breath, which is coming a little too fast. I dial the number.

It rings once, twice.

Please . . .

Three rings, then it stops. Shit.

"Hello." A statement, not a question, in his deep, lovely voice.

"Hi. Joshua?"

"Yes?"

"This is Valentine Day. We met last night at the opera."

"Valentine. Hi." Real pleasure in his voice, and it goes through me like a warm wind, bringing gooseflesh up on my arms, the back of my neck.

I am being far too romantic about this man.

"You asked me to call."

"I'm glad you did. I hoped you would. How are you?"

Ah, a little small talk. I can do this. Even if my pulse is hammering like thunder. "I'm well. And you?"

"I'm fine. What have you been doing since the opera?"

I almost say "working," but I don't want to open that can of worms. "Nothing really." I walk over to my window full of orchids, touch a fingertip to one delicate petal. It's smooth and cool. "Nothing exciting. What about you?"

"Working. And I played hockey this morning."

I can imagine him in one of those bulky uniforms, flying around the ice, getting into one of those angry crushes, a pile of male bodies pressed together. And I'm getting wet.

"Did you win?" I ask him.

"It was just practice for a team I coach. A few of the guys in my league work out with some of the at-risk youth in the city. We figure it helps them to skate off some of their aggressions, learn to work together. No one went home with more than a few bruises; that's always a plus." There is another brief pause and I don't know what to say, but I'm smiling to myself. He's a nice man, this Joshua Spencer. Then he says quietly, "Have dinner with me, Valentine."

"Oh, well . . ." I want to say yes. I really do. I never should have called. My stomach is a hard knot of fear and need. Fear *of* need. "I don't know, Joshua. I'm sorry. I know that sounds stupid. But . . . look, I should go. Okay? I'm sorry."

I start to hang up, but I hear him say, "Don't do it, Valentine. Don't hang up."

His voice is low, yet there is an air of total command in his tone. Maybe that's what makes me pause. I bring the phone back to my ear. "I'm here."

I look out the window at the last remnants of the dying sun. The top part of the sky is already dark as velvet.

"Valentine, I want to see you. I will be a perfect gentleman. But at the risk of making a complete fool of myself, I'll tell you this: I need to see you. I don't know why. No, I don't mean that the way it sounds. Just . . . say you'll see me."

My heart is pounding harder than ever. I should hang up the phone *now*.

"Alright. Yes, I'll see you."

"Dinner?"

"I don't know . . ."

"Drinks, then. I can come and pick you up. Or if you'd prefer, you can meet me. What about the bar at Yamashiro? Do you know it?"

"Yes, of course. Alright. Drinks. When?"

"Tonight?"

But I can't do it. I need some time. To think. To breathe. To talk myself out of it.

"Tomorrow night," I say, not even knowing if I'll have a client. A client I will have to refuse in order to keep this date.

I really must be losing my mind.

"Tomorrow night," he says. "If we're there by seven we

can see the sunset. Unbelievable colors this time of year. It's beautiful from up there; you can see the whole city."

It *is* beautiful. I know this because I've been there with clients a number of times. But I've also been there with friends.

Stop analyzing everything!

"I'll meet you there at seven," I tell him.

Another pause. He's a thoughtful man. Then, "I'm really looking forward to seeing you, Valentine."

I nod my head, even though he can't see me. "Good night, Joshua."

I hang up before I say anything foolish. Before I tell him how badly I want to see him, to watch his lips as he speaks, to feel the heat of his hands on me.

God.

I throw back my drink in one gulp.

What the hell have I done?

YAMASHIRO IS AN OLD Hollywood institution. A bit old-fashioned, a place the Hollywood Old Guard frequents, but more quiet, more intimate, than any of the current hot spots. Great sushi, superb service. It's a sprawling Japanese-style structure perched on top of a hill with big banks of windows overlooking Hollywood. Below the restaurant is a meandering garden built into the hillside, a small pagoda.

The bar has been modernized, with slick wood floors and high bar tables done in black lacquer. Very Zen. Very polished. The tall windows look into the center courtyard, where a pool filled with lilies and koi carp is surrounded by potted bonsai and iris, and a deck where patrons eat in the warm weather.

It's empty out there now, the late September evening cool for us weather-spoiled Los Angelenos. Out of habit I've arrived early, as I always do for a client.

He's not a client.

A small, inexplicable thrill ripples over my skin at the thought.

God, I'm fucked up.

I've gone ahead and ordered a drink, one of their exotic martinis made with saki and lychee juice. Tapping my fingernails against the stem of the glass, I check out the room. There are only a few couples seated in the bar. It's early for the Hollywood crowd. Thursday evenings are party nights in this town; the real action won't begin until after ten.

I sip my drink, carefully set it back on the small paper napkin on the sleek black table. I'm a little chilly. Or maybe it's nerves.

Checking my watch, I see it's still early: five minutes to seven. I should have made a grand entrance, been fashionably late. But old habits die hard.

I tap my nails against the table, notice it and make myself stop. Maybe I should go to the ladies' room, refresh my lipstick?

"Valentine."

That pure pleasure in his voice again, as there was on the phone. It makes my heart pound, makes me hot all over.

I turn and smile at him. "Hi."

He takes my hand, lifts it, and as I stare like some sort of idiot, he brushes his lips over my knuckles. Heat shimmers up my arm, burrows deep into my body. I'm as wet as if his mouth were between my thighs.

Jesus. Can't even think about that now.

"You look beautiful," he says, smiling. Fucking gorgeous, that smile. Absolutely devastating. "Even better than I remembered."

I know I look good. I dressed very carefully in my black crocheted dress. It took me forever to pick my outfit, which is totally unlike me. I wanted something elegant but sexy. Short but not too short. Fitted but not too tight. I don't normally dress like a whore, anyway. I always take care with my appearance, and let's not waste any time considering ego here; this is my job. But tonight it feels nice that he noticed.

That *he* noticed.

"Thank you." I cross my legs, an unconsciously seductive move that I am aware of only after I've done it. But my sex is aching with need already. I can hardly stand to look at him.

He's wearing a pair of black slacks that hang perfectly on his hips, a midnight blue shirt with some tiny, subtle pattern in black. Beneath the collar I notice a narrow chain in silver, or maybe platinum. His watch is a heavy silver Rolex.

I take in all of this in an instant. I am trained to assess a man. I like everything I see. But it's his smile that leaves me breathless, his eyes that make me yearn to touch him.

He orders a cold bottle of the Suishin Tenjomukyu sake without looking at the menu, an excellent choice. The waitress brings it quickly, eyeing Joshua as she sets the bottle on the table, arranges his cup, his napkin. I can't blame her. He is nearly gleaming, all raw male beauty. Or perhaps that's only my own warped perception, seen through the haze of my obsession with this man.

I shift, uncross and recross my legs.

"I'm glad you came," Joshua tells me.

"So am I," I answer, although I'm not really sure yet. What is this going to mean for me later, when I have to go home alone and frustrated? Empty.

He leans forward, fills his cup, sips it, sets it back down. I can't tear my gaze from his hands. They're strong-looking, with long, agile fingers. I bite my lip when he leans closer. "Tell me about yourself, Valentine."

"I'd rather talk about you."

Oh, yes, I'd rather talk about anything else but myself.

"Not every man on the planet is entirely narcissistic, you know." He's grinning at me, a lovely, crooked grin, and I notice then that he has a small scar at the corner of his lower lip.

I can't help but smile back at him. He is charming in some old-fashioned way, and I love it. "Maybe not. But I'd really like to know about you. I'm intrigued by a man who will indulge his mother by taking her to the opera."

"Ah, you think I'm a momma's boy," he teases.

"No, not necessarily. I think it's nice."

He shrugs. Wide shoulders beneath the dark fabric of his shirt. "I'm a nice guy."

"I'm sure you are."

He locks his gaze on mine. His eyes are glittering in the low lighting of the bar. "Oh, I'm not *too* nice," he says, his tone full of dark promise.

I shiver. Clear my throat. "Tell me about your family, Joshua."

"You can call me Josh, if you like. Most people do. Except for my family."

"I like Joshua. I always call people by their full names, for some reason. I get the idea you're close to your family."

"I am. We lost my dad about fifteen years ago, so it's just my mother and my younger sister, Lanie."

"I'm sorry. That must have been hard."

He shrugs again. "It made me grow up a little faster. I had to take over the family business. But I don't regret that part.

Too many young people have no sense of responsibility these days. Turns them into slackers. The world is too easy, in some ways." He pauses, laughs. "I sound like some old man, don't I? Some old curmudgeon bitching about today's youth."

"No, not at all. And I happen to agree with you. The hardest things in life teach us the most."

"Sometimes. Sometimes it just teaches us to be pissed off. It takes more than just the hard part to channel all that into something else."

"Yes, that makes sense."

"You should see these kids I work with. All of them from the worst parts of the city. Broken homes. Drugs. Absent parents. A lot of these boys have spent their whole lives having to fend for themselves. And when they first join the team they're out there trying not to slip on the ice and trying to bash the hell out of anyone who comes near them. But after a while, they get it. Every single one of them. Just having someone give a damn about them transforms them." He pauses, laughs. "I'm sorry. I'll get off my soapbox."

"No, I like it." And I do.

He smiles, nods, and I sip my drink, enjoying the heat of it going down my throat. Enjoying talking with him. He really is an incredibly good guy, which makes me yearn for him all the more in some perverse way. Perverse for a woman like me, anyway.

"So, you became a businessman at an early age," I prompt him, wanting to understand him, his life.

He nods. "Real estate. Dad had been prepping me since I was a kid, and I was already studying business in college, so I wasn't completely unprepared. It was rough for a while, but now it's just . . . my life. I even enjoy my work sometimes, which is more than most people can say."

"And your sister? Are you close with her?"

He pauses for a moment, his gaze wandering, as though he's really thinking about his answer. "In a strange way, we are. Even though she has a tendency to drive me crazy. Classic little-sister syndrome. And she hates that I'm always telling her what to do. Classic big brother syndrome." He flashes a quick, devastating grin at me and I go hot all over. "She's always been spoiled. By my parents. By me, to be honest. Lanie's an unbelievable bundle of energy. Luckily she lives in D.C. with her husband; she's his problem now. He's a great guy; I know he takes good care of her. But I miss her. I don't get to see her enough."

So sweet, the way he talks about his family. His affection for them shines through everything he says.

"It must be lovely to be close to your family."

"You're not close with yours?"

"No."

"Do they live in L.A.?"

"My mother is still here, but my father . . . I honestly don't know. That sounds pathetic . . ."

"No, it doesn't."

I shrug. "I never really knew him, anyway. He wasn't a part of my life even when he was around, so there's nothing to miss."

"And your mother?"

"We're . . . estranged."

"I'm sorry."

"No, don't be. It's fine. Fine."

Don't think about her now. Don't let her ruin this evening.

"So I guess that means you grew up here in L.A.?"

I nod, take a sip of my drink. "In the Valley."

He smiles at me. "A real California girl."

"I suppose. Although my childhood wasn't beach parties and surfing. In the Valley we rode bikes, skateboards, roller-skated. But there were a few kids in the neighborhood who had pools. My girlfriends and I used to slather ourselves in suntan lotion, close our eyes and breathe in that coconut scent, and pretend we were at the beach . . . Isn't that funny, how kids think?"

In my mind I can see the sparkling blue of the water in the neighbor's pool, smell that scent of chlorine and wet cement, along with the suntan lotion.

"That doesn't sound like a bad life, even if you weren't at the beach."

"No. It doesn't sound like a bad life."

Suddenly I remember being about twelve, coming home from one of those pool parties to find my mother passed out on the sofa, her dropped cigarette burning a hole in the cushion. I remember standing there and staring, watching the hole smolder, grow. The sharp odor of burning fabric, smoke filling the room. I remember how utterly sick I felt. Even worse that when I poured a whole pitcher of water on the fire to put it out, she never woke up. And she never said anything about it, as though that hole wasn't there. She just flipped the cushion over.

I look away, tightening my fingers around the stem of my glass.

"Are you okay?" he asks.

I turn back to him. "You're a very nice man, Joshua. You really are, you know."

He reaches out and takes my hand, and the heat is there, enveloping me, my hand, my entire body. And I can't seem to sort it all out—the heat of him, my response, the strange thoughts going through my mind. Thoughts about how lovely it would be to do this, to date this wonderful man. To have a normal life.

There is nothing normal about your life.

No, there's not.

I want to pull my hand back. I start to, but he hangs on to it.

"Am I doing something wrong, Valentine?" he asks me, his voice low.

"What? No. Of course not. I'm just . . . out of practice."

"I find that hard to believe."

"I haven't dated in quite a while."

"I haven't, either."

"It sounds as though you work an awful lot," I say, trying to change the subject. My hand is burning in his.

"I do, but that's not it. To be honest, I broke up with a woman a while ago, and I've been hiding away ever since."

"Ah. You were in love with her."

"That's the sad part. I'm not sure I ever was."

I look up at him. His eyes are shadowed, unreadable. He pours another glass of sake and drinks. "Anyway, it was what it was. I needed to be on my own for a while. Needed to figure a few things out."

"And have you?"

"I like to think so. I'm more clear on what I want." He's smiling at me again. Such a dazzling smile, those strong, white teeth.

I know what I want. I want to kiss him. *Need* to kiss him.

I haven't kissed a man on the mouth in years. We don't do that, we working girls.

I don't want to think about that now. All I want to think about is *him*. I want to continue with this little charade, pretending to myself that I can have him.

"And what about you?" he asks. "You said you haven't been dating. Is there a reason why?"

I pause, bite my lip. What can I possibly say? And why do I want to tell him the truth, all of it? It's not about being self-destructive. I just want to. But of course that's impossible.

"Not that it's any of my business," he continues. "I know that. But I'm curious. You're welcome to tell me to go to hell, if you like."

One corner of his mouth is cocked in a small, crooked grin, and it is irresistible. He is irresistible.

"I just . . . Dating is not a successful venture for me. It never has been." I shrug my shoulders, feel them loosen up. "I can't seem to get it. All the rules, the posturing. I wish the whole dating thing was more honest. I don't understand why people feel they have to lie to each other."

Isn't that what you're doing now?

Yes, but in some way, I'm being more honest with him right now than I have with anyone in a very long time. Other than Enzo, no one really has any idea of what goes on in my head. Not even Regan and Rosalyn, my only real friends, and frankly, I'm not too sure how real they are. A part of me is always hidden away behind the walls I've spent my life constructing. We talk about clothes, shopping, celebrity gossip, my girlfriends and I. Nothing any deeper. This is more truth than I've spoken in years. It's freeing, as clichéd as that may sound. And it's addictive. I want to tell him more.

Get yourself under control.

"I don't get that part, either," he says. "The games. All that shit—and pardon my language, but it *is* shit—about not calling a woman for three days, a week."

"Exactly. And you don't have to worry about language

with me. There was plenty of it in the house I grew up in. I'm used to it."

Damn it. I'm saying too much. But he hasn't noticed.

"I'm going to be honest with you, Valentine." My hand is still resting in his, and he uses both his hands to turn mine over. He strokes my open palm with his thumbs, and I am shivering immediately with lust. Drenched. Aching. "You are the most beautiful and fascinating woman I've ever met. I know you're holding something back from me. But I find it intriguing. I don't mind that little bit of mystery."

I'm nearly blushing now; another first in this decade. When I look up into his eyes they are steady, unblinking. Beautiful, his long, dark lashes.

"Tell me about your life, Valentine. Whatever you want to tell me. You decide."

I nod my head. He understands me, in some strange way. And he's incredibly kind. I don't know what to think of him, this impossible man. Like something I dreamed up.

If only I could fuck him and get off like I do with my clients. But I don't want to think about that part now, that part which will mean an end to this lovely dream. By tomorrow I will have to wake up and understand it's over.

If that's the case, what does it matter if I let him in a little? My mind is reeling with the idea.

"I don't know where to start," I tell him.

"Start with what you like, what interests you."

I pause, thinking. My brain is whirling.

"I always loved going to school, from the time I was a kid, and later, in college. I took classes on every subject. I never earned a degree. I just . . . learned."

He leans in closer. "What were your favorite classes?"

"History. Sociology. Cultural anthropology. If you put them all together, it's like a picture of the world. Of people."

"I loved my sociology classes, too. And psychology. It all seems like such a long time ago, now. But it's come in handy in my business. Knowing how people tick. Or some of it, at least. People are a mystery to me on a lot of levels, which I find interesting. Fascinating."

He pauses, takes a sip of his drink. The ice cubes rattle in his glass as he sets it back down on the table. His lower lip is left a bit damp, and it's all I can do not to reach out and taste that droplet of fine sake, just lick it off with my tongue.

"It's like a window letting you inside," he goes on, "having these odd bits of knowledge. Being made to dissect the way we all think, how we function, what makes us do whatever it is we do."

"Yes, exactly. But I thought you went to school for a business degree."

"I did. But I had other interests. I was young, and I'm sure my dad saw it as lack of focus. But the world was too varied. I didn't want to do any one thing forever."

"And now you've been running the family business forever," I say quietly, then immediately regret it. It seems cruel of me to point that out.

He nods. "Yes." He's quiet a moment, then, "When we're young the world is one big possibility. But then we have to grow up and face reality. This is my reality."

"I never had that," I tell him, realizing suddenly how true it is. "I never felt that sense of endless opportunity. I envy you."

"What did you want to be? When you were a kid? When you were in college?"

I shake my head. "I don't really know. I don't remember

ever having any dreams for myself. It never occurred to me. Even now, recently, I've been taking art history courses just because I love art. There's no definitive end, no plan."

A knot is rising in my chest. This is hitting too close to home.

"I remember we talked art at the opera the other night. But where did it all lead you, Valentine? Do you have a job, a career? I've just realized I don't know that about you."

"I day trade from home," I tell him, which isn't a lie, exactly. I've spent the last several years learning about the stock market and I dabble a bit, enough to make some extra cash. It was Louis who taught me. And it's my standard answer. But he doesn't have to know any of that.

I feel a little sick to my stomach.

"Ah, you're a risk-taker," he says, smiling at me.

I'm not sure if being a call girl for the last nine years qualifies as being a risk-taker. I am as stuck in my job as any nine-to-five corporate hack, if for very different reasons.

I shrug, take a sip of my drink. "Maybe. I do like the thrill of it, the idea of losing all my money, but it's really all a big fake for me. I tend to play it fairly safe."

"I'm surprised." His tone lowers and he leans in a little closer, until I can smell the subtle fragrance of his cologne. That wood and citrus scent that filters into my body, finds an empty place right between my thighs, and I swear it strokes me, teases me. "You strike me more as an adventurer," he says.

There is something distinctly sexual going on in the wicked gleam in his eyes. In the way he is stroking my palm again, in slow circles. The same way his tongue might dance around my clit. Oh, yes, something sexual in my response to his scent, his voice, his touch. The tone of our conversation has shifted with a hard, grinding lurch. I can't help but go loose all over, hot and melting. I manage to smile at him. Actually, I can't help it. My mouth is suddenly not my own. I am about to do something entirely foolish.

I drop my voice. "In certain arenas, yes, I can be very adventurous."

His slow smile spreads. God, his teeth are so strong and beautiful. The need to kiss him, to feel his tongue in my mouth, is nearly overwhelming. I squeeze my thighs together. I'm throbbing, hurting with the need for him to touch me.

He lets my hand go, pulling away slowly, inch by excruciating inch, like a long caress, his eyes never leaving mine. He clears his throat. "I think I need another drink."

He motions to the waitress, orders for both of us while I try to pull myself together. But I am buzzing all over, lust as sharp as knife blades in my sex, my hardened nipples, on my skin. I want him too badly. Too much to handle, and I am about to blow it.

You cannot have this.

I need this. Need him.

God.

"I'm sorry. Please excuse me. I'll . . . I'll be back." I grab my purse and rush downstairs to the ladies' room.

I ignore the attendant, a dark-eyed woman pointing out the perfume and breath mints on the counter, and push my way into the marble-lined stall, slamming the door behind me. My breath is coming in rough pants. I yank up the hem of my dress and press the heel of my hand over my aching mound. My silk panties are soaked. When I slip my fingers under that damp edge, into my cleft, I am as wet as the ocean, slick, needy.

I am absolutely burning. And my fingers are rough as I massage my engorged clitoris. Harder and faster. I need this, need some release, even knowing I won't find it. Dropping my purse on the floor, I slip two fingers inside, pumping, thrusting, searching for my G-spot. I gasp when I find it. Joshua's scent is all over me. His face in front of my closed eyes.

Yes.

I tilt my hips, spread my legs, plunge deeper.

Yes, just fuck me, please . . .

Pressing harder, I circle my clit. I am so damn wet, so full of need, I'm going to explode.

Joshua.

Fuck me, please. Please, please, please . . . let me come. Make me come with your beautiful hands.

And I begin to, that lovely keen edge like a bomb about to go off. And just as quickly, it fizzles into nothing.

God damn it!

I slump against the door with a small sob.

What am I doing here? This is insane. I'm insane.

Joshua.

What is he thinking, left alone in the bar while I masturbate in the ladies' room?

I sit down and pee, get up and stand for a few moments in the stall while I catch my breath. Lust is a hard ache between my thighs still. Unsated. But it's not as if I expected anything more.

Finally, I go out to the lounge area, wash my hands, brush my hair, spray a little perfume on my neck, touch up my lipstick. I tip the dark-eyed attendant when she hands me a paper towel. But it's another minute or two before I can go back upstairs, face him.

He smiles at me when I get back to our table, sliding my drink across the smooth surface toward me. My body surges with lust, a powerful tide. I could drown in this. And I understand now how dangerous this is. How close I am to doing something I'll regret. And drinking more is not going to help. I'm barely hanging on to any sense of control as it is.

"Joshua, I'm not feeling very well. I should go." I hate lying to him. I feel *too* damn good, need desperately to feel better. To come.

Oh, God.

"I'm sorry. What can I do? Do you need me to drive you home?"

I shake my head. "No. Thank you. It's . . . just a headache. I'll be fine."

No you won't.

"Let me ask the waitress for some aspirin."

"No. That's not necessary. I just need to go home."

I don't mean to sound so cold, it just comes out that way.

"Of course."

That easy sense of intimacy is gone, or at least diminished, and it's my fault. But I can't go there with him, can I? Better to cut it off now.

He is all gentlemanly manners, walking me out with a hand at my waist, which I have to grit my teeth against. He gives the parking valet my ticket, insists on tipping him, then hands me into my car. I am so relieved that he is no longer touching me. And empty. Yearning.

"Call me, Valentine. I want to see you again. Hell, I'd like to see you tomorrow."

He is too gorgeous in the silvery moonlight, the amber glow coming through the windows of the restaurant. His eyes are dark and mysterious, his smile sincere, his lips unbelievably lush. My sex gives a sharp squeeze.

Just go, get home.

"I'll . . . I'll give you a call," I say, having no intention of doing so. "Thank you for the drink."

"It was my pleasure."

He reaches into the car, caresses my shoulder lightly, his hand whispering over my skin. I shiver. I want to take him home with me, feel that touch all over my body, fuck him in my bed all night.

You know what you have to do.

It's my heart that gives a hard squeeze now. I really like him. *Fuck.*

"Joshua, I have to go."

"Yes, of course." His hand slips over my shoulder, down my arm. If I turn my head he will kiss me. I don't do it. Instead, I nod, give him a quick, pale, sideways smile, and shift my car, pull away.

When I glance in the rearview mirror, he is standing there watching me.

I feel as though I've survived some sort of test, and I am exhausted. But is this really any sort of triumph? Or am I nothing more than a coward?

Chapter Four

AT HOME I GO immediately to my bedroom, kick my shoes off, tear my dress over my head. My bra comes next, and I fling it onto the bed. I'm angry. Horny. In need. And not all of it is physical, which is even worse. As if the lust ravaging my system isn't hard enough to deal with.

I glance at the clock. It's already after nine. But I grab my purse from where I threw it on the bed and pull out my cell phone, checking for messages, hoping for a client. I already checked at least three times on the way home. But I fucking *need* it tonight. And not being able to get myself off is excruciating.

Pathetic.

There are no more messages than there were when I checked five minutes ago. Tossing my cell phone down, I stalk into the bathroom, glare at my reflection in the big, brass-framed mirror. I look flushed. My bare breasts seem fuller than usual, the nipples two hard peaks of reddened flesh, begging to be touched, kissed, sucked.

Groaning, I bring my hands to my breasts, watch in the mirror as I caress the nipples, tease them. Groan again as I pinch them hard between my fingers. And my sex is absolutely burning.

I slide my panties off, feeling the damp silk as it glides over my legs. I'm soaked. Slipping a hand between my thighs, I touch just the tip of my clit. It's a hard little nub of flesh, a small, aching erection. Unbearable, to be in this much need.

Probing my slick flesh with my fingers, I arc into my searching hand. Playing with my swollen pussy lips with one hand, tweaking my nipple with the other. And my fevered gaze reflected back to me in the mirror: need and confusion and fury! I fuck myself with my fingers, driving harder, using the heel of my hand to grind against my clit. And it feels so damn good.

Joshua's hands would feel infinitely better.

Yes, Joshua.

"Make me come, Joshua," I whisper into the quiet air.

Sensation builds, pleasure pouring through me, scalding hot. I spread my legs wide, watch my fingers moving in and out of my body, imagine it is his hand working my flesh. If I try hard enough, I can conjure up his scent. Imagine his hazel eyes staring back at me in the mirror. I can imagine his cock hardening as he watches me fuck myself.

Oh, yes . . .

I pull in a deep breath, and I can almost feel his warm hands on my skin.

Joshua . . .

I pump my fingers harder, deeper, hurting myself. But I don't care. He is there with me, fucking me. And pleasure is pouring through my body like an electric current, hot and rich. I'm grating hard against my G-spot on the inside, and my clit on the outside. And I could almost come.

Please . . .

Oh, yes, Joshua. Fuck me. Yes. Make me come, into your hands. Into your mouth . . .

Almost there. And my gaze is locked on my image in the mirror. But it is him watching me, stroking his rigid cock now, thick and beautiful in his hand, the tip wet with pre-come. My mouth waters, I need to suck his flesh so badly, to suck his beautiful cock, to feel it slip between my thighs.

Joshua . . .

Closing my eyes, I see him before me, parting my pussy lips with his fingers, massaging them, massaging my clit. I press harder, faster. Pleasure builds, surging through me, small waves that grow, sharper, pounding through me. And I pause on that keen edge. It is painful. Exquisite.

Joshua, Joshua, Joshua . . .

And just like that, I tumble right over. And all the doubt and fear is washed away in Joshua's face, his scent. And I'm coming, hard, into my hand. Into his hands.

Joshua!

Coming so damn hard I am sobbing his name. Over and over. My legs go loose and I fall into the hard edge of the granite counter. But it doesn't matter. *I came.* And it was so good. For the moment I don't care about anything else.

I stand there, stunned, supporting myself on the cool granite, trying to catch my breath. When I look into the mirror again, my eyes are glittering, my cheeks bright, my mouth looks loose and red, as though someone has kissed me for hours.

If only that were true.

I am in shock. No money on the counter. Just Joshua in my mind, and as good an orgasm as I've ever had with a client.

Impossible.

But my body is still vibrating, small frissons of pleasure hot on my skin. It really did happen.

And I realize that as triumphant as I feel about this lovely, solitary orgasm, the first I've ever had this way, I am still as alone as ever.

———

IT'S SATURDAY AND I'VE slept in. Again. I took all of Friday off, skipping my yoga class, my facial, canceling on a client. I couldn't seem to face getting out of bed.

Joshua called yesterday morning. He left a message, his voice deep, certain, telling me he wants to see me again. Asking me to please call him. So polite, yet commanding at the same time. I didn't call. I can't do it.

I cannot do it.

Fucking torture, frankly, how badly I want to simply hear his voice. Pathetic that I played his message half a dozen times during the day. I finally made myself erase it around ten o'clock last night.

I hate when I brood, not that I do it often. I spent all of yesterday pretending not to: not to brood, not to be obsessed with Joshua's voice over the telephone line. I stayed in bed, drank tea, read magazines, watched a few movies on television, as though I were sick. Maybe I am, on some level.

One of the stations was running a marathon of eighties flicks: *Pretty in Pink, The Breakfast Club.* I have a secret love for these films. They're so innocent. Nothing is ever truly ugly, even the hard parts. Total escapism, which is exactly what I needed. But I can never indulge myself for too long. Today I'm hoping for a client. Either that or I'll be reduced to cleaning out my closets simply to prevent myself from picking up the phone.

I get up and shower, being careful to shave, exfoliate, moisturize, in case I get a call. But I don't stay in the shower for too long; something about the steam, the heat of the water, is too tempting.

I am pretending not to think about Joshua. I did a lousy job of it yesterday. I fought the need to masturbate all day and all night. I'm fighting it again today. I'm too afraid it was just a fluke, that it won't work again. I'm too afraid of being disappointed. And today he is with me, just behind my eyes. As half invisible as this vague sense of need that is heavy in my chest, that has nothing to do with my intense physical attraction to him.

I can pretend all I want, but I'm still thinking about him, every moment. I love that he's so honest, how truth slips from his mouth without him really thinking about it; that's just *him*. I love the way my body responds to him, am shocked by it. I am every bit as shocked at how I respond to him emotionally, and I'm not happy about that at all.

He is a danger to me.

One more reason never to see him again.

I slip into my silk robe, a short kimono-style in a deep plum with cranes flying across the hem. A gift from a client who had just returned from a business trip to Japan. It's the finest quality, like everything else in my life. Except for my actual life, of course. I'm still a prostitute. I'm still a girl from the Valley. From a totally fucked-up family. Still a girl who would have had no life at all if it weren't for this faux glamorous job of mine.

Why am I thinking about these things suddenly? I've

gone years simply floating along, enjoying what I have without question.

Stop it.

Yes, I need to stop thinking. I need to get out of the house, out of my own head.

Moving down the hall into the living room, I check my orchids, my babies, then go into the kitchen to start tea and grab my watering can. I take care of the orchids on the kitchen windowsill first, then go back to the living room, water each of them carefully, sparingly. One of the most common mistakes people make in raising orchids is overwatering. They need a good amount of water, but not too much. Too much and it will kill them.

Too much of a good thing is always dangerous.

And suddenly I am thinking of him again. Joshua.

The kettle whistles and I go back to the kitchen, make my tea. I am just adding a small spoonful of sugar to the cup when my cell phone goes off.

My heart is pounding. Could it be him?

Bad idea, Valentine.

Yes, I know. And he doesn't even have my cell number. My cell phone is only for work. Why am I being so ridiculous?

I pick it up, look at the caller ID.

It's Colin Harper. Movie producer, gorgeous bad boy turned good, married to a beautiful young woman. He is a golden boy with a golden life. But he likes to have anal sex with prostitutes because his golden wife won't give it to him. And it's really a fetish for him. He likes it dirty, loves to call me a whore. I don't mind. I even like it. I can be a bit twisted when it comes to sex. Or maybe I'm just jaded. I think the more sex you have, the more stimulation you need to make it exciting.

I've had a *lot* of sex.

And I'm here to serve, aren't I?

I pick up the phone, take a breath, plaster a smile on my face.

"Colin," I say, making my voice deep, sultry. "So nice to hear from you. What can I do for you?"

"Ah, Val, you know what you can do for me. And you do it so well."

He chuckles at his little joke, and I am going warm with need already. Yes, this is what I need. Sex. Sex for money, to be more exact. Everything simple, clean, straightforward.

"Tell me when and where, Colin."

He loves the cheap little motels that rent by the hour. No Beverly Wilshire or W or Roosevelt for him. His hooker fetish must include the proper setting. So he gives me the name and address of some crap hole off Sunset. Fine with me. I don't really care today, although normally I must admit this bugs me a little. What can I say? I'm a snob about good hotels. I've been trained to be. I would never go anyplace without room service on my own. But this isn't about me, is it?

Or is it?

I could swear I'm about to come just knowing I'm going to see a client today. I'm burning, swollen, throbbing with desire as I hang up the phone.

I slip into a slutty dress, a tight, hot-pink number that pushes my small breasts together, forcing cleavage. I skip the underwear. Not my usual fare, but this is Colin's fantasy, not mine. And I always have wardrobe on hand: the black leather dominatrix gear, the little plaid schoolgirl outfit, the nurse's uniform, the gray pencil skirt and a pair of black-framed glasses for the hot-for-teacher fantasy. The wardrobe, the toys. An enormous supply of condoms and lube. I am as prepared as any good Boy Scout. This is my job.

I remind myself of that as I drive through the underbelly of Hollywood, south of Sunset. This is exactly the reminder I need, I think, as I pull into the parking lot of an old motel with peeling blue paint, half the yellow lights on the neon sign burned out. There's a homeless guy curled up on the sidewalk, his eyes closed. I don't even know if he's asleep or if he's dead. And I feel sort of distant from the whole idea. This is how people like me protect ourselves from the ugliness of our own truth.

But despite the shabby building, the homeless guy, the stench of dirty pavement, I can hardly wait to get to the room with the inevitable worn seventies décor and let Golden Boy fuck me.

I make my way upstairs, and Colin opens the door even before I have a chance to knock.

He's hot. Classic Hollywood good looks, with his perfectly groomed wavy blond hair, chiseled jaw, piercing blue eyes. He looks a hell of a lot like Jude Law. But that's not what turns me on. And he knows it.

Smiling, he grabs my wrist, pulling me into the room. He shoves a wad of hundred-dollar bills into my hand at almost the same moment he unzips his fly, and I'm wet instantly. Then he's pushing me up against the chipped dresser, bending me over, lifting the hem of my dress. I can see him behind me in the mirror, pulling his cock out. He's hard as iron already. I shiver. Lick my lips. Spread my legs wide for him.

He rolls a condom over his dick, spreads a good gob of lube on it, then between my ass cheeks.

Good boy.

Using his fingers, he slips a hand between my thighs from behind, over the slick folds of my pussy. Pleasure ripples through me, and I spread a little wider for him.

I love knowing what he's about to do. I love that he loves it. I love the feeling of the rolled-up hundred-dollar bills clenched in my left hand.

He's rubbing my clit now, tugging on it, and I groan. He's great with his hands, this one. He knows just how to get me there. He knows to bring me almost to orgasm before he puts his cock in my ass.

"You are a dirty little bitch. You love when I fuck you with my hand. Just like this. Don't you, Val?"

His voice is harsh, low, as he pushes two fingers inside me, pleasure shafting deep into my body, and I grind against him.

"Oh, God, I'm going to come," I tell him.

"Not yet. Not until my cock is buried in your ass."

"Do it now. Please."

I mean every word of it. I can hardly hold back. I need to come so badly. *Need* it.

He uses his free hand to spread my ass cheeks, and slips the tip of his cock into that tight entrance. I push back against him.

"Come on. I can take it," I tell him. He's still got his fingers deep inside my pussy, but I need more. And truthfully, Colin isn't very well endowed, so taking him is easy. "Please, baby."

"You're such a whore, Val."

"Yes . . ."

He pushes in an inch. I bear down, opening for him, accepting the head, then the rigid shaft. There is that exquisite sensation of being filled, even by his less-than-impressive dick. And then he pushes a little deeper.

"Oh!"

Joshua's face invading my mind again. Beautiful.

And I'm coming, onto his hand, his cock in my ass,

Joshua's, not Colin's. I'm coming so damn hard it hurts. But I don't care. Even in between spasms I whisper to him, "Really fuck me now. Please."

And he does, sliding his cock in, slowly, deeply. I hear his breath quicken behind me. He's still playing with my clit, and the tension is building again already.

"Yes, that's it. Oh, God, yes . . ." I'm moaning, gasping for breath.

He moves a little faster, rubbing my clit hard.

"Make me come again, baby. I need it," I tell him. Beg him.

Yes, so honest. And I know he'll give me exactly what I ask for, what I need.

He's really fucking me now, slamming into my ass, hurting just a little. But I like it. Need it. And his hand doing its magic, pleasure ramming into me with every stroke of his fingertips, every thrust of his cock.

My legs are shaking. I'm coming again, long, hard waves washing over me.

Joshua . . .

And he goes tense, absolutely rigid all over, yells, "Fuck!" as he comes, shuddering. His hand slides up into my hair, pulling hard, and I'm still shivering with the last ripples of my own climax.

Colin pulls out as soon as he's done coming. There's no lingering for him. But that's fine. I'm not his lover, after all, am I? I don't need the cuddling.

Pulling my dress down, I stuff the wad of cash into my purse, give him a wink in the mirror as I go to the bathroom to clean up.

I don't look too carefully in the mirror as I use a wet wash-cloth to clean myself. I don't want to see myself looking back at me, questioning anything. Not now.

When I come back out Colin has disposed of the condom and is reclined on the bed, fully dressed, not a hair out of place. You'd never know he'd just had sex, except for the glow in his pretty blue eyes.

"That was great, Val."

I smile at him. "Yes it was," I say, meaning it.

I feel good. Better than I have in days. Colin was exactly what I needed.

"How about another round?" I ask him.

He glances at his watch. "I have a meeting in thirty minutes. Can't do it. You really are a dirty little whore, aren't you?"

I smile at him. This is our usual game. And while we're having sex it's fine. It's part of the thrill. And I know he likes it. But for some reason it bothers me when he says it now. I try not to let it show.

What the hell is wrong with me?

Be a pro, Valentine. Get it together.

"So, same time next week?" I ask him playfully.

"I have to be in Vegas next week," he says.

"Ah. Well, plenty of hookers in Vegas. You should be in heaven."

He gets up, comes and sweeps a hand across the back of my neck. "Never as good as you, Val." He reaches into his pocket, pulls out some more cash. "I'm feeling generous today."

Smiling, I take the money. Of course I do. "I should almost be paying you today, Colin," I tell him truthfully. "Almost."

I pat his cheek, my good mood back. I can really feel how loose my body is now.

He looks at his watch again. "Gotta go."

He pats me on the ass as he sweeps past me, opens the door, and walks out.

I stand for a moment in front of the mirror, reapplying my

lip gloss. My brown hair is a little mussed, my green eyes as on fire as Colin's. I don't want to see.

I look down at the bills in my hand, bring them to my face, to my nose, inhale the scent of money. Lowering my hand a little, I press my lips to the paper. And feel that thrill race through me, as it always does.

I am aching again. Insatiable. Luckily it's early enough that I can see another client today. It's Saturday; someone is bound to call.

I am praying that someone calls.

I guess Colin didn't give me what I needed after all. Maybe that's just a lie I tell myself sometimes, when questions, doubts, are hovering in the back of my mind. Like the ones I'm trying desperately to ignore right now.

MY PHONE STARTS RINGING the minute I get home. I kick the front door shut behind me, set the take-out sushi I picked up on my way home on the hall table and pick up without checking the caller ID.

"Hello?"

The voice is deep, with a rough edge that makes me think of good bourbon. "Valentine, it's Joshua."

Shit.

But I'm going warm and loose all over at the sound of his voice, my pulse fluttering. I can't help myself. "Hi. How are you?" I'm buying time. I'm a little in shock. I didn't want to talk to him.

No, that's a lie. I'm dying to talk to him.

"I'm fine, great. How are you doing? I hope you don't mind that I got your number from my caller ID after you called the other night."

God, can I make small talk with this man? I feel utterly unprepared for this. When was the last time I did this sort of dating dance?

"No, of course not; that's fine. And I'm fine, thanks. I was just about to eat."

"And I was about to ask you to dinner."

"Joshua . . ."

"Valentine, did I do something the other night?"

"What? No, of course not."

"Because I like you. But something happened that night, and you haven't returned my calls. I'm not admonishing you. Christ, I don't mean to sound like an asshole."

"You don't." I wave my hand in front of my face, as though he can see me.

I feel absolutely backed into a corner. I can't even come up with an excuse. I don't really want to.

A long pause. Then he says, "I'd like to see you again." Another pause in which I don't say anything. He goes on. "I don't even know why I'm doing this. Pushing the issue. I consider myself to be a fairly intelligent guy. I can usually take a hint. But I need to see you, Valentine. Don't make me fight for it."

A line from that Dylan Thomas poem goes through my mind: *Do not go gentle into that good night.* But the poem was talking about not fighting against death. I really am screwed up. This is only a date, for God's sake!

Pure torture, hearing his voice. My body is on fire.

Yes, see him. Just once. Be with him.

"I want to see you, too, Joshua." It slips out before I can do anything about it. But I can almost feel his radiant smile on the other end of the phone. My heart is absolutely pounding in my chest.

"Good. You won't be sorry." He says it in a low tone that reverberates through my system like a caress. "Do you like Thai?"

"I like everything."

"There's a great place in Malibu I'd love to take you to. Tomorrow night, seven o'clock?"

"Yes, sure. I can meet you if you tell me where it is."

"Or I can pick you up. I'd like to. You can relax on the drive out there, we can talk."

I freeze a little at that idea. Too close, to have him here in my house. But irresistible.

I am going to do this.

"Yes, that sounds fine. Come and pick me up, then." I give him the address.

"I can't wait to see you, Valentine."

God, that voice, like warm whiskey going down my throat. My sex is heating up, pulsing with need. And my head is half empty, I'm trying so hard not to think about what I'm doing.

My cell phone starts ringing, and I pull it out of my purse, check the ID.

Shit.

"Joshua, I have another call and I have to take it. I'm sorry."

"No problem. I'll see you tomorrow evening."

I hang up, staring a moment at my phone. It's Deirdre, my boss. The Broker. "Madam" seems much too tame a term for this elegant, steely woman. Deirdre looks a lot like Catherine Deneuve—a tall, pale blonde with classic features—and has that same aura of regal Ice Queen. She's the one who finds my clients for me, and while regulars can book directly by calling my cell, new clients or anyone who wants an out-of-town trick has to go through The Broker.

This is exactly what I need. I know it. But she's the last person I want to talk to right now.

I flip open the phone.

"Hi, Deirdre."

"Val. I'm glad I caught you." Her voice is cool, her elocution flawless.

"So am I. What do you have for me?"

"I hope you're free tomorrow—and for the next few days. And if you're not, make it happen."

A sinking feeling in the pit of my stomach, but relief, too. "Who is it?"

"Zayed. He wants to send you, Regan, and Rosalyn to New York."

"Ah, I love New York." My palms are sweating. I curl my fingers into a tight little knot.

"You know how he is, Val. He'll want to keep you three cloistered in the hotel room. No shopping, no museums."

"Yes, I know. We'll be the perfect harem, waiting for his every command."

"Yes, you will."

Deirdre never did have a sense of humor.

"When do we leave?"

"Be at LAX tomorrow at nine a.m. He's sending his jet for you. You know what to do, I trust?"

"Of course. Any idea how long he'll want us?"

"It's Zayed. It could be a night. It could be two weeks."

I make a mental note to ask my housekeeper to water my orchids. I'm already thinking of what to pack.

"I'll be prepared. Thank you, Deirdre."

"Just keep him happy, Val."

"As always."

She hangs up, and I see there's a message on my cell. It's

Bennett, probably making up for the night he had to cancel on the opera. Which leads me back to Joshua.

Damn it.

This is exactly why I can't do this. This dating thing. Why I cannot have a personal life. I've been perfectly fine with the way things are for over nine years. Why is everything so complicated suddenly?

I pace the floor, back and forth in front of the window, the scenery outside a blur of green beyond my pots of orchids.

I know why. It's because I actually *like* Joshua, aside from the intense attraction. If it was just sex, I could handle it. And I'm not allowed to feel like this. This is the end for a girl in my position.

But why not? I have plenty of money.

It's not about the money.

No, it's not. It's about condemning myself to a life of disappointing sex. And frankly, I like it far too much to do that to myself. It's the sex. Not that I have any craving for a normal life. For a real relationship. I don't even know what that is.

I have to call him.

Shit. *Shit!*

I pace for another ten minutes before picking up my phone and dialing his number. I don't know what the hell I'm going to tell him.

The conversation is as brief as I can make it. I tell him I have to go away on business and I'm not sure how long I'll be gone, all of which is true. He sounds disappointed, polite. I feel like there's a weight on my chest, pressing down, making it hard to breathe. It's not any better when I hang up the phone.

I try to tell myself this is for the best as I head into the bedroom to pack for the trip: slinky little dresses, my sexiest silk and lace lingerie, my highest heels. A few vibrators, indi-vidual packets of lube, condoms. The equipment of a call girl. A nice little reminder.

I'll be away for a while, be distracted. I'll have some time and distance to get things back in perspective. On some level I think the universe has intervened to keep me from doing what can only be destructive for both of us, ultimately. It wouldn't be fair of me to start something I have no intention of finishing.

But sometimes I just think the universe is fucked.

Chapter Five

Zayed Bin Saleh al-Rahman's private jet is about as luxurious as you'd expect from a member of the Middle Eastern
nobility. Plush seats, far better than anything you'd find in
first class on a commercial flight, a cabin staff of three, two
bedrooms in the back. Decorated in damask-striped wallpa-
per, velvet and silk upholstery, marble-topped tables. And
they have everything on this plane: the best champagne and
liquor—not that I ever drink when flying. The food is gour-
met, the service impeccable. I'd never fly any other way if I
could help it.

We've all brought a good supply of fashion and gossip
magazines and are dressed in our yoga pants and slippers.
We've done this routine before, Regan, Rosalyn, and I. Flown
in Zayed's jet, worked together.

Regan and Rosalyn are my best friends. They're not the
kind of friends I had in elementary school and high school.
No, I left those girls far behind me. Those kinds of innocent

friendships. And of course, I never had sex with any of those girls. But that's part of this business.

I'm not really into girls, although Regan does have a wicked tongue. But I couldn't get into it without the requisite payment. That makes everything work for me. And these girls are hot, I have to admit that. Both gorgeous blondes, Rosalyn with big blue eyes, Regan with almond-shaped green eyes, and both of them with the full breasts I lack. They pose as sisters, but I've always doubted the truth of that. Still, they look enough alike to get away with it, and frankly, the clients love the idea too much to question it.

Like me, they both seem to actually enjoy the work, which makes them popular. We three are the cream of the crop, even in Deirdre's outfit, which is saying a lot. That's why Zayed asks for us. Perfection for our Arab sheik, always.

They're both curled up on the curved couch in their matching pink outfits. Regan is idly paging through a British fashion magazine; she has this idea that the European editions are classier than the American ones. As though reading classy magazines is going to have any impact on what we are. But I never bother her about it. Let her have her illusions.

Rosalyn is painting her nails a pale, shimmery pink that sets off her lightly tanned skin. Her hair is piled on top of her head in a sexy tumble, her head bent, showing a sensual curve of neck. Oh, yes, I can appreciate their beauty. Any woman can feel the beauty of another female, whether they want to admit it or not.

I'm bored. We've only been in the air an hour and I'm restless already, unable to relax. I usually plug in my iPod and drift on the music, but it's not working this time. Pulling off my headset, I sift through the pile of magazines, but nothing interests me until I find an article about a woman in Detroit working with teen girls recovering from drug addiction. I don't know why this particular article touches me, but it does. These girls are so sad, so alone. I know how that feels. And maybe some of it has to do with Joshua talking about the boys he works with on the hockey team. When I get to the part about some of the girls walking the streets for drug money, I go cold all over.

"Someone should help them," I mutter.

Regan looks up from her bright fashion ads. "What?"

I tell them about the article. "Someone should help them. I mean, there's the woman in this article, but how many girls are out there, all over the country? How many of them will end up on the streets?"

"Too many," Rosalyn says, nodding.

"I can't stand it, the idea of it. That there's no one who cares about them. That they're so completely neglected. How many of them will end up pregnant? Dead? It's too awful."

"Why are you getting so worked up, Val?" Regan asks. She's looking at me like I've lost my mind. Maybe I have.

"I don't know. I guess . . . I can see myself in them. And I wish . . . I wish I could help."

"No one would let people like us near their kids."

"Yes, you're probably right. But still . . ."

"Honey, don't worry yourself about it." This is Rosalyn, trying to soothe me. But she always sees the world through the most incredibly rose-tinted glasses. Her personal form of denial that makes this kind of life possible.

I look back down at the magazine, at the pictures of these young girls, their eyes dark, hollow, even as they smile for the camera. I can imagine what they must have been through.

No one would let people like us near their kids.

Yes, Regan's right, I know. And what would I do for them, anyway?

Maybe what Joshua does. Just be there. Listen. Help them to see something of the beauty of the world. I sometimes think that's what saved me from going in an even worse direction. Loving art. Learning about it. Appreciating the beauty.

A quick flash of the pleasure on Joshua's face as he spoke about the boys he works with. One of the things I admire about him.

I flip the magazine closed and stand up, sigh, walk the length of the plane, lean over a seat and stare out a window, watching the earth glide by beneath a thin layer of clouds.

I cannot stop thinking about him.

Stop it!

Shit.

I straighten up, push the closest call button, and ask the girls, "Anyone else want a cocktail?"

Rosalyn glances up from her nails. "A cocktail? We never drink in the air, Val. It makes us puffy. What's up with you?"

I shrug. "I just need to relax, that's all. Come on, drink with me."

"Maybe a small glass of champagne wouldn't hurt," Regan says. "Especially you and your sour mood. Ooh, I feel like a college kid sneaking booze into the dorm." She grins.

"You've never been in a college dorm in your life, Regan," Rosalyn says.

"I have a good imagination. Have a drink with us, Ros."

She sighs. "Okay. I'm sure it won't kill me."

The steward arrives and after some discussion we order champagne. He brings it back within moments, a nice Mumm's

Cuvée. I settle back onto the sofa and take a long sip, feel it loosen my limbs right away. I'm not a big champagne drinker; the bubbles always go right to my head.

"So," Rosalyn asks, "when are you going to tell us what's wrong, Val?"

Jesus. Is it that obvious? Or is it only because these women are my friends? They know me as well as anyone does. As much as I let anyone know me aside from Enzo. And even he only knows so much.

I shrug, pulling up my shoulders, aware suddenly of how tight they are, despite the champagne. "I don't know. Nothing is wrong, really. I've just been . . . a little reflective lately."

Regan shakes her head. "That's not necessarily a good thing for us, Val. We're the live-in-the-moment girls. You know it works better that way."

"I know. I know." I take another sip of the champagne, savor the mild bite of the bubbles on my tongue.

Rosalyn, always the more gentle of the two, asks, "Do you want to tell us what brought this up?"

"I don't know." I stop, let out a long, sighing breath. If there's anyone in the world I can talk to, it's these two women. Why am I so scared? But I need to tell someone before I really do lose my mind. "It's . . . a man."

"A client?" This from Regan, her golden brows shooting up, arching over her green cat-eyes.

"What? No. God, no. Not that this is any better."

Regan asks, "Who then, Val?"

"He's someone I met at the opera. A client canceled last minute and I was there already . . . He was sitting next to me."

I remember that night, how spectacular he looked in his crisp suit. Rugged and elegant at the same time, all calm, cool male. The way he smelled.

"Tell us about him," Rosalyn prompts.

I twist a strand of hair around my finger, take a breath. What is there to say? What do I want to say? There is something sort of lovely about keeping Joshua my little secret. But perhaps something even better in talking about him

"There isn't a whole lot to tell. Joshua is . . . he's beautiful. I don't mean in a pretty-boy way. He's extremely masculine. And he's smart, which always gets me. Kills me, really. Smart and generous. He has this gorgeous, smoky voice . . . We went out once, for drinks, talked. And I could barely concentrate on the conversation. He makes me . . ." I stop, tug on the end of my hair. "God, I don't know. It's better that I've hardly seen him, hardly talked to him. I know I should keep it that way. I should cut things off right now."

"Yes, you probably should," Regan says quietly.

"I know you're right. And I tried to. But I can't seem to do it. I'm too . . . intrigued. He's gotten under my skin somehow." I pause, sip my champagne. "To be honest, I can't stop thinking about him. Like some teenager with a crush. How pathetic is that?"

"Maybe that's all it is," Rosalyn suggests. "A crush."

"Maybe."

"Look, Val," Regan says, her voice urgent. "You cannot be thinking of seeing this guy, starting something with him. We don't do that, have relationships. Date. Real dates, I mean. You cannot reveal yourself to someone not in this business. It's dangerous to you personally, and to the rest of us."

"I know," I say quietly, staring down at the glass in my hand for a moment. But suddenly I'm angry. I raise my gaze to hers. "Don't you think I know all that, Regan? But I can't seem to help myself with this guy. You have no idea how I feel! I barely have a grasp on it myself. But it's not as though I'm trying to start a relationship. I just want to *see* him. Be with him once. Don't I deserve that much? Or are we such damaged goods we deserve nothing just for ourselves? Jesus!"

"Okay, Val. Calm down, honey," Rosalyn comforts, a hand on my arm. She's right. I need to calm down.

"Val, I didn't mean to upset you," Regan says. "I really didn't. I'm just trying to be your reality check. Forgive me for saying so, but it seemed like you needed one."

"I know. God." I run a hand through my hair, my fingers tangling, and pull hard, until my scalp burns. I squeeze my eyes shut for a moment, then open them and find both girls watching me. "I'm sorry, Regan. I didn't mean to snap at you. It's just . . . this guy has done a number on my head. I'm sorry."

"It's okay, hon. Don't worry about it. Just . . . watch yourself, okay? Don't get in any deeper than you already have. You need to protect yourself, Val."

"I will." I nod, sip my champagne, letting the bubbles and the alcohol go to work, loosening my shoulders again. But inside I know it's all bullshit. Because it's too late. I'm already in deep. And I'm not going to stop until I see this thing to whatever sad end is in store for me. Because I know it'll be sad. Fucking story of my life, after all, isn't it?

THE PLAZA IS LIKE no other hotel in the world. Old-world elegance, done even better than in Europe. This, of course, is where Zayed has his New York apartment.

We take the elevator up and the bellman lets us in, turning on lights, opening curtains to the view of Central Park South, with the small lake, the sweep of green lawn. It's late in the afternoon, and the sun is just beginning to lower in the sky, to change colors, going soft and gold and watery.

That pale golden light illuminates Zayed's apartment, which is done in classic Plaza style: everything in deep blue and cream damask, heavy gold braid, ornate King Louis pieces everywhere, crystal chandeliers suspended over the enormous, high-ceilinged rooms. The drapes look as though they weigh a ton, the fabric is so heavy and lush. The room is perfectly silent, nothing but the whisper of the brass luggage carts rolling over the plush carpet behind us.

The room steward asks, "Shall we run a bath for any of you?"

"Yes, please," Rosalyn says, and I nod agreement.

"Not for me, thank you." Regan flops down on a creamy sofa perched on delicate, carved legs. "I'm starving, though. Send up a pot of black tea and some of those currant scones, if they're fresh."

"Right away, miss."

The white-jacketed steward nods sharply, and one of his team goes off to run our baths, while the third makes a note; the food order, I imagine.

"May I get you anything else, ladies?"

"Tea for me, as well," I tell him. "Thank you."

There is nothing more luxurious than a pot of tea at the Plaza. I don't know why. It's English, rich and delicate all at the same time. It's a favorite indulgence of ours.

Since Zayed owns a suite here, there is no need to tip the bellmen; everything is taken care of. They finish their business and leave.

I pull a few items from my cosmetics case, including my favorite lilac bath salts, a special brand I get from France.

Mostly I adore it for the beautiful packaging, but it does smell lovely, and it makes my skin soft. In the white marble bathroom I strip off my plane-weary clothes, pour a handful of the salts into the tub, and slip down into the steaming water.

The bathrooms at the Plaza are truly spectacular, everything done in slabs of snow-white marble, the fixtures covered in fourteen-carat gold. Even the deep, enormous tub is trimmed in golden scrollwork, like something you'd see at Versailles.

I love this kind of luxury. My life has accustomed me to it. On the inside, though, there is still a part of me that sometimes can't believe I'm here. Maybe that makes me appreciate it more?

Maybe. When I'm not busy questioning how someone like me could possibly deserve it, which I do all too often.

But today I don't want to linger on that thought pattern. The warm, scented water feels too good. And these next days will be pure decadence. No, the thing to do is to immerse myself in the experience. This is the good part of my life: the luxury, the sex. Why shouldn't I enjoy it as much as possible?

I take a sponge, squeeze some liquid soap onto it, and run it over my skin. The soap is like satin, all cool and slippery. Lovely. And as I lean my head against a rolled-up towel thoughtfully arranged by the room steward, I can't help but see Joshua's face, his dark, gleaming eyes, his lush mouth.

I'm getting turned on simply imagining his face; that and the silky sponge gliding over my skin, the heat of the water. And in my mind he is there with me, naked, wet.

Oh, yes.

He reaches out and strokes the curve of my shoulder, then lower, over the swell of one breast, and my nipples tighten.

Joshua . . .

I slide the sponge over my breasts, my nipples hardening quickly. There is an insistent ache between my thighs, a craving which grows sharper and sharper. Moving the sponge down between my legs, I stroke my swelling sex with it. And it's too good: the gentle touch of the sponge, his face in my mind. I need to come, so badly it's like a knife blade pressing against the throbbing lips of my sex.

I rub harder, pressing the sponge onto my clit, moan softly.

The door swings open and Regan is there, a cup of tea in her hand.

"Here, I thought you might want your tea. Just a little sugar, right?"

"Oh, right. Thanks."

I sit up, dropping the sponge into the water. Regan's green eyes take in my hardened nipples, but she doesn't say anything. Not that I care; it's nothing she hasn't seen before.

She sets the cup on a small vanity stool next to the tub. "I'm going to take a quick nap. See you later, okay?"

"Yes, sure."

"I have a feeling this is going to be a busy night. You know how Zayed is. You should be . . . rested, Val." She grins at me, and I understand she knows exactly what was going on in here before she came in.

She's right. Zayed will keep us working for hours, and I'd better have that keen sexual edge to feed on. I pick up my tea instead of the sponge, which is what I'd really like to do. Yes, slide that sponge over my still-aching mound, bring myself to orgasm with Joshua's beautiful face, his voice, in my mind.

But I'm a professional. That means something in this business, regardless of what most of the world might think. I refuse to disappoint.

I sigh softly, sip my tea. It's perfect, as always. As I should be. As I *will* be, for Zayed tonight.

I push thoughts of Joshua to the back of my mind. I try to, anyway. But the warm water is too much like silk against my skin. I swear I can feel it moving between my thighs like some lovely, ghostly tongue.

I stand, get out of the bath, and dry myself off.

Joshua Spencer has ruined everything for me. But I'm not angry. I'm simply yearning, in a way I never have in my entire life. I am helpless against it, this yearning. And I don't like it one bit.

AT EIGHT O'CLOCK THAT night we are all three lined up in the living room of the suite, ready for Zayed to come through the door. He's been in his room freshening up, having used a private entrance, and we have been instructed to wait here for him. A lavish meal sits on a table behind us. We are all dressed in Zayed's favorite lingerie, all jewel-toned silk trimmed in lace, our hair up, exactly as he likes it. We are his perfect little harem.

I am trembling already, my body humming with pent-up lust ever since my bath. I can smell Regan's perfume, Rosalyn's shampoo, as they stand next to me, clean and beautiful, and lush, female curves.

I wonder which one of them will use her mouth on me tonight?

Zayed comes into the room, smiling. His face was handsome once; now it is a bit weathered, but his teeth are still a glorious flash of white against his brown skin, and his eyes, so dark they are nearly black, sparkle with intelligence. He is not a large man, but he radiates power, something I always find attractive. He is in his early sixties, I would guess. Elegant, as most of my clients are. He carries himself like royalty, which apparently he is, in his country. He wears American suits, always dark, formal, with a bright silk tie, but he's removed it now in order to relax and enjoy his meal with his private *houris*. His head is uncovered, which happens only in privacy.

I like Zayed. We all do. He's kind to us. Demanding yet gentle. He's a true sybarite, and he loves nothing more than to shower that opulence on us.

"Good evening, Zayed," we all say, like wind-up dolls, making him grin widely.

"Good evening, ladies. Come, let us eat."

We sit down at the table, with me on his right, Rosalyn on his left looking lovely in her deep purple silk. Regan pushes Rosalyn's plate over and places her bottom right on the table by Zayed's arm.

"Let me feed our tired sheik," she says, saucy, flirtatious.

Zayed's eyes twinkle, and he pats her smooth, tan thigh. "You know just how to please me."

And we do.

We spend the meal feeding him tidbits of meat, tiny, tenderly cooked carrots, dates, and goat cheese, and feeding each other, which he particularly loves to see.

Zayed is an unashamed voyeur, which is mostly what we're here for. Luckily, being watched thrills me. Even having him watch us eat is exciting: the widening of his eyes as Rosalyn slips a date between my lips and I suck on her fingertips, holding her hand there with my own.

Her hands are soft, her skin fragrant, and my sex swells in anticipation of the night to come.

The meal is festive—food, wine—and we listen as Zayed tells us of his day. It's all international business, and I must admit I don't listen too carefully tonight. My mind, my body, are preoccupied with the sensuality of the feast before us, the brush of Regan's breast as she leans over to pick something from my plate.

The meal lasts for well over an hour before Rosalyn stands up, moves behind Zayed's chair, and gently slips his suit jacket from his shoulders.

"How about a little entertainment for you, Zayed?"

"That would be excellent."

He stands and leads us all into the bedroom. The bed is an enormous affair, all done in the purest white linen and piled with golden pillows, with a tall golden scroll-worked headboard reminiscent of the boudoirs of kings and queens, and flanked by those heavy blue and gold damask curtains. Truly a bed for royalty. But tonight it will hold three whores while we entertain our royal client.

I shiver all over, just a small trembling beneath my skin.

The three of us move to the bed while Zayed settles into a large, plush armchair which has already been pulled to one side of the bed. We kick our shoes off but don't strip down just yet; that's something Zayed will want to draw out, savor.

Rosalyn, ever passive, lays back against the pillows, and I step out of my black silk G-string before crawling onto the bed. I go to her on my hands and knees, my naked sex peeking out from beneath my emerald green silk chemise; I can feel the warm air whisper over my flesh, teasing.

Rosalyn opens her arms for me and I press up against her, my small breasts crushed against the lush flesh of her chest. Her nipples grow hard as I hold still for a few moments, smiling at her. Then her eyes close and she leans her head against the pillows, offering her long, lovely throat to me. I lean in, trail soft kisses over her skin. Skin like a doll's: that fine, that smooth. I dart my tongue out, taste her sweet flesh, feel a ripple of excitement course through me as I hear a soft moan from our client. I lift my head to peek at him and see Regan standing by his chair, massaging his shoulder with one hand. His arm is looped around her narrow waist, his hand caressing her thigh beneath the hem of her pale blue silk slip. He grins at me, nods his head.

"Please continue, my lovelies."

I turn back to Rosalyn, and her blue eyes are open once more. I press my lips to hers, raspberry lip gloss mingling in a sticky warmth. Kissing a woman is so very different from kissing a man. So much softer. Although it's been a long time since I've kissed a man. We don't do that with our clients. But we do kiss each other, during these sorts of little orgies. The clients love it. I enjoy it, myself. And Rosalyn knows how to kiss, her mouth all soft, moist heat, her tongue gentle, teasing as it slides between my parted lips.

My body is heating up, my sex going wet, just from kissing her, from her breasts crushed against mine, from the knowledge of Zayed watching us. Lusting for us. From knowing I'll be generously paid for what I am about to do.

Oh, yes.

I open my lips wider, really go in, probing her mouth with my tongue, thrusting as though my tongue is a small, pumping cock, which I know she loves. Her hands come up and slide my chemise up my thighs, baring my naked ass, my pussy, to Zayed's view. I wiggle a little for him, for her. It's all the same already.

Her hands are cool and smooth against my skin. And suddenly there is another pair of hands on my bare flesh, soft as only a woman's can be, and I know Regan is touching me. Taking her cue, Rosalyn pulls my chemise over my head, breaking our kiss for a moment. Then I'm back on her, one hand going to the firm mound of her breast. Her nipple is hard, and I tease it through the bright purple silk for a few moments, pinching, pulling. She moans, a sound low in her throat, and beneath me I feel her hips arc up toward my body.

Regan's hands are moving over my skin, lighting up the nerves all over. My sex is slick, pulsing with need already. And when Regan moves her hands in between my thighs, parting the lips of my sex with her thumbs, I gasp into Rosalyn's mouth. That only makes her kiss me harder and push her breast into my hand. I slide her shoulder straps off, one at a time, baring her beautiful breasts.

"Ah, yes," Zayed murmurs behind us.

Pulling away from Rosalyn's mouth, I lower my head and bury my face between those smooth mounds of flesh. I inhale her perfume, feminine, subtle, fill my senses with it, with that taboo feeling I always get when I fuck a woman. I'm shaking a little all over, with Rosalyn's flesh before me, Regan's fingers massaging my pussy lips. I surge back into her clever hands, and she pushes one fingertip inside me.

"Oh, that's good," I moan, and she moves deeper.

"Come on, Val," Rosalyn begs me, her voice soft, breathy. "Come on, suck my tits. Pretty please, Val."

I bend to my task, pulling one taut nipple into my mouth. Rosalyn has lovely, large, pink nipples, so pale normally, but they go all dark and rosy when she's excited. Her flesh fills my mouth, and she squirms beneath me. It's hard to concentrate with Regan working my pussy with her fingertips. I almost want to come already. I feel like I could come forever tonight.

Regan adds another finger, then another, filling me, and suddenly I am transported back to my bath earlier tonight, and Joshua's face fills my mind as, bit by bit, Regan's fingers fill my sex, going deeper, harder.

I groan against Rosalyn's breast, pull away and move to the other side. I pull the nipple in, taking it between my teeth. Her hands go into my hair as I suck, pulling, pulling, lengthening her hard pink flesh.

"Yeah, Val. Harder," she gasps. "I need you to fuck me, Val. Please."

I think of saying this to Joshua as I reach down and pull her silky slip up around her waist and immediately plunge two fingers into her wet heat. Her sex is all warm velvet as I thrust into her, using my thumb to massage her clit.

"Oh, yeah . . ."

Her voice is low, her breath catching as she tilts her hips into my hand, just as I would if it were Joshua working me the way I am Rosalyn, the way Regan works me with her softly rough hands. We are one female organ now, all nipples and pussy and drenched heat.

"Come, my ladies," Zayed orders us. "I want to see you come."

I focus, sucking hard on her nipple, which has become almost impossibly long in my mouth. And I pump my fingers into her. Her hips are moving, her rhythm the same as my own as Regan thrusts inside me. I am so damn wet, I can feel my juices trickling down my thighs. I arch my back, pushing onto those impaling fingers as I work Rosalyn harder, grinding onto her clitoris with my thumb.

Then she's panting, gripping my hair tightly, and I know she's about to climax. She lets out a long keening moan, her body arches into mine, and she's trembling, her sex clenching around my thrusting hand. I suck hard on her tit; I know she loves it when she's coming, loves it to almost hurt. A few more cries and she goes limp. I let her nipple slip from my lips and fall onto her breasts, pillowing my head on her fragrant flesh, my ass high in the air. Regan renews her efforts now, using both hands: one to hold my pussy lips wide open for Zayed to view, one hand thrusting inside me.

"Beautiful, Val," Zayed says quietly, his voice raw with lust.

I arch harder into Regan's hand, and once more Joshua's face comes into my mind. I don't know why it happens now. I don't care. Pleasure is arcing through me like some inevitable electrical current. And I can't stop the climax that comes hammering down on my body like thunder: that powerful, that relentless.

"Oh! Oh, oh, oh . . ."

And I'm coming and coming, my sex dripping onto Regan's lovely hands . . . Joshua's hands. I'm pushing back against her, needing to be filled, needing to be fucked. By him. By *him!*

"Oh, yes!"

Pleasure, intense, keen, shafting into my body in wave after wave. I am left shaking, weak. But Zayed is not done with us.

"Our poor Regan is left out," Zayed complains. "I want to see your lovely face between her legs, Val," he tells me, his voice rough with need, a sensation that reverberates through me as I hear him speak. "I want to see you make her come."

There is a shifting of bodies as Rosalyn rolls to one side, and in a moment Regan's naked body is laid out beneath me. I part her thighs with a shaking hand and lower my face, breathe in the fragrance of her excitement, like the scent of the ocean.

I move up, tugging at her silky blue slip, and she helps me to pull it over her head. She has a truly spectacular body. Her breasts are a bit smaller than Rosalyn's, yet still quite lush and full, with tight, dusky nipples. She's all long, lean limbs, a bit on the athletic side, without Rosalyn's rounded curves. More like me, but with those gorgeous breasts. I find I can hardly wait to touch her.

I lean in and run my tongue between those lovely, fleshy mounds, following with my hands. I pause to tweak her nipples, hard. She likes things a little rough, and I am all too happy to oblige. She reaches up and grabs my breasts in her hands, squeezes my nipples until I wince, making Zayed and Rosalyn laugh.

I grin at Regan. "Oh, you're in trouble now," I tell her, hearing Zayed chuckle.

"You must punish her now, Val," he tells me.

Straddling Regan's body, I sit back on my knees, watching her face. Her green eyes are absolutely glowing.

"As you wish, Zayed," I say, turning to smile at him over my shoulder.

Reaching for Regan's breasts again, I squeeze them in my palms roughly. She's squirming beneath me, but I know it's all show. She's smiling, and her nipples have gone dark and hard as two large pebbles. I grind my naked sex against hers, feel the slick heat that is as much hers as it is my own. Oh, yes, she loves this, the rough play. So do I.

"With your beautiful mouth, Val," Zayed instructs me.

Shifting once more, I lay my body over Regan's, skin to skin, breasts to breasts, and she lets out a groan. She is every bit as hot as I am; I can feel the need coming off her body in undulating waves. I feel it as though it is my own, and it is.

Sliding down, inch by inch, I trail my tongue between her breasts, over her rib cage, her taut belly, until I am at the apex of her thighs.

Her sex is mostly shaved, nearly as naked as my own, with just a narrow strip of silky blond hair in the center. Her lips are pink and swollen, glistening with her juices. My own sex clenches in response as I bend to my task.

First a gentle blowing as she spreads her thighs for me, wider and wider, opening herself to me, and to Zayed's view. A quick glance at him and I see Rosalyn is perched on the arm of his chair, naked, her hand working in his lap. Good girl. Our poor Zayed has an erection issue and it can take him a very long time to get off, if he is able to at all. But I think we will be able to take him there tonight.

I turn back to Regan. Inadvertently, my pause has been a tease for her. But I like to torture her a little.

I blow on her flesh again, and she squirms. I smile before letting my tongue dart out. Just one small taste before I pull back.

"Oh, come on, Val. Don't torture me."

More laughter from Zayed, but that husky edge is there in his voice. Oh, yes, he's as turned on as we are.

Using my fingers, I pinch her pussy lips together, then begin to tug on them, hard. She groans, and I pinch harder, until I know it really hurts. I also know how much she loves this. She's drenched, her juices soaking the pure white coverlet beneath us. I bend my head and lick her slit, one long, torturous stroke, pinching still. She groans louder. And my own sex is full, needy. Needing to come again.

I really go to work then, pinching the lips of her wet sex, lapping at her clit with my tongue, hard and fast. Soon she is moaning, panting, writhing.

"God, Val, make me come. Yes, that's it. Make it hurt. Make me come. Oh!"

I plunge three fingers deep inside her, still pinching one

side of her swollen labia and sucking hard on her clit now, imagining that hardened nub of flesh is Joshua's cock in my mouth.

Oh, yes . . .

And I can almost come myself, just from this: Regan's hard little clit in my mouth, her moans, imagining the smooth flesh of Joshua's cock, his come spurting down my throat like liquid pearls . . .

I feel a hand between my legs suddenly, and as Regan comes, Zayed pries me open with his strong fingers, pulling on my clit expertly. My body explodes as Regan and I shatter together, fireworks going off behind my closed eyes. And it is as though Joshua is here with me, doing these things, as though it is *him* making me come like this. And in some sense it is. Always, lately. But it's too hard to think about it now.

I roll over onto my back, gasping, trying to catch my breath.

"You bitch," Regan whispers, not unhappily.

I glance over at her, and she's grinning, her face glowing. She looks as used as I feel, but we're not done yet. Rosalyn has helped Zayed to undress, and he is climbing onto the bed, leaning against the pillows. And we all descend upon him and his poor, half-hard cock. But we can make him come without a full erection. We are experts, after all.

Regan takes the lead, as she so often does, taking his cock in her mouth. Rosalyn is pinching his dark nipples between her fingers, tugging and rolling them, and I go in and massage his balls with my hand.

We all whisper words of encouragement to him, and after a while Regan and I change places. I pull his cock into my mouth, which is mostly hard now and really rather pretty: all deep golden brown and finely shaped, even beneath the condom Rosalyn has put on him. I suck hard, moving in a smooth, steady motion. And again it is Joshua's cock in my mouth. And I could almost come.

Yes, come for me, Joshua . . .

It's really working tonight, luckily for us, and it's not long before Zayed goes rock-hard between my lips, his body stiffening all over, and he comes, all heat and thrusting need, his erection hitting the back of my throat. My eyes watering, I take it, not wanting to disappoint him.

After, we all lie on the bed together while Rosalyn goes to get a warm towel for our exhausted nobleman. And he has been noble tonight, which makes me happy.

Except for a strange sensation of emptiness. Because what I really want is for it to be Joshua Spencer lying here beside me, naked and sated.

I try to shake off the sensation, but it won't go. And I feel . . . sad. Sad that I can no longer be happy with this life. Sad because I know I could never be happy with Joshua—and he could never be happy with a woman like me.

Which leaves me with what?

Nothing.

I roll onto my side, hiding my face from Zayed and the other girls as they talk softly. I squeeze my eyes shut, willing this feeling to go away.

I want to talk to him, see him.

No.

Yes!

This is hopeless.

"Val, I'd like some wine," Zayed says to me.

"Of course. I'll be right back."

I get up, naked, go into the other room to get it, and

just like that I am back on duty. Simply doing my job, as I always do.

The thing is, something is different. Something is missing. Despite my endless ability to climax, despite the postorgasm buzz still moving through my body, I no longer love being here.

My stomach tightens into a hard, grasping knot and a wave of nausea sweeps over me. I find the bottle of wine, grip it in my hand until my fingers hurt.

What the fuck am I going to do now?

Chapter Six

"JOSHUA?"

"Yes, this is Joshua."

God, his voice! Like cool water sluicing over my skin, making me shiver.

"It's Valentine."

"Valentine. I thought you were away working."

"I am. I'm in New York." I'm lying in bed in my room in Zayed's apartment. It's nearly midnight and everyone else has gone to sleep. I should absolutely not be doing this, calling Joshua when I'm working. When I am basically some other man's property. When my time is paid for. But I can't help myself. "I hope I'm not calling too late."

"No, not at all. It's still early here. How are you?"

"I'm fine." I pause. Why do I need to tell him the truth? "Actually, I'm not fine."

"Tell me what's wrong."

I can hear the sincerity in his voice, and it makes my pulse flutter as much as the subtle tone of command.

"I just . . . I needed to talk to you. I know that sounds silly. But I just . . . did."

He's quiet a moment. "I like that," he says, his voice low, flirty. "I'm glad you called. I was disappointed you had to cancel our date."

"So was I. I mean that. I'm sorry."

"No need to apologize. You're here now, calling me. And not because I asked you to, which is even better. What have you been doing?"

God, if he only knew. What am I going to say? That I've spent my evening in bed with two girls and an old man? That I've come over and over thinking of *him* while my friends go down on me? That I'm here because I make a ridiculous amount of money fucking and sucking everyone?

As much as I don't want to lie to him, as much as I am oddly compelled to tell him the truth, there is no way I can do it.

"I had a late dinner with some people, and now I'm in my room. I feel . . . alone here." That much is true. I pause, twist the braided trim on the edge of the silk duvet between my fingertips. "I've been thinking about you."

"I've been thinking about you, too. Can't seem to get you out of my head. I hope you don't mind my telling you that."

"I don't mind at all. I'm having the same problem, actually."

Am I really admitting these things to him?

"Ah, you know how to get to me, don't you, Valentine?"

"Do I?" I'm not being coy. I really need to know.

"Ever since the first moment I laid eyes on you, as corny as that sounds."

I'm blushing. I can't help it. "So, what was your day like?" I ask him.

"Too long. I spent hours on the phone today trying to

work out issues with this project in Sacramento. But you don't want to hear about that. I'd rather talk about you."

"There isn't much to talk about."

He's quiet again, but I can hear him breathing, a slow, steady cadence.

"Valentine," he says quietly, "please don't do that again. Shut me out. Okay?"

Shit.

My fingers tighten on the phone. But even though my stomach is in knots, I know this is exactly what I wanted. To talk to him, *really* talk to him. Maybe I'm testing him a little. Maybe I'm testing myself. But I want him to know about me. To know some things, anyway.

"I'm not the kind of person who's used to opening up to people. I have a tendency to . . . keep everyone at arm's length."

I can't believe I'm saying even this much.

He's quiet, thinking. "There were a few moments when we were at Yamashiro the other night when I felt you letting me in."

"Yes."

"Was that terrible? Did you go home and regret doing that?"

"To be honest, part of me did, yes. But I was also glad. At least, I was when I thought about it later." I pause, pressing the phone hard against my cheek. "Joshua, I don't mean to sound like some . . . like I'm completely neurotic. I'm just . . . a bit shut down. I can admit that much. The nature of my life has made me close off on a lot of levels. But something about you makes me feel as though I can talk to you. Makes me want to. I think that's why I called tonight."

That, and my total sexual obsession with this man.

"That's good, isn't it?" he asks.

"I think so. But it also feels dangerous to me."

"It's good to live outside the boundaries that make us feel safe sometimes. It's important. We have to challenge ourselves. That's what living life is all about."

"Maybe I haven't been living life, as you say. Not in the way I should be."

"It's not too late, Valentine. You can change any time you decide to. It's all about choosing to do it. That's something I've learned in the last few years."

He's right. God, he's right. But talking about all this makes me feel as though there's a weight on my chest, making it hard to draw a full breath. Still, it's all sort of pouring out now. Terrifying. Necessary.

"Change is so scary for me. I spent most of my childhood never knowing what to expect from one moment to the next. I think as an adult I've set up my life so that I have total control over it. I don't like to leave too much to chance."

"Maybe, in doing that, you've closed too many doors," he suggests quietly.

"Maybe. No. It's true." I pause, take a sip of water from the glass the room steward set beside my bed when he came to turn down the covers earlier. "I think you're a very wise man."

"I don't know about wise. But I think about these things. Too much, my sister always tells me. It drives her crazy, my analyzing."

It feels good, talking with him. Even going over some of the scary stuff. I realize my body has relaxed. It's as though he and I are in some secret place, hidden away from the rest of the world.

"Let's change the subject, Joshua, okay? I want to hear about what it was like for you, growing up."

"It wasn't all that interesting. I had a pretty standard-issue childhood. It was happy. But happy doesn't make for a great story."

"It does for me. That's like some sort of fantasy to me, people who had a normal life, an intact family."

"Alright. Okay." I hear some faint sound in the background: liquid swirling in a glass.

"What are you doing, Joshua?"

"Pouring myself a drink."

"Ah. A good scotch, single malt."

"How did you know?"

"I remember from the opera."

"You're very observant."

"It's my job to be." Damn it! I've slipped. I quickly redirect his attention. "So, tell me about your childhood, your family. I want to know what your life was like."

"We had a good life. Nice house, good schools. My parents were great. Dad worked a lot, but when he was home he was really present." He stops for a few moments, as though he's considering his words, and I can hear the gentle rhythm of his breath if I listen carefully. "I guess I didn't think about it at the time, about how lucky I was. I know other people's fathers weren't as involved as mine. He spent time with us. He'd take me to ball games, fishing. That was his thing, fishing. I didn't like it all that much, but I didn't care, as long as we got to spend time together. He taught me a lot. He taught me to be hardworking. To be a good person. To be a man. I've tried to follow his example. It's important to me."

"And your mother?"

"Mom is an amazing woman. She's strong." He's quiet

again, and I can hear the ice cubes sliding in his glass as he sips his scotch. I remember the scent of it on him at the opera, and a surge of need washes over my body as he continues. "The thing with my parents, though, was that they loved each other. I mean, they were crazy about each other in a way you don't see too often."

"I don't think I've ever seen that. I don't know that I really believe it's possible, that sort of true, lasting happiness."

"Oh, it's real. I think it's hard to find, but one thing I learned from them is to believe in that kind of love."

"Have you ever found it?"

I hold my breath, waiting for his answer. Why does it feel so important? I want him to tell me he's never loved a woman before. At the same time, he deserves that, if anyone does.

"I thought I had a few times . . ."

He trails off, but not before I've heard some trace of pain in his voice.

"You don't have to tell me," I say. "We all have our secrets."

"No, it's no secret. I've been through a few serious relationships, and they've all ended badly." He pauses a moment. "Not badly, exactly. They've always just ended in . . . indifference. But that's the saddest thing to me. That's what hurt the most. That I've never found what my parents had. And that it was probably my own fault, because of . . . who I've been in those relationships. So I guess the answer is no, I haven't really been in love. Not like that. Other than my last girlfriend, the women I've been with have always been the ones to break things off, because I . . . I wasn't really there. Not in the way I should have been. I can't blame them. I took a long time off relationships before this last one. And then I realized how unfair it was, for me to be with this woman who loved me when I didn't feel the same way. This time, I made the decision to end things. I wanted us both to have a chance to find that kind of love." He's quiet again for several moments. "Maybe I'm aiming too high, trying to live up to this iconic love my parents had. What they had was . . . beautiful. I don't know. I can't help wanting that, at some point in my life."

We're both quiet for a few moments. My head is spinning. He is the most amazing man. So sincere. So honest.

Far too good for a whore like me.

Stop it!

I don't want to think about that right now. I simply want to enjoy getting to know him.

"Thank you, Joshua. For telling me all this."

"You're easy to talk to. I can't wait to see you, to talk to you in person again. When will you be back in L.A.?"

"I'm not sure yet."

"I wish you were here with me now," he says, his tone lowering. That husky edge is back, and that warmth I felt earlier kicks up a few notches, my nipples going hard beneath the Egyptian cotton bed linens.

"I wish I was, too. I like talking with you. You make me want to tell you . . . everything."

"Then tell me something." His voice is full of need, matching my own.

I think back to that evening in the restaurant bar, that rush of lust reverberating through my veins, his scent, his eyes on me.

"When we were at Yamashiro the other night . . ."

"What? Tell me."

"I could barely stand to sit so close to you."

"I know exactly what you mean. I was so damn attracted

to you. When you left I thought I was going to lose it. I couldn't stop thinking that I never got to kiss you."

"I'm sorry. I had to go."

"I know, you weren't feeling well—"

"No. That wasn't it. I had to leave because . . . I wanted you too much. And it scared me."

He's quiet while I lie in the big bed, my heart hammering, my pulse hot, needy.

"Jesus, Valentine." A small groan. "I wanted you so badly. I still do. So damn frustrating that you're so far away. If you were here . . ."

"If I was there . . . what?"

He lets out another groan. "What I would do if you were here . . ."

I smile, move my hand down between my aching thighs, brushing the swollen lips of my sex, teasing.

"I'll tell you something, Joshua. That night, when I rushed off to the ladies' room, I locked myself in a stall and slipped my fingers beneath my panties . . ."

"God, you're killing me, Valentine." A long pause, then, quietly, "Did you come?"

"No. But I wanted to. Needed to."

"I've always fantasized about having sex in a public bathroom. Quick and hard up against the wall, then sneak out like nothing ever happened. Thinking about you in there, touching yourself . . . that image is going to be in my head for the rest of my life."

"I've fantasized about you ever since I met you." Saying it out loud is so good, I can barely breathe. "What else have you fantasized about?"

"Turning you over my knee, slipping your dress up, maybe

spanking you a little while I drive my fingers into you." I can hear his ragged breath. "Valentine, are you wet?"

"Oh, yes . . ."

"Are you touching yourself?"

"Yes . . ." I slide my fingers over my soaking slit, push two fingers inside, feel my own body clenching. "Are you?"

"Yeah. If I close my eyes I can almost feel your skin. I can almost feel myself inside you."

"God, Joshua." I'm stroking harder now, my thighs falling open, my fingers alternately dipping inside, then rubbing my clit. I'm shivering with desire, my hips arcing. "Talk to me, please."

"I'm so damn hard. And you are so God damn beautiful, Valentine. I just want to thrust into you, to feel you inside, all soft and wet. Jesus . . ."

"Joshua, I'm going to come."

I can hardly believe it. But his voice is in my head, in my body, making me shiver with need, desire coursing through me like liquid fire.

"Yes, come . . . I'm coming . . ."

I moan as a wall of pleasure hits me, shuddering as it flows through my veins, hot and electric. His groans drive me on, and I'm coming, coming, into my hand, into his hand . . .

"Valentine!"

Still trembling, I close my eyes, picture his face behind the brilliant flashes of light beneath my lids. "Joshua . . ."

For several moments there is no sound but our joined, panting breath. My head is spinning. How is it that I can come, suddenly? Something about Joshua, but I can't figure it out right now. I'm afraid if I question it, it'll go away, these lovely, unpaid orgasms. But I know if I ever feel his hands on me, I will come with him. Terrifying. Wonderful.

"Tell me you'll call me when you get back. Tell me you'll see me." There is a gasping desperation in his voice.

"Yes. I'll call you, see you. I need to see you."

"I want you. I don't know if I can see you again and not touch you. Not after this."

God, his voice goes through me like a hand stroking over my bare flesh. I am burning with need simply thinking about seeing him, imagining his face, his scent.

"Joshua . . ." But I don't know what to say. My voice is so shaky I can barely speak.

"Do you still want to see me?" It's more a command than a question.

"Yes!" My voice is a quiet hiss. I've never wanted anything so much in my life.

"Good." I hear him take a sip of his drink. "When you get back, you'll know what to expect."

There is so much in that simple remark, in the implication in his tone. Oh yes, I'll know what to expect. My skin is going damp and taut all over, my sex filling, swelling once more. I ache for him in a way I have never ached for any other man.

"Joshua?"

"Yes?"

"I can hardly wait to see you."

I don't care that I sound desperate. I *am* desperate.

"I can't wait to see you, either, Valentine."

I love the sound of my name on his lips. I love the tone of his deep, husky voice. I'm shaking all over now, wishing for his touch. I need to feel his hands on my body.

"Do you need to go, Valentine? It's late there."

It is. But I don't care.

"I just want to talk to you," I tell him. I don't know where all this honesty has come from.

"What do you want to talk about?"

I laugh a little roughly. "Oh, I don't think I can do this again already."

"Ah, Valentine." His tone drops, going deeper, softer. "I really cannot wait to see you. To touch you. Kiss you."

"Oh, don't do this to me," I groan, and he laughs on the other end, so far away in California.

"Why don't we leave it here for now?" he says. "It'll make it even better when you get back to L.A."

"I'll call as soon as I'm back."

"Yes, I think you will. Have a good night, Valentine. Sweet dreams. Mine will be."

"Good night, Joshua."

I don't care that what I've done, calling him, having phone sex with him, for God's sake, is entirely forbidden. I don't care that my client sleeps in the next room. All I care about is seeing him, being with him.

Joshua.

I am a woman obsessed. I am risking everything. None of that matters.

For the first time in my life, I am being completely self-indulgent. I will deal with the fallout later. And I know there will be fallout. I'm scared to death. Out of control. But I can't help myself. I'm going numb, trying to figure it all out, and still in a sex coma from my climax. There's so much going on in my mind, in my body. Everything is changing, and it's happened so fast, it's making my head spin.

Fuck it. This is just for me. Even if it means losing the life I've spent years building. And it just may mean that. It probably will.

THE TRIP HOME TO L.A. seemed to take forever. We had weather problems in New York and it took hours to get clearance for takeoff. Finally at home, I dump my luggage in the bedroom; I'll unpack tomorrow. I'm far too tired tonight, too travel-weary.

The rest of the trip and the journey itself was unremarkable. Zayed kept us with him for another four days. Nothing notable. Not for me, anyway. Nightly orgies, the occasional midday blow job between meetings and lunches in which it took all three of us to get him off. All three of us locked in the hotel suite like the favorite pet cats. Here, kitty, kitty. Come suck my dick.

Shit. When did I become so bitter?

I'd wanted to call Joshua again. Every day. But I didn't dare. I knew it was far too much for me, trying to exist in dual lives like that. That one night had me thinking about him too much, too desperately, caused lapses in my focus.

I didn't talk to Regan and Rosalyn much on the flight back. I slept a bit, pretended to doze the rest of the time. I was too afraid I'd admit my sin to them. Talking to Joshua. Thinking about him. I was afraid to give the matter any more importance than it already holds for me. I was afraid they'd see through whatever half-truths I told them. Better to say nothing at all.

I take a quick shower and change into a pair of yoga pants and a T-shirt, settle on the sofa and check my messages. There is only one, from Deirdre, asking me to call as soon as I return. Which means now, not tomorrow, when I've had a chance to sleep off my jet lag. I dial her private number.

"Hello?"

"Deirdre, it's Val. You left a message for me?"

"Yes, I did. Thank you for being so prompt in returning

my call." She is absolutely polite, as always. And as glacially cold as ever. "I'll get right to it, Val. There's been a complaint about you."

"What?"

But I'm not nearly as shocked as I pretend to be.

"You know I always follow up with our clients. Zayed mentioned you seemed a bit distracted. He was quite nice about it. But we cannot have that at the level of business at which we operate. I believe you understand."

"Yes. Of course." My heart is hammering. This is not good. "I'm sorry, Deirdre."

"I don't know what's going on with you, Val, but obviously something is."

"I'm sorry. It won't happen again. I can handle it, I promise."

"How long have you been doing this, Val? You've been with me for eight years. How long before Enzo brought you to me?"

"Maybe a year. A little less."

"So, nine years of this life. That may be enough for anyone."

"No, Deirdre. Not for me."

But am I as certain of that as I was even a few weeks ago? I grip the phone in one hand, pull an embroidered throw pillow to my chest with the other, and hold on tight.

"As much as we'd all like to think of ourselves as irreplaceable, none of us really is," she goes on, her voice as smooth as glass. "Not the girls, not the clients. Not even me."

"Yes, of course, Deirdre."

I see where this conversation is going. I understand the implied threat to get me back in line.

"We are of a caliber of women who cannot make mistakes, Val. We are at the top of the food chain in our industry. You've been with me long enough to know that."

My palms are going damp. She's a hard woman. I have no idea how far she'll go with this, what she'll do, exactly. "Deirdre, I'll handle this. I will."

The Broker is silent a moment. "I want you to go see someone. Will you do it?"

"See someone?" It takes me a moment to understand what she's suggesting. "You mean a shrink?"

"Yes. That's exactly what I mean. This woman is someone I trust, someone who has worked with working girls before. She'll understand. She's very special. And I believe you need her."

God, I hate that she's right. But that doesn't change the fact that she is. I'm not going to fight her on this. I'm not in any position to. Whatever The Broker says is the word of God in this business.

"Alright, yes. I'll go see her."

Why do I feel defeated somehow?

Deirdre gives me her name, Lydia Foster, and an address in an upscale section of Santa Monica.

"Check in with me after you've seen her next week. I'll expect to hear from you. And, Val, I'd prefer not to send you on any overnights until you've spoken with her. Do you understand?"

"Yes, of course. I understand." I pause, not wanting to say it, needing to. "Thank you, Deirdre."

A pause on her end. Surprise, perhaps? "You're most welcome. I prefer not to lose one of my best girls to burnout."

Is that what this is? Maybe. Or maybe it goes a lot deeper than that.

I am about to find out.

I SPENT ALL OF Friday night mentally wrestling with myself: call Joshua, don't call Joshua. But after my little wake-up call with The Broker, I needed some time to sort my head out. I went to bed with a glass of wine—okay, a bottle—and now the morning sun shafting through my bedroom windows is making my head ache. I'm not a good drinker. In fact, I suck at drinking, which has been my way of avoiding turning into my mother. But I'm doing a bit too much of it lately. Need to put a stop to that, fast.

The wine didn't help me come to any conclusions, either. My mind keeps spiraling around the idea that once I go to this therapist, I'll have to make a choice. I'll have to choose my career. After all, it's Deirdre who is sending me to this person. It makes me feel desperate. To see Joshua. Be with him. Before it's all taken away. Before I take it away from myself.

My mouth feels like the Sahara Desert. I get up, slip into my short kimono robe, and brush my teeth before padding into the kitchen. Too damn bright in here, but my darling orchids love the morning sun. I squint as I put the kettle on for tea, pull the sugar bowl from the cupboard.

I wait for the water to boil. My heart is racing.

Just call him.

Yes, why not? Why not call him, talk to him? See him, while I can? This lovely little dream will shatter quickly enough.

A sharp wrench in my chest at the thought. I quickly push it to the back of my mind.

I make myself wait until my tea is ready, carry it back into the living room, fragrant steam wafting from the cup. I don't even stop to check the orchids in the window seat before grabbing the house phone and dialing.

I know his number by heart already.

"Joshua Spencer."

His voice is clipped.

"Hi, Joshua, it's Valentine. Am I calling at a bad time?"

"Never."

Real pleasure in his voice. It goes through me like a warm shiver up my spine.

"I just wanted to let you know I'm back in town."

"Are you jet-lagged?"

"Not much. I slept on the plane."

"Good. Tell me where to pick you up for dinner. Never mind. Let's make it lunch."

That air of command again. But I can't wait to see him, all of my doubts melting away, like liquid, like rain. Even lunch seems too far away. My body is going hot all over, my pulse fluttering.

"Yes, lunch would be perfect. Do you still have my address?"

"I wouldn't think of losing it. I'll pick you up at twelve."

"I'll be ready."

I'm ready now. Soaked, aching.

We hang up and suddenly I feel disoriented, as though I don't know what to do first. I have two hours. Two hours in which to get ready. To luxuriate in the idea of seeing him again.

I take a long, hot bath scented with my favorite fragrance, wash my hair, rub oil into my still-damp skin, making a ritual of my preparation. I can hardly stand the sight of my own naked body in the mirror: the flush on my skin, my erect nipples, look infinitely sexual to me. Vanity, yes. Perhaps a form of narcissism, even. I've always enjoyed the sight of my own body.

I've never thought there was anything wrong with that. But even more, it's the idea of him seeing me like this, looking at myself through his eyes.

Will I sleep with him? Oh, yes, after that night on the phone.

When was the last time I even questioned such a thing?

I slip into a simple navy cotton knit slip dress edged in satin, a pair of red strappy heeled sandals: casual but sexy. And the entire time I'm looking at the clock every ten minutes, my heart hammering. I can't stop the hot pulsing between my thighs.

I have a plan. I am going to pretend, just for today, that I am a normal person. That this is a normal date. That I can have this.

I feel like a total bitch because this is utterly unfair to him. Dishonest. But I need this in a way I have never needed anything before in my life. I'll live with the guilt. I always have, anyway.

When I was a kid and my mother cried for hours, I knew it was because my father was gone, off with some other woman. I knew this from the time I was four or five. But still, I always felt responsible for it. For her loneliness, her despair. And when they argued, voices shouting from the next room, I was frightened by it, but overcome by guilt, too. When you're a kid, the universe revolves around you. You have no true sense of cause and effect. And so I took it all on. Really fucked me up; I know that. But there it is.

I do not want to think about this now.

Stop thinking, Valentine. Stop analyzing. You're seeing a real shrink soon enough; she can analyze you.

No, all I want is to enjoy this exquisite anticipation as I

slide my favorite raspberry gloss over my lips. I stand back, look at myself in the mirror. I look good. Great. I'm fucking glowing. And all because of him.

Joshua.

When the doorbell rings I nearly jump out of my skin, but in a good way. I don't know how to explain that.

I open the door, and there he is, smiling. Dazzling. He looks better to me each time I see him.

"Joshua, hi."

"Hi."

He's wearing dark slacks, a short-sleeved button-down shirt layered over a T-shirt. Very hip. Very European. And I see for the first time that he's tattooed on his left biceps, just below the hem of his sleeve. It's MC Escher: that famous image of the hand drawing the hand. Before I can stop myself I reach out and touch it. His skin is hot.

"It's beautiful."

"I'm glad you like it."

"What does it mean? Tattoos should mean something, right?"

"It's about how we create ourselves. Our lives. We make choices and those choices determine what happens to us."

I nod. I don't know what to say. His words have hit a little too close to home.

I recover a moment later, shaking my head to clear it. "I'm sorry; I'm leaving you standing on the doorstep. Come in."

I take his hand and bring him into my house. That in itself is some sort of epiphany. I never, ever, bring a man to my house. But his hand is so warm, I hardly have time to think about it, hardly have the breath to think at all. His skin is pure heat on mine, just that hand-in-hand contact. And suddenly he is bending down and kissing me, like every single fantasy come true.

Just a small brush of lips against lips, but I am on fire. Burning.

He pulls away.

"Jesus, Valentine."

He brushes a lock of hair from my face, and now the warmth from his hand seems to permeate my chest. I don't understand what I'm feeling. Lust, yes, but something else. Something more. Totally unfamiliar. I am on shaky ground. I don't know how to deal with what's happening.

I must have been standing there, mute, senseless, for several moments. He tugs on my hand and leads me farther into the living room.

"I was perfectly serious about what I said to you on the phone the other night."

I nod. He pulls me closer. His thumb is running over the back of my hand, and that quiet touch is pure sex to me. That and his hazel eyes staring into mine. They are dark with desire.

"I could hardly stand you being away after I talked with you," he tells me. "There's something about you . . . I'm not sure yet what it is. I want to find out. I intend to find out."

"Yes," I say, my voice a breathy whisper.

There is no point in pretense. I've already answered my earlier, ridiculous question. I will sleep with him. I will do whatever he wants, frankly.

He leans in again and moves so slowly, I have time to wonder when his lips will touch mine, to feel that anticipation coursing through my body like a wave of heat. Closer, closer. And finally his mouth meets mine, and his lips are so damn soft and sweet, it goes through me like some kind of gentle shock.

Immediately, I am lost.

This is exactly what I was afraid of.

This is exactly what I've dreamed of.

Chapter Seven

I DON'T REMEMBER A man feeling as good to me as Joshua does. Maybe it's the kissing—making out like a couple of teenagers. Like I haven't done since high school. His mouth is warm, sweet. God, I've forgotten how good it feels to kiss a man. Really kiss him. I am shivering all over.

His mouth is all heat and need, his tongue gliding like silk on mine. When his hands go into my hair and grip, a small gasp escapes me, slipping in between his lips like a plea for more.

Yes, more . . .

He kisses me harder, and I am dizzy with pleasure.

I press up against him. I can feel every hard plane of his body through our clothes. Too many damn clothes. But lovely to have to wait to feel him all over, to know his skin. Excruciating.

He has the hard-packed body of an athlete. And I know athletes. Pro basketball players, football players, soccer players from Spain.

No, don't think about them now. Only him.

Joshua.

He pulls me in closer, just roughly enough to let me know I am his at this moment. I am, anyway. My body knows. I am shaking. Needing him.

His hands slide down, briefly cupping my face, so gentle it nearly makes me want to cry. But I don't have time to question it. His hands glide over my bare shoulders. Just him touching my naked skin, so innocently, and my sex fills, swells. I arch harder into him, and his thigh moves in between mine, pressing onto my mound. I am panting into his mouth, breathing him in. My heart is racing.

Have I ever wanted anything this much?

He pulls his mouth away. "Bedroom, Valentine."

A command, not a question. Not that I have any notion of refusing.

I take his hand and lead him down the hallway, into my little sanctuary. The few moments it's taken to get there feel far too long.

He takes me in his arms, and once more I have that strange awareness of how alien this all is to me, being with a man simply because I want him. This sense of truly needing *him,* not just the sex itself. Yet I am as turned on as I've ever been in my life. I look up at him. His hair is a bit mussed, his eyes dark and glossy. I reach up, trace the small scar on his lip with one fingertip. He groans softly and takes it into his mouth, sucking. Pleasure ripples through me like water, undulating, liquid, making me go loose all over. And his eyes are still on me, glowing gold and silver and green. I don't know if it's fear or excitement that has my heart hammering in my chest, as thunderous as a freight train. I can't figure it out. I don't want to.

He lets my finger slide from his mouth, takes my hand in his and opens it up, kissing my palm. Something in my chest is softening, swelling, even as my sex swells with desire. There is need in his steady gaze, a stark intensity. And it is like being shocked over and over. I can hardly stand to look into his eyes. I can't look away.

He slips one of the straps of my dress down, letting it fall off my shoulder, leans in and lays a soft kiss there. I am shivering again, my head falling back. He kisses my throat with his silken lips, small ripples of pleasure moving over my skin. I am overcome by his touch, and he has barely touched me yet. How will I stand it when we are naked? When he is inside my body?

"Valentine," he says, his voice quiet, full of smoke.

"Yes . . ."

"I want you."

"Yes. Please . . ."

He fills his hands with my breasts, my nipples peaking against his palms, hard and hurting with need.

More . . .

He tears the straps of my dress down, and my breasts are bared.

"Touch me, Joshua. Don't make me wait."

His hands on my naked skin are hot, lovely. His palms glide over my flesh, and my whole body bows into him. I can't help myself. I can barely think.

When he takes my hardened nipples in his fingers, tugs gently, pleasure washes over me in small, sharp ripples. When he pinches them, hard, demanding, I am nearly coming already. Scary, how much I want him, how my body responds, betraying all sense of self-control.

"Joshua . . . please . . ."

"Tell me, Valentine. Tell me what you need."

"I need you to touch me. I need your mouth on me. I need to feel you."

"Oh, I plan to touch you. To taste you."

He slips my dress over my head, leaving me bare, other than my navy lace panties and my high sandals. He stands back, pulling his shirt off, then his undershirt. His chest is solid, muscled, his nipples dark and dusky against his light golden skin. As hard as my own. I want to touch them, to take them into my mouth. I bite my lip, waiting, my gaze going to the narrow line of hair from his navel to the low-slung waistband of his slacks. Abs like steel. He is too beautiful. My hands go to his broad shoulders. His skin is smooth beneath my palms. And beneath that beautiful skin his muscles bunch, then loosen. My mouth waters, my thighs tensing.

"Joshua . . ."

"You are so God damned beautiful, Valentine. I knew you would be." He shakes his head. "But not like this. Jesus."

He reaches out, runs one fingertip down the front of my body, between my breasts, over my belly, stopping just above the lacy edge of my underwear. And I am trembling with need at the way he touches me, looks at me, as though I am something special. Precious.

Standing back, he watches me, his eyes going from my breasts, to my mouth, to my eyes, and back again, roving every inch of me. He is *really* looking. I don't know if any man has ever looked at me in quite this way before. It's making me hot all over. I need to touch him more than ever. But I don't want him to stop what he's doing: looking at me, worshiping me with his eyes, somehow. Making my body surge with desire, making my chest tight with a need I don't quite recognize.

His voice is low, almost a whisper. "Valentine . . ." he says, before wrapping his hands around my waist and pushing me roughly onto the bed.

The embroidery of the duvet cover is a little coarse against my bare skin. I am keenly aware of everything: the earthy scent of my imported wood furniture, the faint heat of the sunlight coming in through the half-closed shutters, Joshua's intense, unwavering gaze on mine. He reaches out, grasps my hair, pulling hard. And it is this way he has of being tender and rough with me at the same time that has me melting.

He slides his slacks down, leaving him in a pair of black boxer-briefs that outline the strong muscles of his thighs, the ridge of his erection. I can hardly wait to wrap my hands around that rigid shaft, to take him in my mouth. To bring him pleasure.

Yes . . .

He leans over me, and the heat from his body is incredible. Pulling him in, I finally feel the length of his hard frame against mine.

"Ah, Joshua, you feel too good."

He is smiling down at me, looking nearly as dazed as I feel, his full mouth soft and loose with desire. I want him to kiss me again. I want him to do everything. Anything. But I am lambent with my own need for him, my body buzzing, half paralyzed.

I have never felt so helpless with a man. I have never felt this dazzling yearning. I have never felt this sense of absolute connection.

I don't let myself think about that.

He leans in, kisses my throat, my shoulder once more, then lower still, until his soft lips are on my breast. And when he takes one nipple into his hot, wet mouth, I cry out, the pleasure so sharp it nearly hurts.

"Ah, Joshua!"

Arching into him, he pulls my flesh in deeper, sucking, sucking. And it is as though his mouth is everywhere at once: lighting up my skin, in that musky, wanting place between my thighs. I hold his head to my breast, my fingers digging into his thick, soft hair. Taking a long breath, I inhale his scent, that deep, woodsy citrus he wears, and beneath it, his own musk, his own heated skin.

He lifts his head, murmurs, "You like that."

"Yes."

He smiles, bends once more, lapping at my nipples with his moist tongue, first one, then the other, over and over until I am squirming, my sex swollen with an exquisite, hurting need.

He stops, looks up at me. "What do you need, Valentine?"

I am gasping, making it difficult to speak. "I need . . . I feel like I could almost come just from this. I need to come. I want you to touch me, to make me come, Joshua. Please."

"I will. But not yet."

Again he leans in and, using his hands to push my breasts together, begins his assault on my nipples once more. Now his mouth is rough on me, sucking hard, biting my hardened flesh. And he uses his fingers, tugging, pinching. And it feels so damn good, I can barely take it. I'm really squirming now, my hips arching, my sex needing to be filled, my clit throbbing. And I am soaking wet, tears of desire spilling onto the bed beneath me.

Just when I think I can no longer stand it without losing my mind, he pauses, lifts his head, brushes a kiss across my lips. Then taking my wrists, he pulls my arms over my head, pinning them hard with his strong hands. He is watching me again, his gaze deep, dark on mine, searching.

I feel . . . I don't know what, exactly. Lust, yes. An overwhelming craving for him: his body. For *him*. I don't know how to explain it. But I know he reads it in my eyes, that I am at that moment totally transparent to him. And the idea makes my heart beat even faster, my pulse racing with desire and emotion I can't understand. The tinge of fear running just beneath that current makes it all more intense. But I don't want to think about it now. No, all I want to do is feel.

"Valentine, I am going to take you now. With my hands. With my mouth. And then I'm going to push inside you . . ."

"Yes. Do it. Do it all."

He licks his lips, making me want to reach up and touch his pink tongue with my fingertip. His mouth is so fucking beautiful to me, I can hardly stand to look at it. But I am just as eager to have him do the things he's talking about. I am burning for him, my body on that lovely, keen edge.

He lowers his body over mine once more, and his cock is hard against my leg, hard and long and so good. But in moments he is sliding down, trailing kisses over my stomach, scorching my skin. Then lower, his strong hands tearing my panties down over my thighs before he parts them.

There is no resisting him: my legs fall wide open for him. I wait while he looks at me, his gaze searching my sex.

With one hand he reaches out, brushes at the swollen lips, whispers, "Beautiful."

Then his mouth is there, his breath warm against me for one lovely anticipatory moment before the soft touch of his lips. He is kissing me there, just as he did my mouth! And it is some sort of revelation to me, the tenderness of his mouth and his hard hands on my thighs. I have never felt anything like it. Pleasure shafts into me, deep and slow, like liquid heat.

And he is kissing me and kissing me with his soft lips. I am squirming, panting as he holds me down.

His tongue flicks out, whispering across my clitoris.

"Ah!"

Then again.

"Joshua!"

"Are you going to come?" he asks, his voice muffled.

"Yes!"

And it's true. I *am* going to come, despite that small part of me that struggles to hang on to some last shred of control.

"Not yet," he commands.

I take in a deep breath, wanting to please him, to do as he asks, even more than I need to come. Knowing that I will come exactly as he wants me to. And that knowing gives me permission, somehow.

Yes, I am in his hands now. I can let it go.

He uses his hands then, pressing the lips of my sex closed with his fingers, and it feels so damn good, and it hurts maybe a little. But the pleasure is not the point; the point is that he is letting me know he is in command, and I understand it. I love it.

I am about to go out of my head.

"Take a breath, Valentine."

I do, drawing the warm air into my lungs, along with the heady scent of desire: his as well as my own.

"Again," he tells me, and once more I obey.

He holds the lips of my sex open with his fingers and bends down once more, his tongue driving softly into my body.

"Oh!"

He stops. "Not yet, Valentine. Hold back. You can do it."

"Yes."

Anything for him at this moment.

He begins again, his hot tongue moving inside of me, slipping out, like wet silk, like some small, lovely erection. And all the while his fingers massaging the lips of my sex. My swollen clitoris is left waiting, needy. I know he knows this. He knows exactly what he's doing.

The pleasure builds, a hard knot of need in my belly, my sex, my breasts. It's all I can do to hold the tide back. His tongue is sliding in and out of me, his fingers rubbing, pinching just hard enough.

"Joshua, please . . ."

I feel him shift, his tongue pulling out of me. Then his fingers drive inside, hard. My body arches against him, and he plants his mouth right on me, drawing my swollen clitoris into his mouth and sucking.

I explode, my body tensing, pleasure shafting into me like a blade. Lights ignite behind my closed eyes, a million stars going off in my head. And I am calling his name.

"Joshua! Joshua! Ah, God . . ."

Writhing against him, his lovely mouth still sucking, sucking, his fingers deep inside me, drawing my climax from me, milking my body for every last drop of pleasure. *Making* me come.

"Joshua, I need you. Please," I gasp.

"Yes, now," he says.

He moves away from me, and I am vaguely aware that he is pulling a condom from the pocket of his discarded slacks. He kneels on the bed, pulling me upright, then into his arms, so that I am straddling his lap, my knees on either side of his.

His cock is as beautiful as the rest of him, golden and strong. Reaching down between us, I brush the silky tip with my fingertips, watch him sigh in pleasure, his eyes fluttering closed. Taking him in my hand, I wrap my fingers around the hard length of him. He is big, thick. Lovely to look at, like solid velvet in my hand. I stroke him and his hips pump into my touch. Then his hand comes down over mine.

"I need to stop." His voice is low, rough with need. And the sound of it is intensely sexual to me. My sex gives a hard squeeze. "I need to make love to you, Valentine."

Has any man ever said those words to me?

But I am shaking with desire; I can't think about it. Can't think about anything but him.

I help him roll the condom down over his rigid flesh, then he lifts me. I spread my thighs wider, and he grips my hips, lowering me onto his cock, impaling me, his dark hazel gaze never leaving mine. Pleasure drives into me, deep, hot, nearly paralyzing.

I am going to come again.

"Jesus, Valentine. You feel so good. So damn good."

We hold still, his hands gripping my hips, pleasure dancing like electricity in the air between us, in our joined bodies. And there is a strange intensity to the moment that has as much to do with the way he's looking at me, with the way he makes me feel, as it does with his cock deep inside my body, his fingers digging into my flesh.

Then he begins to move, pulling me in close until my breasts are crushed against his chest, rocking slowly. The sensation is exquisite, his cock moving in and out of me, a gentle thrusting, the hard planes of his body against mine, so close I can feel the wild beating of his heart against my own. He moves his lips over my neck, sending shivers over my skin. And he is thrusting harder now, deeper, my hips moving to meet his. My clitoris is rubbing against his pubic bone, the pressure exactly where I need it. Desire is like heat lightning in my body, arcing into me with every stroke of his cock, every touch of his lips on my throat.

His hands are holding me so damn tight I know they'll leave bruises as he pumps into me, harder now. But I don't care. I need it, to be possessed like this. And I am hovering at that edge of climax, yearning for it, but waiting for him.

"Valentine . . . I'm going to come."

"Yes. Please . . . come, Joshua."

He drives hard into me, pleasure moving deep, and I feel him tense all over. And as his hips jerk hard, then harder, as his groan escapes, pleasure fills my body in a hot tide, like the ocean: that heavy, that powerful, as if drawn by the moon. And I am lost, my mind gone, as I come in long, shuddering waves. Over and over, and I can barely breathe. Doesn't matter. I'm coming and coming. And he is coming into me, moaning, our panting breath mingling in the pale afternoon sunlight.

And I feel something I have never felt before in my life. Something warm and light and frightening as he pulls me tighter into his arms, whispering my name into my hair.

"Valentine, Valentine, Valentine . . ."

Heat is seeping into my chest, expanding. How will I ever let him go? I can't do it.

I cannot do this.

Tears fill my eyes. I know this is more than I can ever have, this beautiful thing between us. More than I deserve.

But I have it now, *right now*. Fuck it. This moment is mine. Even *I* deserve to have this much.

———

I DON'T KNOW HOW I managed to sleep, but I did. Even with my mind whirling. How lovely to wake up in the late afternoon light, Joshua's body resting beside me.

His breath is shallow, slow, rhythmic. His face is almost

innocent as he sleeps. And so damn beautiful to me, my chest tightens, and I have to make an effort simply to breathe.

I shake my head.

Get it together, Valentine. He's just a man.

But I know that's not true. Joshua is so much more. It would be so damn simple otherwise. The fact that I can climax with him is only an outward sign of something that runs much deeper. It's something I'll need to figure out at some point: what it means for me, exactly, what it says about him, about the kind of person I am with him. But I can't do it now. I am so filled with wanting I can barely think straight.

I run my hands through the tangles in my hair, pulling hard on the knots there, needing that pain to center myself. I draw in a few deep breaths. Focus once more on his face, on the lines of his body, the way the shaft of light coming through the wooden shutters casts striped shadows across the smooth, bare skin of his chest.

I find myself wishing I had a good camera, some black-and-white film. He is art to me. He has somehow become this almost iconic figure of desire. His mouth is all soft and loose, his lips so plush. And I can't help myself; I lean in and kiss him. He comes awake, breathing into my mouth, sweetly. His arms go around me, pulling me to him. Absolutely unbelievable how good this feels: his mouth, these simple, sweet kisses, being held by him.

I realize I am happy. *Happy!*

A sharp tug in my chest once more, but I ignore it.

"Are you hungry?" he asks me.

"I'm starving."

"I'm a terrible date. I made you miss the lunch I'd offered."

"Mmm . . . this was better."

"Better, yes. Amazing."

He strokes a lock of hair from my face, and I am caught up once more in his steady gaze, trembling beneath his touch. I want him to make love to me again.

Make love.

Like some alien language.

He turns, until we are on our sides, lying facing each other, our legs tangling. His hard cock presses against my belly. My sex stirs with desire, hot, thrumming through my body.

"How hungry are you?" he asks me.

"Fainting from malnutrition. But I can wait a little longer."

He flips me over, pinning me beneath him, his cock slipping between my thighs, tempting at the entrance to my pussy.

"I'll make it fast, then."

"Oh, yes. Fast and hard, please."

He smiles at me.

"Condoms, Valentine."

"In my nightstand."

I don't even know why I keep them there. I never have sex in my own bed. This is my place. My haven. But it is his now, too.

Don't even think that . . .

No, too much to think of anything but watching him sheath his gorgeous, golden cock, feeling him slide into me as easy as water, sensation flooding my body.

His hands slip under my ass, and he lifts me a little, angling deeper, and begins a hard, pumping rhythm. I love this, the way he holds on to me, so hard it hurts, his fingers digging into my flesh.

Possessed, yes.

I am breathless immediately, panting, gasping with plea-

sure. Drowning in it. He's going so damn fast and deep, burrowing into me. And desire builds inside me, driven by his
thrusting cock as he holds me tightly, every surface of our
bodies pressed together.

And still, I need more.

"Deeper, Joshua."

"Yes . . ."

He presses into me, until there is a small flash of pain. But
I need it. Need him to fill me this way.

My climax is waiting for me, hovering, and when he lowers his beautiful face to mine, sucks my tongue into his mouth,
it's too much for me. I come, shivering, gasping into his
mouth, between those lush lips.

In moments he tenses, and I swear I can feel his cock pulsing inside of me as he cries out, shudders.

We are covered in sweat, the scent of sex heavy in the air.
Like some lovely, intoxicating perfume.

He rolls off me, and we lie on our sides again, facing each
other, both of us trying to catch our breath. His hand goes to
my face, traces my cheek.

"I'll feed you now, I promise."

He smiles, dazzling my already dazed brain.

"Alright." I slide a hand over his shoulder, his chest, loving his silken skin on my palm. Does any other man have skin
like his?

I know I need to eat. But all I want to do is kiss him.
Touch him. I am obsessed. Reaching up, I trace the scar on his
lower lip. Such a contrast to the lush flesh there.

"How did you get this, Joshua? Let me guess; it was something innocent. A bicycle accident when you were eight."

"Why would you say it had to be something innocent?"

"There's something a bit innocent about you. Even about this scar." I touch it once more, feel the texture beneath my fingertip.

He grins. "Oh, you think so? You have no idea how funny that is to me. To anyone who really knows me."

"Then tell me what's not so innocent about you. Let me know you. Tell me how you got your scar."

He shrugs one shoulder. "In a bar fight when I was eighteen."

"Really?" Why does this surprise me so much? Why does the idea turn me on?

"It was a stupid college thing. Classic young, angry guy. That was before I realized I didn't have much to be angry about. I was still young enough to think the world owed me."

"What else? What else about your life is less than innocent?"

He pauses, silent for several moments. Then, "When Dad died I took off and went to Europe. And I don't mean the usual tour of Paris, London. I wanted to explore the underbelly." He pauses, runs a finger over my jaw. He's not really looking at me now. "It was a bad time for me. I went to Prague and drank absinthe until I puked. In Berlin I drank whatever was available, whatever they had in the clubs. Berlin is a hard place. I drank with strangers who stole my wallet while I was passed out cold on the floor of some girl's apartment. Who knows, maybe it was the girl who stole it. I went to Amsterdam and smoked hash. I went to the red light district and bought hookers."

I clench my teeth against the gasp that wants to come out.

I look up and he's focused on me once more, watching me very carefully. I nod for him to continue. "Go on."

"Are you sure you want to hear this?"

"Yes. I do."

I need to hear it, maybe.

"I didn't go to the shiny girls in the windows. I looked for the cheap ones, but not because of the money. I sought out the pale girls all strung out on heroin, and let me tell you, there were a lot of them. That's what finally got me. That's when I realized I'd worked off enough anger, when I saw these girls for what they really were. How fucking sad it all was.

"I went home. Went back to make a life for myself. To take responsibility for myself. To be a man. But I stopped off in San Francisco first and got my tattoo."

He pauses, and I touch the dark lines on his biceps.

"Creating your own life," I murmur.

"Yes. It's all about choice. I could have chosen to be that pissed-off guy, wasting my life because I felt helpless over my father's death. Over the sense of responsibility I felt to be the man of the family at only twenty. Or not. I realized that."

"And you stepped up, took care of the family, the business."

"Yeah, I did."

"Do you ever regret that?"

"No. Not for a minute. But I also know I had to go through that, had to be that pissed-off guy. And it was probably better that I did it in Europe instead of in front of my mother, my sister. Most of it, anyway."

"What do you mean?"

"Europe didn't cure me. It helped. But I still had issues to work out. Stuff I've been working on since then. Making that choice was only the beginning. I have to keep reminding myself."

He glances away, gazing past my shoulder.

I touch his arm. "Joshua?"

It's several moments before he brings his eyes back to mine.

"I should tell you something, Valentine."

"Tell me anything."

He's watching me, smoothing his thumb along my jaw. Then, "I've spent most of my adult life running. From my father's death. From that sudden responsibility I had to take on too young. From my own expectations."

"But you've been there, working. I don't know what you mean."

"Running can come in a lot of different forms. For me, it was sex."

"Sex?"

"That part didn't stop with those sad girls in Amsterdam. Not that I paid for it again once I got home. But I used sex for a long time. I went from one relationship to the next, looking for something I felt was beyond my reach. And I never found it. And when I didn't, I cheated. Over and over. That relationship break I talked about? That was two years. No women. No sex. Two years in which I dealt with my addiction."

It's difficult to know what to say. I don't judge him; of course I don't. But it is a revelation to me, this flaw in the knight's shining armor that is Joshua now. It makes my heart ache for him.

"Shit. Maybe I shouldn't have told you. But you deserve to know."

"No. I'm glad you told me." I reach up, stroke my fingertips over his scar once more. "I'm glad."

And I am. The fact that he's overcome these things makes him more real, more desirable, more noble.

He smiles, pulls my hand to his lips, kisses the tender skin of my fingertips. Lovely. But my chest is tight with guilt. There is so much I should tell him, that he deserves to know. But I can't do it.

We lie together for a while, watching each other's eyes. It is the most amazing yet simple thing. My heart is pounding still.

"Come on," he says eventually. "Let's get some food. There must be someplace that delivers around here."

He goes into the bathroom off my bedroom to clean up. Back a moment later, he pulls me up, and we go naked into the kitchen. His body is so beautiful, I'm distracted. He looks delicious surrounded by the stark granite counters, the shining brushed steel appliances. His cock is soft, lying golden and warm against his thigh, and even now it is beautiful. I dig around in a drawer for my small collection of take-out menus.

"Here, there are a few Chinese places, some Thai, pizza. Pick whatever you'd like." I hand him the small pile of paper menus.

He takes them, takes my hand, and leads me to the counter, where he spreads the menus out.

"Which one is your favorite?" he asks me.

"My favorite?"

I am too unused to a man asking me about my preferences.

He waits for me to answer.

"I love this Szechuan place. The food is pretty Americanized, but they have the best lo mein noodles in town."

"Then that's what we'll have."

He finds my phone, orders, then we stand in the kitchen while I make some jasmine tea, serving it in one of a small collection of teapots. I've been collecting for several years; they are all lined up on a high shelf in my kitchen, beautiful objects in porcelain and clay. This one is a stark clay piece from Japan, something I picked up on a job there last year.

Don't think about work. Nothing else exists now.

The food arrives and Joshua pulls his slacks on to answer the door, pay the delivery guy. He takes them off again while I make two plates and carry them back into the bedroom on a tray.

We eat in bed, naked, surrounded by the aroma of sesame oil, soy sauce, and the perfumed scent of the tea. I don't even care when I spill on my good sheets.

"Valentine, tell me about your orchids. They're beautiful," he says between bites of Mongolian beef.

"I love them. I've been growing them for years. It's a bit of an obsession, really."

"I'm not sure I would have expected that of you."

"What do you mean?"

"You seem far too controlled a woman to become obsessed by anything."

Is he teasing me? And God, if he only knew.

"Am I really . . . controlled?"

"Except in bed." He moves closer, brushes a fingertip over my breast, his tone lowering. "There's nothing controlled about you in bed."

And just like that I'm hot all over again, needing him. But the bed is covered in food. Perhaps I can hold off for a few more minutes. And it's too good, simply being here with him like this. Like normal people.

"Don't you have any obsessions, Joshua?"

"Currently, a new one," he says, picking up my free hand, lifting it to his mouth and kissing my fingers before sucking them in.

"How can I eat when you're doing that to me?" I'm smiling, desire darting through my body.

Letting my hand go, he picks up a few noodles and holds them to my mouth. "I'll feed you," he says as I open my lips, take the noodles in, tasting his fingertips along with them.

God, he is too much, this man. And I am aware once more of how unreal this all is. How magical. How fragile. This feels almost kinky to me. It's wrong, somehow. But it's also right for the first time in my life. My shallow life. How can I trust this?

Just be here.

Yes, I can do this. It's far too good to stop. I cannot send him away; not yet. I want to keep pretending. Isn't that what I've always done, pretended that what I do is okay? Convincing myself that being with this lovely man must be easier, surely. And I'm good at pretending.

The harder thing will be knowing when to stop.

Chapter Eight

WE SPENT THE WHOLE weekend together, leaving the bed only long enough to eat again, to shower together. He made love to me over and over—enough times that I finally believe in making love, that I've forgotten to question it. Enough that I understand on some very deep level the way he handles me, that combination of rough, commanding touch and soft, sweet kisses, is what making love is really about.

He has been inside my body for hours, touching me, kissing me. In my big bed, in the shower, in the kitchen while I was making omelets. They burned. It didn't matter. All that mattered was his hard cock inside me, his steady gaze on mine, his strong arms wrapped around my body.

I have come so many times I've lost count. And I am amazed every time.

We stayed up late last night watching rather horrible old monster movies, an entire marathon of Godzilla, Mothra, all those old Japanese cult classics. They are truly awful. But Joshua loved them, told me how it reminded him of being a kid, staying up late on a summer night. And I cannot resist him at those moments when I can see that child in him, beneath his sophisticated surface. Beneath the bad boy hovering behind that sophistication.

I cannot resist him at all.

I am getting to be far too sentimental. Something I have never been before in my life. Something I cannot allow myself to get used to.

Too late.

Oh, yes, those are the words, the doubts, that fill my mind as I sit here in the predawn light, alone. Joshua had to leave early to get ready for work. He has a late meeting, so I won't even hear from him until tomorrow night. I shouldn't talk to him at all, I know that. I should just let him go. But kissing him good-bye was like a blow to the chest.

What the hell is wrong with me?

Now all I feel is a sharp yearning to have the weekend back again. To feel that wonderful light sensation of pure happiness. Panic at knowing I can't really have this lovely dream.

I cannot have this.

Fuck.

The air is cold on my skin, and I pull the blankets up, covering my breasts, my shoulders. I realize that for the first time in a very long time, since the early shock of turning my first tricks, I can hardly stand to be in my own skin.

I try to go back to sleep, but it's impossible. By eight o'clock I give up, get out of bed. It's a gray day, which is fine with me. The usual L.A. sunshine would seem far too optimistic today. Snow White and her smiling fucking woodland animals.

Oh, you are bitter.

Yes, I am. Why shouldn't I be? I have let a man touch me, in all the important places, for the first time in years. Maybe the first time ever. And it was fucking wonderful. And I cannot allow it to happen again.

I consider taking a slug of gin rather than my usual tea, but that's getting to be too pathetic for me. The drinking crap has got to stop. Instead, I go through my morning routine: brew my Earl Grey tea, water my orchids, shower. I throw on a pair of jeans and a T-shirt and remember that I am supposed to make an appointment with the therapist Deirdre is sending me to. I wonder briefly what I'll talk about with her first. There is so much to choose from. My fucked-up childhood? My fucked-up current life?

Just make the damn call.

I dial the number The Broker gave me, talk to a receptionist. She can see me tomorrow afternoon.

I hang up and immediately my stomach is in knots. I am already thinking about what I'm going to say to this woman. Because I know damn well I'm not going to a shrink because I'm too distracted to work. No, that's too simple. I'm going because I am lost. Because I feel as if my life is about to come crashing down around me. And I don't know how to stop it. I don't think there's an easy answer out there for me. Maybe there isn't one at all.

My cell phone rings and I check the caller ID. Bennett. Damn it. I can't handle him today. I can't handle anyone. I shut my phone off and take my tea, get back into bed. I turn on the television, channel surf, looking for an old monster movie, but all I find are talk shows and soap operas. I turn it off, burrow under the covers with my bag of gummi bears, and sulk.

LYDIA FOSTER'S OFFICE IS in one of those quaint old brick buildings in Santa Monica. As I ride the elevator to the third floor, I check my cell phone before powering it off. There are three messages from clients, but I don't even want to think about what they want from me.

Her receptionist is one of those fresh young girls you see so often in this town. She's just filling the chair until she lands a good acting job. A film, a television show. Maybe on a soap. Half these girls end up in my line of work eventually.

I give her my name and a door on the other side of the room opens and my new therapist walks out. She's fiftyish, with shoulder-length strawberry blond hair, a bit frizzy and wild. Large, kind blue eyes peer out from an elfin face. She is dressed conservatively, in a navy skirt and an ivory blouse.

I'd expected her to be intimidating, more like Deirdre, for some reason. She is the exact opposite. Still, my hands are fisted at my sides and I have to force myself to uncurl my fingers to shake her hand.

"You must be Val. I'm Lydia."

"Yes, nice to meet you."

"Come into my office."

She stands and lets me slip through the door, follows me, shutting it behind her.

Her office is all soft neutrals. A light wood bookshelf lines one wall, full of books, small pieces of pottery. A large bronze Buddha is displayed in the center. She gestures for me to sit on a soft sofa piled with throw pillows. I sit with my purse in my lap, as though I'm at a job interview.

What the hell is wrong with me? I set my purse on the floor, try to breathe normally.

Lydia settles into an armchair across from me.

"So," she says, "tell me why you're here."

I laugh, a small, harsh sound. "I thought you were supposed to tell me that."

I immediately feel like an idiot. But she just smiles at me. "That's not my job. My job is to listen, to prompt you to figure things out yourself, in a way your psyche can accept."

"Oh . . ." I shift, cross my legs, tug on the end of my hair, twining a strand around my finger. "What do you want to know?"

"What do you want to tell me?"

"Do you always answer a question with a question?"

She smiles once more. "I'm here to be a sounding board. You only have to talk about what you want to talk about. I'm not going to tell you what to do, what to say. You get to decide that, okay?"

I nod. "Yes, sure."

Taking a moment, I let my gaze settle on the shelves behind her chair. There are art books there, among the self-help and psychology titles, books on spirituality.

"Well . . . you know that Deirdre referred me to you, so you know what I do for a living."

"How would *you* describe what you do for a living, Val?"

I look up at her, meet her watery blue eyes. "It's Valentine. If I'm going to be honest with you, open, you should call me Valentine."

"Alright. Valentine."

I can tell she is the kind of person who will remain calm no matter what I say, what I do. Frightening and reassuring all at the same time.

I lean forward a fraction of an inch. It's really more a flexing of tight muscle. "I'm a call girl. A prostitute. I sell my body for sex. A hooker. A whore."

"You sound bitter."

"Do I?" I can feel my pulse racing. I have no reason to be angry with this woman. "Maybe I am. Maybe that's why I'm here."

She's quiet a moment, then, "Was there some incident that sparked your interest in therapy?"

"I had a complaint from a client and Deirdre sent me to you."

"I meant, did something happen to you personally?"

"What? No." I curl my fingers into my palms, the nails biting into the soft flesh there and say, more quietly, "Yes."

She waits for me to elaborate.

"I don't know how to do this," I tell her. "This one-way conversation thing. Am I supposed to just spew my guts while you listen?"

"Sometimes, yes." She leans forward, resting her elbows on her knees, clasps her hands together. "I'll tell you a secret, Valentine. I can already see your intelligence. I have no intention of bullshitting you. Part of what we therapists look for, particularly on a first meeting, is body language. Your comfort level, or lack of comfort, in talking about yourself. It's part of how we get to know a client."

"So this is a test."

"No. This is me observing how you respond to this environment."

"And?"

"And it's too soon for me to come to any real conclusions. We're just getting started. Why don't you talk about what brought you here?"

"Oh, well . . ." I uncross my legs, cross them again. I'm glad I wore jeans, something I rarely do. I don't want to look like a hooker to this woman. "It's a man. How cliché is that? But that's what made me stop and think about . . . everything. My work. My life."

"A client?"

"Oh, God no."

She's quiet again, contemplative. She sits back in her chair. "What is it about him that makes you question everything, as you said?"

"He's so damn perfect." I push my hair away from my face. I want to pull it, to make it hurt. Instead, I keep talking. "He's too beautiful and too good. A real person. He's not like me, you know? He has a real life. A man like that could never be with me."

"Because you're not a real person?"

"Something like that, yes. My life is a totally surreal existence. I know that. I've been living it for nearly a decade. There's no room in it for a man like Joshua. And there's certainly no place in his life for a woman like me."

"And you find that difficult to accept?"

"It's fucking impossible." I shake my head. "I'm sorry."

She shrugs, smiles. "I've heard worse."

She really is awfully nice, this Lydia Foster. But I'm not ready to let my guard down completely yet.

It strikes me that my guard is never down; it hasn't been since I was maybe five years old.

"I have a terrible habit of swearing," I tell her. "I grew up around it. I've never gotten over it. But I can usually keep it under control when I have to."

"You don't have to here."

I nod, look away. There's a window to my left, sectioned into small panes. Outside the sun glances green and gold on the leaves of a tree. Behind it the fall sky is blue, marred by a thin layer of smog. I've known that sky all my life. One of the few constants.

"I had this weird childhood. Dysfunctional."

"In what way?"

"In every way."

"Oh?"

I shake my head. "I'm sorry. I was drifting."

"I don't think you were."

"Maybe. I guess I'm supposed to talk about my childhood. Isn't that what Freud would say?"

"Probably."

"What would you say?"

"I like to let the client set the pace. Why don't you just talk for a while, and we'll let it go wherever your mind chooses. Okay?"

"Yes. Sure."

"You were talking about your childhood."

"Yes." I pull on my hair again, wrap my fingers up in the ends, take a breath. My childhood is the one thing I try to avoid thinking about as much as possible. But if I'm not going to go there, what the hell am I doing here? Why bother? I'm not supposed to like it. I'm just supposed to do it.

Shit.

But I am going to do it.

Why do I feel like this is some sort of last chance for me?

"My mother was an alcoholic."

I have to stop, breathe. I've never actually said that out loud to anyone. It's never been necessary. I didn't know it would feel like this. Like a small knife slipping between my ribs. I didn't know it would feel like *anything*.

"How did that affect you, growing up?"

"How didn't it affect me? She was depressed. Insecure. A real mess. And my father, he couldn't stand it. I can't blame him. That's why he was gone all the time, off with other women. My mother was pathetic. I always knew that, even when I was very young."

"How do you think that's influenced how you see yourself as a woman?"

"Oh, I'm completely opposite from her. I take care of myself, keep my life under control. I rarely have more than a drink or two."

"Do you ever experience depression?"

"No, I don't think so."

"And your self-esteem?"

"It's fine. I'm fine."

"And yet you believe this man, Joshua, is too good for you."

It's like being socked in the chest. The air just rushes right out of my lungs.

Fuck.

I say, "Yes." It comes out in a small, hissing whisper.

She sits quietly, waiting. Finally she says, "Let's go back to your childhood. Tell me about your father."

I take a few moments, finding my breath. "He wasn't around much. I never really felt that I knew him. I felt . . . separate from him. Maybe my mom had something to do with that, kept us separate. He'd leave for days, sometimes weeks at a time. She would spend most of that time on the sofa, a bottle in her hand. There's a reason why it's called stinking drunk." I have to stop, to shake the memory away. It's too awful. "I took care of myself. I ate a lot of cereal until I was old enough to figure out how to cook. After Mom passed out I could change the channel and watch the cooking shows. That's one thing I have now; I love to cook when I get the chance."

"You became self-reliant."

"Yes. I always have been. I've always had to be."

"What was it like when your father was home?"

"It was worse. They'd lock me in my room. Well, it was my mother who did that. I doubt he even remembered I was there half the time. I doubt he knew I existed."

Why does it hurt to say these things? Things I've known

all my life. My chest aches as though a heavy weight is pressing there. I draw another breath in, hold on to it a moment, as though it might keep me afloat.

"What I know about relationships comes from those nights. Being locked in my room, sometimes without any dinner, and the two of them fucking like crazy in the other room. Their moans. Their laughter.

"He'd bring gifts on those nights. Well, for Mom, mostly, but sometimes for me. He never once apologized, for any of it. But my mother seemed to think those little gifts were everything. She'd tell me how hard marriage was. What a burden the sex was, how she only did it to keep him. How the gifts made it all worth it for a while. And the better the gift was, the more crap she'd put up with." It's pouring out now, like the proverbial broken dam. It hurts, but I can't stop it. I don't want to badly enough. "She told me how sex was the only time she had any control over him. She told me far too much, frankly. And she was so damn grateful for whatever small pleasure she got out of him, and believe me, it wasn't much. Even when he was gone, she was never angry enough. Just so incredibly sad. I hated her sadness. I hated them both for it, but her most of all, because I knew it was what drove him away."

I stop, trying to untangle all those ugly bits and pieces from my brain. I want to tear them out. I want them all to be gone. But this is part of who I am. It will always be there.

"And what about your teen years, Valentine?"

"That was better. And worse. I'd gotten too old for my mom to drag me around anymore, to lock me in my room. I was pretty much left to my own devices by about age thirteen. I stayed out late, did what I wanted to. I got into smoking cigarettes for a while, drinking beer with my friends, but it reminded me too much of my mother, so that stopped pretty quickly. I became hypersexual, sleeping with all the boys in school, the occasional college guy. I never had a real boyfriend, not even then."

"What about it was bad, exactly?"

"Well, the sleeping around itself, I guess."

"You guess?"

"I mean, I don't think sex itself is bad, even at that age. But it was just so fucking . . . empty. I was looking for something to . . . fill me up. But it never did. Oh, I got that momentary thrill of male attention. That validation. But no one really cared. Even I didn't care."

I think back for a moment to that article I read on the way to New York, about those girls. So abandoned. So like me. A small wrenching sensation in my chest. For them. For myself. What difference might it have made if someone gave a shit?

"I think my early sexual behavior was a culmination of all that happened prior to that, in my childhood, with my parents. And then my sexual behavior as an adult . . . I think I've partitioned my life in my mind, separating the two. The time before I got paid for sex, and the time after." The words are just streaming out now, the thoughts forming milliseconds before translating into language. "But ultimately, it was all the same thing, wasn't it? Because there's always been this issue with my orgasms. And it's all got to be connected."

"Yes?" Lydia prompts.

I look right at her, watching for her reaction. "I've never been able to have an orgasm without getting paid for it. I can't even masturbate successfully."

And there it is, laid out on the table. I feel naked. Raw.

"What do you think that's about for you?"

"Oh, I know what it's about. It's about control. Isn't that what it always is? Classic control freak."

I'm being snotty again, and I really don't mean to be, but my chest is twisting into a hard ball, like a stone.

"It's not important to define anything here for anyone but yourself, Valentine."

"Okay. Okay." I nod my head, pause. My voice is a thin whisper. "That's all changed, though. With him."

"Joshua?"

"Yes."

"Do you think that's a positive sign?"

"Yes. No." I tighten my grip on my hair. I hadn't even been aware I was still holding on to it. "God, I don't know. Everything is different with him."

"Why do you think it's different?"

"Maybe . . . maybe because it's the first normal relationship I've allowed myself to have. And I use the term 'normal' lightly. But it's more than I've ever had by a long shot. He lets me . . . I can let go of some of the control with him. Like the orgasm is my own. It doesn't belong to anyone else. And that's scary for me. I don't know if this is making sense."

Lydia is quiet a moment. "Do you think if you'd had what you call a 'normal' relationship before now, you might have been able to work through this orgasm issue?"

"Maybe. I don't know. So much of what's happening right now seems to be about Joshua. About the kind of man he is. My response to him. But I also think sometimes things happen only when you're ready for it to happen. Big changes."

"So this is a time of change for you. Of transformation."

"Yes." My pulse is racing. "Yes. That's why I'm here, isn't it? That's why I'm so fucking scared." I look at Lydia. "Is this even going to help?"

"I hope so." She smiles at me again. There's warmth there, and sincerity.

I realize that I hope so, too.

"To answer your earlier question, I don't exactly know why I'm here. I don't know what I hope to get out of this. I don't know what I *can* hope for. But I want . . . something."

Something just for me, for once.

"I think that's a good place to start."

I can feel myself warming toward this woman. Opening up. Softening a little on the inside. And I also know it didn't start with her, here in this office. It started with Joshua. But I need to try to put him aside while I'm here with Lydia. I need to figure myself out before I can even begin to decide where he fits into the equation, if he fits at all. I'm still doubtful. But also, for the first time since he came into my life and began to change it, I have some sense of hope.

I don't know yet what I'm hoping for, as I've just said to Lydia. But a woman like me has to hang on to whatever she can.

AFTER THE THERAPY I feel . . . strange. As though all of my nerve endings are on high alert, sensitive. My muscles are tight; my *skin* is tight. Restless, I go to the Century City mall for a while, wandering the shops, but nothing catches my interest. And I can't stand the people today, everyone so damned polished and pretty. It's all so fucking artificial. I get in my car and head home, cutting over to Wilshire and heading east, into Hollywood.

It's smoggier here, inland, than it was in Santa Monica. And simply seeing that familiar sky brings me back to my earlier musings about my childhood.

I do not want to think about this.

Regardless, images flash through my head: the half-darkened living room, my mother sitting on the couch, her hair askew, the air thick with her hot cigarette smoke, the stench of stale booze. And me on the couch next to her, trapped while she goes on and on about what an asshole my father is. While she tells me that men are supposed to be good for fucking, but my father, that useless bastard, isn't even good at that. How much she hates having to sleep with him, how hard it is to smile and play along, letting him do what he wants to her, just so he won't leave again.

But he always did, didn't he?

I feel sick, suddenly, my stomach churning. Unbearable.

I pull over, right in the middle of the perfect emerald lawns of Beverly Hills, and throw up on the street.

After wiping my mouth with a Kleenex pulled from my purse, I take a swallow from my water bottle, sit a moment to catch my breath before I pull back onto the road.

What the hell is wrong with me?

All I want now is to get home. To crawl into bed as though I'm ill. Maybe I am.

I'm shaking by the time I get to my house and make it through the front door. Tossing my keys and my purse on the table in the entry hall, I kick my shoes off, start stripping off my clothes. And see the blinking light on my answering machine. I don't feel like talking to anyone.

Except Joshua.

I punch the button.

"Valentine, it's Joshua. When can I see you?" A pause, then, "I want to see you tonight. I want to see you *now*. Call me."

My stomach flutters. Relief rushes through my body, leaving me weak-kneed. I am dying to see him, in a way that frankly scares the hell out of me. But I'm too shaken up to talk to him now.

I get naked and crawl into bed, pulling the covers up

over my head. I don't care about anything but hiding away for a while, sleeping off this sense of shock. The rest of the world can go away. I can't deal with anything. Not even him, as much as I want to see him, talk to him, touch him. Feel his arms around me.

Oh yes, I want that more than anything.

I curl into a tight ball beneath the weight of the covers, reach over and grab the bag of gummi bears from my nightstand, pop one into my mouth. And with the sugar melting on my tongue, sweet and comforting, I drift off.

IT'S DARK ALREADY WHEN the phone wakes me. I make a grab for it, fumbling, drop it on the floor and have to get out of bed to retrieve it.

"Hello?"

"Valentine. It's me."

His voice is like a hand caressing my naked skin in the dark.

"Joshua?"

"Are you okay? Were you sleeping? It's only eight-thirty."

"No. I mean, yes, I'm fine. I was asleep." I run a hand through my hair, silently ordering my brain to function. "I think I slept most of the day."

"Are you coming down with something?" Concern in his voice. Lovely. Soothing.

"What? No, I'm fine. I was just . . . tired. What are you doing? How are you?"

"I'm dying to see you." He laughs. "I guess that's obvious."

I smile to myself, warming all over. "That's okay. I like it."

And I do.

"Come out with me tomorrow night. I promise to buy you dinner this time."

"Why don't you come over now?"

Yes. Get him here, in your bed.

"Now? Really?"

"Yes. Please. Just come here. Can you do that?"

"I'll be right there. Don't go anywhere."

"I won't. I can't. I'm naked."

"I may get a speeding ticket, Valentine." He chuckles softly, desire lacing his voice. "Stay just as you are."

I nod as though he can see me. "Alright. I'm waiting for you."

We hang up and I curl up on top of the covers, letting the cool night air breathe over my skin, bringing up goose bumps. But I don't care. I don't want to cover myself. He said to stay here, naked, and I will. And I will take a deep pleasure in doing exactly what he asks of me. Doesn't matter why.

I am in an almost meditative state by the time he arrives. His knock at the door is a solid thud that echoes in my empty chest.

When I pull open the door he's smiling, a crooked, lustful grin. And my body is on fire even before he pushes through the door and takes me in his arms.

He kisses me, those long, lovely kisses again. And I am aching for him, longing, *needing*. His hands are everywhere, stroking my bare skin, that hard, demanding touch that makes me swoon. The darkness is like a cocoon around us as he sheds his clothes, pulls me up against his body, naked now, as I am. His erection is like a velvet-sheathed weight against my stomach, pressing, pressing, until I can hardly stand it.

Heat radiates from him, warming me, all but my bare feet

on the cool floor. And then he is pushing me down on the long sofa, his body covering mine. The weight of him is erotic to me, just his big body holding me down. I want it just like this, need it: that sense of him being the one in control, of turning myself over to him, to my need for him.

My pulse is racing as he brushes his cheeks over my breasts, nuzzling them. My nipples are hard already. Wanting. My thighs are spreading as if of their own accord, opening up my body to him. And his hand slips down between us, stroking the wet flesh of my aching sex. Stroking, stroking, making me shiver all over with pleasure. God, he knows just how to do it, two fingers sinking savagely inside me while he circles my clitoris with his thumb. And when he pulls one nipple into his mouth, his teeth grazing the tender flesh, then really biting, I arch, my hips straining. His fingers sink deeper, his mouth sucking me in, one hand on my hip holding me down, pressing my body into the cushions. And my sudden climax is like an eruption of pleasure in my belly, in my sex, my breasts.

"Joshua!"

"Yeah, come for me, baby."

I am coming and coming; I can't stop. He's working my clit still, his fingers pumping as he whispers encouragement against my parted lips.

"Oh, yeah, baby. Come for me. So good . . ."

With my climax still shimmering through my system in small, lingering waves, I wrap my legs around him, beg him, "Please, Joshua. I need you inside me."

"Wait . . ."

He reaches over the side of the sofa, comes back with a condom pulled from his pocket, I imagine. I'm just grateful he's thought of everything. Then he's kneeling up over me, slipping the condom on while I run my hands over the taut muscles of his stomach. He is watching me in that way he has as he lowers his body over mine. So slowly, making me need him even more, and his hands holding me down, pressing onto my shoulders, in that way he has which makes me feel completely taken over. That intensity is there, in the way his eyes glitter in the half-dark, in the tension in every muscle of his beautiful body, in the electric current in the air between us.

When his cock probes at the opening to my body, I pull in a deep, gasping breath, my hands going to his hips, trying to pull him in.

"Wait, Valentine. I want to enjoy every moment of this."

"Yes . . ."

Yes, he's right. I am in too much of a hurry. I can't help myself. I know he'll make me come again.

Oh, yes.

He presses, and the tip of his cock slides right in, like steel over silk, I am that wet. My entire body throbs with pleasure, with anticipation. Then a little deeper. He stops, his expression one of exquisite pain, except that it is pleasure.

"Jesus, Valentine. You feel so good, I can barely stand it."

My hand goes to his cheek; he is too beautiful at this moment for me not to touch him. Pleasure is like a thousand stars, burning into my body as he begins to move, just the tiniest surge of his hips against mine. And my chest feels tight, drawn, simply watching his face. My fingers trace along his jaw, over his lips, and he smiles. Then one hard, lovely thrust, and we are both groaning, panting.

His hands bear down on my shoulders, really using his weight, until I am unable to move. I love this sensation of being held, of being helpless beneath him. Of being *his*.

I am losing my mind.

But when he starts to move, really pumping inside me, I

am too lost in sensation to think anymore. It is just his body and mine, the lovely friction, the scent of him, the power of his touch, his dark gaze, and his smooth skin beneath my grasping hands.

And as he thrusts into me, he moves one of his hands to my throat, presses just a little, just enough to constrict my airflow the tiniest bit, to make my body surge with alarm and hot, sharp pleasure. But I know so deeply that he won't hurt me. And I'm a little dizzy; desire acute, exquisite, incredibly intense. As intense as his gaze hard on mine, glittering. Bottomless.

Pleasure courses through me in brilliant, stinging currents, burrowing deeper and deeper. It builds within me, taking me higher than I have ever been, before dropping me into that abyss, into his dark gaze, into *him*. And I shatter, coming so damn hard I am blinded, breathless, shaking.

He tenses, pumps harder into me, so deep I can feel him hitting my cervix. Pain and pleasure all mixed together, and the hammering beat of my heart, the throbbing of my own climax still heavy in my body.

I am spent. But so content to lie here with Joshua's weight on top of me, with the scent of sex in my nostrils. We are both damp, breathing hard. He lifts his head to brush a kiss across my lips. I want him to keep kissing me, but I truly cannot move, cannot speak.

I am so afraid of what I'm feeling at this moment.

I decide not to think about it.

No, it's too good to think about *him*. About his softening cock still inside me, the warmth of his big body against mine, that lovely pressure holding me down, holding me together in some strange way. His skin is so incredibly soft for a man, with that hard-packed muscle underneath.

I run my hands over him, feeling the texture of his body. And he begins to kiss my cheek, tiny, soft kisses that flutter over my skin like air. Only it's his warm lips on my cheek, then on my mouth. And as I sink into his kiss, my heart fills, warms, and I am crying. I can't stop. Quiet tears that slip down my cheeks.

"What's this, Valentine?" he asks, his voice soft and sweet.

"I don't know."

And I don't. It's all so damn confusing to me. I don't know why I'm crying, what I'm feeling. But the strangest part is that I don't want to run away from it, from this moment. I'm fine, with Joshua whispering to me, wiping my tears away with his hand. I really am.

He doesn't ask for more explanation, and I'm grateful. I couldn't give him one right now.

This is alien territory for me. And I'm afraid, yes, but also accepting of it. For now. There will be plenty of time to dissect it all later, in the safety of Lydia's office, perhaps. But for now, I just need to be here with him. It makes me feel strong, somehow. It's enough. It's more than I've ever had before. This moment is mine—*ours*. I'm not giving it away to the past. For once.

Chapter Nine

I COME OUT OF sleep with warm hands on my cheeks, his lips on mine. I don't want to open my eyes, don't want this to end, this lovely dream state where the world can't intrude, where everything is fine. And he is kissing me so hard I can't think.

Finally, he pulls away.

"Valentine, baby, I have to go."

Fuck. And there it is. Inevitable reality.

"I know," I tell him, my lashes fluttering open, my fingers curling around his wrist. His flesh is warm.

"I wish I could stay with you all day. Just stay here in bed with you," he tells me, his voice quiet, husky with sleep still. I can smell the soap from the shower on him. His hair is damp when I reach up to pull his face in for another kiss.

He groans. "I really have to go to work."

"I'm sorry. I don't want to make you late."

"I'm sorry I can't stay." He pulls back, his eyes on mine. "I don't want to leave you now."

My chest hurts, just looking at him, listening to his tone,

his words. If he doesn't leave right now I feel like I'll crack, just break apart. I can't figure it out. He just gets inside me and it's suddenly too much to handle.

He leans in, kisses me again, his fingers going into my hair. Ah, so nice. Too nice.

Please go.

I can't believe I'm even thinking this. But I need some time to assimilate everything that's happening inside me.

"I'll call you tonight, okay?" He smiles, laughs a little. "Hell, I may call you at lunchtime. I don't know if I can wait until tonight."

I just smile at him, nod my head. I can't talk to him now.

But he seems satisfied. He gives my hair a playful tug and then he's gone, leaving me alone with my whirling thoughts.

I keep coming back to this confusing, frightened place. I can't calm down enough to really think. My body, my mind, crave the safety of sleep, but I know I'm too worked up to fall asleep again. Totally impossible, with my heart pounding, my pulse racing. Instead I get up and get right into the shower, blasting the hot water.

It scorches my skin as I get in and stand under the spray, but I need it, need something that intense to get my mind off what I'm feeling. Something to focus on. I pick up my favorite bottle of liquid soap, squeeze it out onto my palm and run it over my skin until I'm slippery all over, smelling like orange blossoms and vanilla. Then I move under the water, letting the heat rinse away the soap, along with some of my anxiety.

I really need to calm down. Just calm down so I can think this through.

But even as that idea flits through my brain, the water hits my nipples, and they immediately go hard. And in moments I am thinking of Joshua, of his clever hands, his lovely mouth on my body, his cock inside me. I am wet, inside and out, swollen with need, needing him again. My hand goes between my legs, finding my throbbing clitoris. So damn sensitive, a little sore from my night with Joshua, but ready for more.

Taking the handheld sprayer, I spread my thighs and aim it at my clit. Warm and wet, pounding against that tender flesh, pleasure sweeps through me. The water from the ceiling-mounted showerhead washes over my body, and the sprayer pulsates against my aching mound, and I can see his face, his lush mouth, that small scar that makes me want to kiss him over and over.

Oh, yes . . .

My hips are pumping now, fucking the water, fucking his invisible hands, his mouth, his cock, milking him for pleasure.

My orgasm hits so quickly, with such sudden intensity, I gasp aloud. Sharp, powerful, making my body bow, my sex pulse.

Joshua!

Oh, yes, it's always him, only him.

I shove two fingers deep inside, driving my climax on. My sex clenches hard, and I am nearly crying with pleasure, with need. And then I am crying, my tears mingling with the water. I sink to the shower floor, unable to stand. Unable to understand what's happening to me. Unable to bear it.

I don't even know what I'm crying for. Nothing. Everything. Because I'm finally happy and I don't know how to deal with it, maybe.

Fuck.

The water turns cold, finally, shocking me, and I stand, shut it off, get out and dry myself. As I run the towel over my skin, the postcrying numbness fades away, and I realize I feel less conflicted. Stronger. As though the tears have emptied something toxic from my system. I realize I am going to have to deal with this. I am simply going to have to find a way. I can't spend my life masturbating, or curled up on the shower floor. Fucking ridiculous.

Calmer, I take my time doing my makeup, drying my hair, getting dressed, finding comfort in the daily ritual. I don't even know who I'm getting dressed for, what I'm going to do with my day. I don't know what I want to do.

I slip into a cotton knit dress, a mossy green I've always thought looks good with my green eyes. A pair of gold hoop earrings, a few bangle bracelets to match, and a new pair of boots in a deep chocolate suede with high heels.

I'm ready. I just don't know what for.

When I move into the living room I see my purse sitting on the table in the entry hall. I'd turned my cell phone off yesterday. I know I should check for messages. I don't want to. I don't want to deal with anything. I am too at odds in my own body right now. But, being the good little hooker that I am, I pull the phone out of my purse, turn it on, retrieve my messages.

It's Colin, wanting to see me today. Colin, of all people. My pretty, dirty boy. Filthy dirty. But perhaps he's exactly what I need to pull me out of this bubble in my head.

I feel stronger today. Confident. A little more in control. And working will make me feel even more so. It always does.

I dial his number, and we agree to meet at ten-thirty. He often likes to meet in the morning, rather than waiting for lunchtime or evening for his sex, like most clients do. Anything that makes the event seem a little more tawdry.

He's given me the address of a small motel in the Valley this time. I have a cup of tea and some toast, water my orchids, watch the morning news, and then it's time to go. I get in my car and pull away from my house, from my little safe haven that no longer feels quite as safe as it once did. Nothing does.

I follow the twisting road down from the hills and head for the 405, take it north into the San Fernando Valley. It's a bit of a trek, but everything in Los Angles is far from everything else. Taking the 101 cutoff, I head west, exit at De Soto, follow it north, up into Chatsworth.

Chatsworth is the capital of the porn industry. I have no idea why so many porn studios film here. It's a thoroughly middle-class area. Too damn close to where I grew up, the street names all too familiar: Victory, Roscoe, Devonshire. But I can't think about that now.

I swing onto Devonshire and follow it for a few blocks, until I find the motel. It's not nearly as bad as the last one off Sunset, but still sleazy enough to make Colin happy.

I pull in and park, and Colin is standing by the door of a room on the first floor. He whistles as I get out of the car.

"Classy today," he says.

Damn. I forgot to change into one of my slutty outfits for him.

"Just trying to mix things up for you," I tell him, trying hard to smile.

Get into the groove, Valentine.

"No problem. It's all coming off, anyway." He takes my hand and pulls me inside.

The room is nothing special: faded paint, an even more faded floral bedspread. Everything just a little ugly and old. Except the pretty and shining Colin himself.

"You could have been an actor, Colin," I tell him. And it's true. He's that pretty.

"I would have made a lousy actor. I can't lie. Can't play anything off."

"Really? Where do you tell your wife you've been when you're fucking me in some sleazy motel?"

Shit. Why am I baiting him?

But he doesn't seem to notice. "I don't say a damn word to her about it. I save all the talking for you. So I can tell you exactly how I'm going to fuck you, Val. How hard, how deep. Whether I'm going to fuck your pussy or your amazing ass. Have I told you how amazing your ass is?" He moves in, puts his hand on my shoulder, dips his fingers beneath the fabric of my dress. I feel a shiver, but it's not anticipation, not the usual pleasure.

Get it together!

"How do you want it today, Colin?" I say, trying to work the usual purr into my voice.

"Get naked and I'll figure it out."

I pull my dress over my head, feeling oddly exposed in my bra and thong in front of him.

"All of it," he says, his brilliant blue eyes gleaming.

Why do I feel so uncomfortable? Every nerve in my body is screaming, my muscles tight all over as I reach back to unhook my bra.

I cannot do it.

Fuck.

I stop, shake my head. I reach for my discarded dress, picking it up off the floor, and slip it back over my head. "I'm sorry, Colin. I don't know what's wrong. I'm not feeling well. I'm sorry."

His face hardens for a minute, his brows drawing together. But then his features relax, and he looks almost concerned. Maybe he sees me shaking. Maybe I'm pale. I feel pale.

"You alright, babe?"

"No. I'm not. I'm sorry. I have to go. I'm sorry."

I'm out of there so fast, I don't even remember how I get to my car, but suddenly I am sitting in it, leaning into the leather seat. My breath is coming in hard pants.

Breathe. Just fucking breathe.

When I look up Colin is standing at the open door of the hotel room, his cell phone against his ear. Maybe calling Deirdre. Maybe calling for another girl. I don't care right now.

I start the car and pull out of the parking lot, heading back toward home. But what am I going to do there? Crawl back into bed, spend another day sleeping, dreaming, when my life is falling apart around me? While I let it happen?

I am totally out of control. The strength I felt earlier, the strength Lydia talks about, was apparently just an illusion.

I make it to the 101, my mind almost blank, a weird rage surging through my system, before I realize what I need to do. Pulling my cell from my purse, I call Deirdre. Her assistant puts me through right away.

"Yes, Val?"

Cool as ever. Cool as a cucumber. Cold as ice.

"Deirdre, I need to talk to you."

"Alright. Let's set up a time, shall we?"

"No, it can't wait. I'm sorry. I need to speak with you now."

"What's going on, Val? Is there a problem?"

"Did you get a call just now from Colin Harper?"

"No. Should I have?"

"Maybe. Probably." I pause, pull in a deep breath, concentrate for a moment on changing lanes to get back on the 405. "I just left him and . . . I walked out on him, Deirdre."

"What?" Anger in her voice, beneath that slick surface. "Explain yourself, Val."

"I think . . . I think I need some time off."

She is quiet for a moment. I can almost hear her brain working, a faint click and whir, computerlike, assessing the situation in mere moments. "Yes, I agree. That's an excellent idea."

"I'll call all of my clients."

"No, I'll have Cynthia call. If you need time off, then you shouldn't speak with any of them."

She's right. "Yes, of course. But, Deirdre, when she talks to Louis—"

"We will handle it, Val. You do whatever you need to do. Are you seeing Lydia Foster?"

"Yes. I had my first visit with her and I think . . . it brought up a lot of old issues . . ."

God, I do not want to explain myself to this woman.

"Very good. Keep seeing her. I'll be in touch. And, Val, do not contact your clients directly, do you understand what I'm saying?"

"Yes, of course. I understand completely."

I don't want to talk with any of them, anyway. What could I possibly say? No, better to let The Broker and her staff handle it. More professional. And we are nothing if not professionals.

Of course, currently, I am not even that anymore.

I expect to feel some sort of dread, but all I feel is relief.

We hang up and my next call is to my therapist. I tell her I have to see her, that I'm having a crisis, and it's true. She agrees to see me right away.

Exiting the freeway, I make my way to her office. When I get out of the car I am struck by the ocean scent in the air, the quiet solidity of the greenery climbing up the old brick walls of her building, and I feel the tiniest bit better simply knowing I am here.

I go upstairs and she ushers me into her inner sanctum, waves me to the chair. The moment I sit she hands me a box of Kleenex. I take it without protest.

"Tell me what's happened, Valentine."

"I just . . . I think I . . ." but before I can get the words out I'm crying, tears washing in a mad torrent down my cheeks. I haven't cried this much since I was ten years old! But no matter how disgusted I am with myself, I can't seem to stop.

It all comes out between choked sobs: my time with Joshua, the realization of my feelings for him. The epiphany of sex—no, making love—with him! The epiphany of being happy. Then today, my failed meeting with Colin, the absolute need to stop working for the first time in nearly a decade. How absolutely broken I feel. And how certain I am about the need to change my life.

Finally, I am wrung out, empty. She lets me sit quietly for a few minutes, catching my breath as I wipe my damp face with the tissues.

"Okay," she says, drawing in a deep breath herself. "This is a lot, isn't it?"

"Yes. Too much."

"Is it too much, Valentine?"

I look at her, uncertain of what she's asking.

"Because you're here," she says. "You came for help so you can handle this. You made the decision to stop working. And I don't believe that was any sort of snap decision. If it really was too much, you would have simply turned away from Joshua and everything his presence in your life means for you."

"I can't do that!"

She nods. "Exactly. What does that tell you?"

"You really make me work for it, don't you?"

"You need to find your own answers. I'm here to help you

do that. But if I hand you everything on a silver platter, it won't be worth anything. And I can't know what the answers are for you. They're different for everyone. But I think right now, yours are staring you in the face. And by quitting work today, it's obvious that you've figured some of it out already. What's next, do you think?"

I shake my head, but I know what she's getting at.

Fuck.

Fuck!

"I need to . . . I need to tell Joshua. What I do. Did. What my life has been about. I need to be honest with him."

She nods once more. There's no need for her to say it out loud, and I'm grateful to her for not rubbing my face in this stark, cold reality. I already feel like I'm going to throw up, as I did after my first visit here.

"God, I don't know how . . . and it's going to be a mess. He'll never speak to me again."

"How do you know that?"

"Any sane person, any normal person, would react that way. Why would he want to see me, be with me, once he knows the truth? It's impossible."

"Maybe you're not giving him enough credit," Lydia suggests. "Maybe you're not giving yourself enough credit. There is more to you than what you do for a living, Valentine."

Her blue eyes are soft, sympathetic. I understand she's trying to be encouraging, because this is the right thing to do, and therefore I *must* do it. I fucking hate it. But I will do the right thing.

"How can anyone forgive me this if . . ." My voice breaks, emotion welling in my chest, choking me. But I will not cry anymore.

"If what, Valentine?" she asks softly.

"If . . . I can't forgive myself?"

"Sometimes you just have to take a risk. Jump blindly off the edge, trusting the universe to catch you."

"It never has before."

"Maybe you've never given it a chance."

I nod. It's possible, I suppose. But it's awfully hard to believe. People like me don't get those kinds of chances in life, although things could be worse. I know I am lucky for what I have, lucky not to be some streetwalker with knife wounds on my face, addicted to crack, dead in an alley off Sunset Strip.

But what have I got to lose? I will lose Joshua one way or another. If I lie to him I don't deserve to have him. I don't know why this makes me feel better, more resolved, but it does.

"I suppose I should try to redeem myself any way I can. For myself, if nothing else. I need to before I can . . . I don't know. Move on. If that's even possible. But it's going to be the end of everything."

"Valentine, everything is changing for you, but that doesn't mean it has to be the end. Look at this as a time of transformation, as an opportunity."

"I'm trying. But to be honest, it scares me to death. I hardly know where to start."

"But you already have. Trust what you know to be true. And move forward."

She's right. And what else can I do?

You can lie like a coward. Keep him as long as you can.

Of course, the longer I'm with him, the harder it'll be when he goes.

My chest twists in pain as though a knife has been plunged in. Sharp. Cutting. Deep.

My fingers dig into the sofa cushions. "I'll try, Lydia. I'll do it, tell him."

"I think it's the only way. I wish there was an easier solution for you."

"So do I."

"But you can do this, Valentine. I believe in you. I believe in your strength. How else could you have survived your life?"

I'd always thought it was sheer desperation, a lack of other viable options. I like her view on it better. A part of me even believes her.

"Call me if you need to talk, when you'd like to set up another appointment."

"I will."

Our time is up. I leave her office, stepping back out onto the street. That ocean smell is there again, clearing my head a little. Maybe I should find a house close to the ocean? Change everything. Because I know already I'm not going to be able to hang on to any aspect of my old life. I'm changing already. I've taken that first step and begun to look at my life, look inside myself. Considered having a future different from my present. This is not a sabbatical. It's over.

I break out into a sweat as those words echo in my head. *It's over.*

What the fuck am I going to do now? What am I going to *be*?

The only anchor I have now is Joshua. And I am about to lose him. But some small part of me is whispering that I can do this. Survive this. And as I make my way down the street, back to my car, I hang on to that voice as tight as I can.

Maybe I have to be my own anchor.

—

JOSHUA HAS LEFT TWO messages, but I avoid his calls all evening, sitting on my sofa in the dark in my favorite pale pink satin pajamas. They are the color of old roses. Not the best shade on me, but the softness of the color itself is soothing. The sound is turned down on the television and I have a gin and tonic in my hand. I'm not drunk yet, although this is my fourth. Or is it my fifth? I'm just buzzed enough not to care that this drinking binge is far too reminiscent of my mother. I'm buzzed and I'm fucking miserable, which is what being drunk is all about in my mind.

I am my mother's daughter. Not just that I'm using booze to drown my sorrows. But she was as much a whore as I am. She had sex with my father for the gifts, the attention. Isn't that what I do? Although for me, the orgasms have always been as crucial as the money, even if the money has been damn nice.

I've found the cure for the orgasm issue. The cure is Joshua. Or at least, he is some sort of powerful catalyst. I still don't understand it. But I know he is crucial to what's happening to me, the orgasms, everything.

How ironic that it's about to be over, leaving me with nothing?

I am not drunk enough to prevent myself from being thoroughly disgusted with my little pity party.

I am not delusional enough to think I can continue with Joshua without telling him the truth.

Looking at the blue glow of the TV, I flip through the channels. I'm not really paying attention until *Pretty Woman* flashes on the screen.

I laugh, a harsh, barking sound that hurts my ears. I almost want to watch it, to punish myself with those glamorized

Hollywood images of the utterly impossible. Instead I shut the damn TV off, set my glass down, get up, and wander to the bay window. My orchids are there, their purple and white petals washed with silvery moonlight.

Below me Hollywood sparkles, like a handful of diamonds strewn carelessly over the dark landscape. But that's life, isn't it? All of us so careless, ultimately, driven by our own selfish needs. At least, it comforts me to think I'm not the only one doing it.

Joshua is possibly the only human being I've met who isn't entirely selfish. He may have had some rough times, been foolish, been self-indulgent in the past, but he seems to have truly worked through it all. Come out intact. Self-aware. Unshakable in his beliefs. He is the best person I know.

My whole body surges with longing for him, and I have to wrap my arms around my waist and hold on tight, staring out the window. He is out there somewhere, and I can hardly stand it.

Be with him. Tell him. Take a chance.

No. I cannot do it.

When the phone rings I know it's him. I tell myself I won't answer it, but by the third ring the receiver is in my hand.

"Hello?" My voice is breathless. I am breathless.

"Valentine? Have you been out? Did you get my messages?"

"Yes. I got them. I'm sorry. I should have . . . I should have called you. I know that. I just . . ."

"Are you alright?"

I pause to draw in a breath, blow it out slowly, pushing my hair from my face with my free hand.

"No. I'm not."

"What's going on? Can you tell me?"

"I've been drinking . . . I don't know if . . . I don't know how clear I can be."

"Valentine, what's happened?" Real alarm in his voice now. I feel like shit.

"I don't mean to worry you. I'm just . . . I've been thinking all day. Reviewing my life. Actually, I've been doing that since the night I met you."

"Is that a bad thing?"

I have to stop and think about it. I go back to the sofa, pick up my glass and drink, really gulp it down, letting the gin burn as it slides down my throat. Sharp edge of revulsion along with the burn, but I am too scared tonight to do anything else. "If you look at something," I tell him, "really look, and discover that every aspect of it is wrong, what can you do but start over, change everything?"

"We talked about that, in relation to my life, anyway."

"I'm just realizing how it applies to me, to the way I've lived, perceived myself. And so much needs to change." I pick up my glass once more, but the scent of the gin stings my eyes. I don't want it anymore. "I've always thought I had it all figured out. Now all I know is that it was just a lie I told myself, one I've been telling myself my whole life. And I can't do it anymore."

"Valentine, I'm coming over, okay? Will you just stay there? Wait for me?"

"Yes." It comes out as a whisper. That's all I have the breath for. He's coming and it will all be finished soon. Too soon.

We hang up and I wait for him, numbly flipping the TV on again.

Julia Roberts' fresh face lights up the screen, wearing that red gown as Richard Gere fastens the diamonds around her neck. That famous laugh. Everything so damn clean and shiny. But I know that's not what life is like. No, life is hard and dirty, no matter how much money you have. No matter what kind of car you drive. There will be no *Pretty Woman* scenario for me. No limousine and declarations of love. There will just be the end.

Chapter Ten

It seems as though only a few minutes have passed when he knocks on the door. I am acutely aware of how different this is from the last time I opened my door and he came into my house.

Still, my skin tingles as he moves in past me, shutting the door behind him. As he takes my hand, leading me to the sofa.

He sits down next to me, close enough that I can smell him. I pull in a deep breath of his scent, filling my lungs with it. Hoping to have at least that to hang on to when this is done.

His hands are on my shoulders, those gold and green eyes of his are cast in silver from the silent, flickering TV, as intense as ever.

"Talk to me, Valentine." His voice is low, commanding.

I nod. I need a moment before I can begin. I can feel the alcohol in my system, but it is not numbing me nearly enough.

"I have something to tell you, Joshua. Something . . . crucial."

"Has something happened?"

"No. Yes . . . Yes." I can't tear my gaze away from his, but it hurts to look at him. Fucking painful, how beautiful he is to me. "What's happened is that I've led this strange life. It's strange even to me if I let myself think about it. Something I have not allowed myself to do. Until I met you. Then I couldn't help it. And now that I have to look at it, look at myself, I see it for what it really is. And it's unacceptable. And I am stopping right now. I'm done with the way I've lived for almost ten years. I swear I'm done."

The tears are stinging at the back of my eyes, making my throat feel thick, tight.

He's shaking his head. "Please tell me what you're talking about."

"Joshua . . ."

So hard to say the words out loud to him!

Just do it. Get it over with.

I try again. "Joshua. For the last nine years I've been a prostitute."

"What?" He flinches, just the slightest bit, but I feel it like a blow to the head. To the heart. "What the hell are you saying to me?"

"I've been working as a call girl. Most of my adult life."

He's shaking his head again. His hands drop from my shoulders, leaving them cold. He runs both hands through his thick hair, blows out a long breath.

"Is this the truth, Valentine?"

I nod my head. "Yes. It's true. Please, Joshua . . ."

He puts up a hand. "Just . . . wait. Give me a minute to absorb this. Fuck."

He gets up and begins to pace, back and forth in front

of the window, in front of my orchids. I'm shaking all over. I don't dare say anything.

He keeps pacing, running his fingers through his hair, pressing on his eyes. And I'm getting more and more scared.

Finally, he comes and sits down again.

"Okay. Tell me. Tell me everything. I want to know how you started doing this." His voice is so tight I could cut myself on the edge of it.

"God, Joshua, don't make me tell you that." I'm shaking my head. "Don't do it."

"I have to know. Don't you see that? I have to know what your life has been like if I'm ever going to be able to accept it."

"Accept it? How can you . . . how can you even think that's possible?"

"I don't know yet. I don't know how to feel. I don't know anything. Talk to me. Tell me."

"God . . ." The tears are starting, trickling down my cheek. I wipe them away, angry, heartbroken. But I am going to do exactly as he's asked.

"I was twenty years old. I was in a bar. I shouldn't even have been there, but the doormen, the bartenders, will always let an attractive female in. No one ever bothered to check my I.D. And I met this girl, Jana. I don't even know if that was her real name. It probably wasn't. She knew a guy who had this house, and he was always looking for new girls."

I have to pause for a moment. I cannot believe I'm telling him this. No one knows the whole story, except Enzo. But it's too late to stop. "They told me I could make a lot of money, which was something I'd never had. And to be honest, the idea of that kind of attention was attractive to me.

"I was scared the first time. But the guy was okay. And . . . and . . . fuck. I can't do this!"

"Tell me, Valentine. You owe me that much." His voice is low, urgent.

I shake my head back and forth, staring at the floor. I cannot say these things and look into his eyes. He's too hurt. But I start talking.

"Until that night with my first trick, I hadn't ever . . . I had never had an orgasm with a man. I'd slept around, but it had never happened. And I knew right away that it was the act of him handing me that wad of cash that got me off so spectacularly. And it's worked every single time since then. As long as I get paid for it. But it's never been about the money. It's about control. Control."

I'm going cold all over. A little hard. It's the only way I can do this. Too fucking awful, this whole thing. But I have to finish.

"So . . . that became my special talent. My marketing angle. And it wasn't long before I was discovered by a man who knew exactly how to market me. Enzo. He took me out of that place, sent me to school, polished me up, taught me how to dress. He did a real Pygmalion number on me. He made me what I am. But I don't . . . it was the best thing that could have happened to a girl like me. I'll always be grateful to him, because the alternative would have been much, much worse."

I am desperate that Enzo not be blamed. I look at Joshua and he's watching me in that way he has, with total concentration. But I can read the shock all over his face, in his tight features.

"Yes, I can see that," he says quietly.

He gets up then, begins the pacing all over again. I'm quiet, watching him. I have no idea what to expect.

He stops in front of me, his eyes blazing. "Tell me what you've done. All of it."

"What? You want a laundry list? Joshua, why do you want to put yourself through that? Why do you need to know?"

"I just do. Tell me."

"Okay. Okay." I run a hand through my hair, squeeze the strands between my fingers. I feel sick. "I don't know where to start."

"Have you had anal sex with these guys?"

I nod my head.

"Talk to me, Valentine."

His voice is harsh. My heart breaks a little more. But I answer him.

"Yes."

"What about group sex?"

"Yes."

"Sex with other women?"

"Yes, all of that."

"Kinky stuff? Bondage?"

"Not much kink, no."

"Did you like it?"

"God, Joshua . . . you already know . . ."

"I need you to say it."

"Yes. I liked it. Most of it, anyway. Is that what you want to know?"

"Yes!" he hisses. He rubs a hand over his jaw, says more quietly, "Yes. Because . . . it makes it seem less wrong if you weren't compromising every bit of yourself to do these things."

This is shocking, not what I expected him to say at all.

He's still angry, though; I can see it in the clench of his jaw, in his burning eyes. I'm on the defense; I want to explain myself to him, even if he can never truly understand.

"So, do you really day trade, or is that just a cover?"

"I do some trading. I'm not dependent on it, but I make some declarable income that way."

"And have you really been to college? Have you been taking art history courses?"

"Yes. Yes! That's all true. The only thing I kept from you was my . . . occupation. The rest is all true."

"What else, Valentine?"

"I'm not hiding anything else from you. There's nothing left for me to hide. But you should know that I've been tested for HIV every six weeks the whole time. I'm clean. I don't want you to worry about that. I know that's not . . . normal. To have to live this way.

"There's been nothing else to my life, really, for the last nine years. I'm either working or I'm alone. There is nothing in between. I've tried dating a few times, but it's always horribly disappointing. The sex is such a letdown. And I can never be myself, because no one who is not a client can ever know what I do. And so I gave it up, finally, the dating. Trying to have any kind of normal life. I suppose I was resigned. Numb. And then I met you."

"And?"

I know what he's asking.

"And I knew from the first moment I met you that something was different. That things could be different. And they have been. Everything is different with you, Joshua. The sex is . . . amazing. A revelation, if you want to know the truth. For the first time in so long, ever maybe, I'm feeling . . . *something*.

Everything! But it's turned my life upside down. Maybe that needed to happen. I know it did. But now I'm just . . . I know what I need to do. I just don't know how to go about it."

He nods his head a few times. "Okay." He gets up, starts the pacing all over again while I sit there with my heart pounding out of my chest, my fingers clamping together so hard it hurts. "Thank you for telling me."

Ever the gentleman. Even now.

My heart is thudding like a series of hammer blows in my chest. I'm almost sober again. I watch him pace, wait for the verdict. I already know what's coming: that he will walk out the door, walk out of my life. But like some twisted masochist, I have to hear the words from him. I have to hear him say it's over.

Finally, he sits down again, asks, "So, what happens now?"

"You're asking me?"

"Yes."

I shake my head, unable to grasp what he's saying. "Are you telling me I have some choice here?"

"Don't you?"

"Joshua . . ." But my throat closes up. I swallow, hard, forcing it open so I can talk to him. "Are you saying you're not . . . walking out? Walking away from me?"

"That all depends on where you'd like to go from here. If you want to try."

"I . . . I've quit work. Is that what you're asking?"

"Partly. Yes. It's necessary. If you hadn't told me you'd quit, without me having to ask, I would have been out that door already."

"I'm not going back. No matter what. I swear it."

"I believe you."

"You do?"

"Christ, Valentine. If I didn't, how could we possibly have anything?"

"You're angry."

"Hell, yes, I'm angry. I'm angry that you didn't tell me, even though I understand why you didn't. Why you couldn't. I'm trying to imagine what it must have taken for you to tell me now. But, yeah, I'm angry. Because there's something beautiful and intense between us, and I don't want anything to fuck it up, and this very well might. It sure as hell should. But I'm not sure I'm willing to let it. Not if you can really stop. If you're willing to change your life. But you can't do that for me. You have to do it for yourself, or it won't work. It won't mean anything."

My hands are twisted together in my lap, my fingers biting into each other. "Joshua, so much of this is about you, in that you were the starting point. The point at which I had to stop and question what the hell I was doing with my life. But the answer is that I have no life. Not really. And I need to change that. I *want* to. I can't do it anymore; it's become impossible. So while you may have been the catalyst, it ultimately comes down to the fact that I'm done. Even if you walk out the door this very moment . . ." I have to stop, catch my breath. I don't want that to happen. I want him to stay. More than I've wanted anything in my life. "I'm not going back. I can't. That part of me has changed already."

He's quiet, watching me once more. My face is hot. My head feels as though there is an immense pressure, in my brain, beneath my skin.

Finally he says, "I needed to know that."

I nod. The tears are back, waiting for me to let them fall, but I clench my jaw, refusing.

He takes my hand, looking down at it as he runs his

fingers over the knuckles, turns it over, rubs his thumb over my palm.

He says very quietly, "You're shaking."

"Yes."

He looks at me, and I cannot believe what I see in his eyes: sympathy. Understanding. Pain.

The tears fall then. I can't stop them. Fucking awful that he's watching me cry, my face contorting. But fucking wonderful that he's still here with me.

"I can't believe you're willing to do this. To even try," I tell him.

He lifts my hand, lays a soft kiss on the palm. "Maybe I can't, either. I don't understand it all yet. But there's something so deep between us, Valentine. I'm not ready to let that go. And I have to admit that all of my sleeping around, all those years of fucking everything in sight, wasn't any different than what you did. Except that I didn't get paid for it."

I want to throw my arms around him. But I feel too undeserving. If I am to find any comfort with him, he has to be the one to offer it.

"What now?" I ask, even though it scares me to think about what his answer might be.

"Now we just . . . spend some time together. Try to work through this. If you're willing."

"I want to. But, Joshua, I have to tell you, I don't know what the hell I'm doing. I've never had a normal relationship."

He smiles then, just a small, crooked smile. "I don't know that this will ever be a 'normal' relationship."

A small sob escapes me. "No. I suppose it couldn't be."

"It'll be whatever we make it."

"Okay."

"Come here."

He grabs me, his hand snaking around the back of my neck, holding me hard, and he kisses me. His lips are firm, insistent. They taste like my tears.

How can I be so incredibly sad and hopeful and hot for him all at the same time?

But he presses closer, his other hand grasping my hip, pulling me toward him. Holding me tightly, he stands, lifting me to my feet, then he picks me up and walks down the hall to my bedroom.

"No, Joshua."

"What?" I can feel his body tense.

"Not in my bed. Take me into the shower. I . . . I have to be clean."

How can I explain that I need some sort of ritual to mark this moment? I hardly understand it myself. But he seems to understand. He takes me into the bathroom, sets me on my feet. I reach in to turn on the shower while he leaves for a moment, coming back with a condom package, which he sets on one of the small shelves built into the big red granite shower stall.

I wait for him, as passive as I've ever been with any man.

I don't want to think about other men.

He begins to undress me. Slowly, carefully, as though he's never seen me naked before. Maybe he hasn't. Not like this. Not with my entire being open to him.

When I'm bare he strips his own clothes off quickly, takes my hand, and leads me into the water.

We stand under the rain showerhead for a long time, our arms entwined. I can barely think. I don't want to. I simply want to be here with him, in the wet, steamy heat. He holds me, tighter and tighter, until I can barely breathe. I don't care.

Then he starts to kiss me, his lush mouth on mine. Tender kisses, like nothing I have ever felt before, not even from him. I don't know if he's different, or if it's about what's happening inside me, or both, maybe. And my chest is filling with some sort of dense warmth. Like honey: that thick, that heavy.

His kisses are so lovely. And as his hands grip me, his strong fingers digging into my flesh, *owning* me, my body is heating up, a slow burn that is almost dreamlike in the misty steam. And the sensation of his wet skin against mine, the water seeping in between our closely pressed bodies, is more real than anything I've ever felt in my life.

His hands begin to roam over my skin: my back, my buttocks, the back of my thighs. He pulls his lips from mine and dips his head, laying open-mouthed kisses on my throat, between my breasts. And my hands go into his wet hair, pulling him closer. He kisses my breasts, my nipples coming up hard. And once more I'm amazed at how I can burn for him, physically and emotionally all at the same time.

"Valentine, I can't wait."

"No, don't wait. I need you."

In moments he's rolled the condom over his rigid cock, and he lifts me, pushing me up against the wall of the shower. I wrap my legs around his waist, and he sinks into me, sweet and smooth. Like the water coming down on us. Like everything I have ever needed.

He pushes in, his cock sliding deeper. And already my body is arcing into his, clenching, pleasure sweeping through me in long, undulating waves.

He kisses me again, our mouths pressed together, tongues twining, that sweet, wet heat, the taste of him, filling my mouth, my mind.

Pleasure rises in my body, higher, higher, as he presses his hips into mine, his cock thrusting harder and harder, slamming into me, and his grip on me tightening, hurting, possessing. But this is exactly what I need from him. My muscles go loose, and I am his. *His.* We move in perfect rhythm: our mouths, his cock in my sex. My body is filled with him; my heart is filled in a way it never has been in my life. And as I come onto him I am too caught up in how good he feels, how good we feel together, to be scared.

WE SPENT ALL OF last night and the entire day today in bed. I couldn't stand to be away from him, too afraid that if he left my side for even a few moments, I would start to think. I admitted this to him, and he canceled all of his work appointments, just to stay with me.

I still can't believe anyone would do this for me. For *me*!

It's late now, the night all around us, like some dark blanket, hiding us away from the world. He has made love to me over and over. We've talked about meaningless things, both of us being careful not to address the really important issues. After the shock of my revelation yesterday we need things to be as simple as possible between us for a little while. We both have too much to absorb; it can't be done all at once.

He's in the other room now, checking his messages. I don't want to check mine. Even seeing there aren't any will remind me of how my life has emptied out. I know I can't fill it entirely with Joshua. That wouldn't be fair. I'll have to figure out the rest of it.

Not now.

No, there will be time for that later. If I have to think about it now, it will ruin everything.

He comes back into the bedroom, climbs into bed with

me. I love it when he looks like this: his hair spiky, a little beard stubble on his cheeks, his eyes sleepy. Smelling like sex. Like love.

My heart stutters, and I swear it skips a few beats.

Love?

Is that what this is? How can someone like me even know?

We have known each other two and a half weeks. This is not possible.

What else could this warmth be expanding in my chest, filling me, making me weak as he takes me into his arms? It's not sex. Oh, no. I know what that feels like. This is something else entirely.

But love?

Too much to deal with right now. I can't do it. No, just be here with him, lie in his arms, listen to his breathing grow shallow as he slips into sleep.

And wonder for the first time about the limitless possibilities before me.

Absolutely terrifying. I have been such a sexual adventurer. But maybe the truth is that in every other area of my life, I have been hiding, too scared to take any real chances.

Turning to Joshua, I concentrate on the slow cadence of his breath. Careful not to wake him, I slide my hand onto his bare chest, feel the rise and fall of it. I need to know he's really *here*. I need him to ground me.

He draws in a deep breath, mutters, but he's still sleeping. Part of me wishes he'd wake up, make love to me again. But I've hidden behind sex for far too long already, haven't I? Perhaps that's actually been my specialty all these years.

I slip out of bed, finally, go into the kitchen and make a cup of tea. The floor is cold beneath my bare feet as I pad back into the living room, curl up on the sofa under a blanket. The tea is too hot to drink, but the mug warms my hands, the fragrant steam comforts me. Still, I think of the small plastic bag of gummi bears in my nightstand drawer. I want them, but I don't want to risk waking up Joshua. I need a little time to myself, despite the constant craving to be near him, to touch him.

It's one of those pitch-black nights outside, no moon to illuminate the sky. Just velvet darkness and the distant stars. That same sky I watched as a child. But I'm not the same, am I? Maybe some part of me has never let that child go, on the inside. Have I ever really grown up, gotten over my past? Have I ever really let it go? Or have I just shoved it down deep where I don't have to deal with it?

I'm going to have to deal with it now, or nothing will really change.

I sip my tea carefully and let myself think for a moment about my clients, my regulars. Bennett, Colin, Zayed, Louis. Enzo. I'll have to talk to him eventually. Tell him I won't see him anymore. I can't decide whether any of them will truly care, beyond their own selfish need for the sex. I hope some of them will. Sweet Louis. Enzo.

How ridiculous is that? I'm a prostitute. They pay me for sex. I am not a wife. Not even a mistress. Why do I care?

But I do. And maybe, just maybe, that was part of the magic, too. Maybe it wasn't just that I got off on the sex. Maybe I can allow myself that much credit. Perhaps I can even allow myself to feel a little sad. To grieve.

I am tight with grief, like a cord strung to the breaking point.

Almost. Because I'm not breaking, am I?

I don't know how long I sit in the dark before Joshua

comes into the room, so quiet I don't even know he's there until he is sitting next to me, pulling me into his arms.

"What is it, baby?"

"I'm just . . . feeling everything, you know?"

"Yes." He holds me tighter. "It's okay."

"Joshua, I feel like . . . I'm some sort of emotional infant. Trying to figure it all out. I'm trying to find my strength here, but it's hard."

He squeezes my hand. "I'm having a hard time with this, too. I'm trying to process it, but when I stop to think about it . . . Fuck, I don't mean to make you feel worse, but it's hard, you know? I have to be able to say that to you."

"Of course."

I know it's not his intention, but it does make me feel worse. Even though I am also deliriously happy that I have this chance, that he is here with me.

"Maybe we need to get you out of here? Change your environment? Maybe we both need to get out of here."

I nod.

"I should take you to my house. I'll take another day or two off work."

"When? How soon can we go?" Suddenly I want nothing more than to leave this place.

"We can go tonight, if you want. We can be there in twenty minutes if I drive fast enough."

"Yes, please, Joshua. Let's just go."

He pulls me up with him, pauses to tuck my hair behind my ears.

"Go and pack a bag and we'll do it. We'll leave right now."

I feel an enormous sense of relief. I know it's only a temporary solution. But I feel like all I can do right now is survive this with him. It has to be that basic.

I leave him to go into the bedroom, throw a few things into an overnight bag: a silk nightgown, a pair of loose linen drawstring pants and a pair of jeans, a few cotton tank tops, my favorite cashmere sweater, a pair of sandals. I take my toothbrush and hairbrush from the bathroom, a bottle of lotion, throw those into the bag.

When I come back into the bedroom, he's dressed. He's holding a dress for me that he must have pulled from my closet, a soft gray knit piece with long sleeves. He goes to my drawer and pulls out a bra, underwear, and helps me into them, handling me as though I'm fragile. But for the first time in a long time, I'm not. Whether I ever wanted to admit to my own weakness, it's been there, beneath the smooth veneer. Now I've dug deeper and found something more, something better.

He sits me down on the bed, slides my feet into a pair of black boots. Then he takes my hand, picks up my bag, and leads me into the living room. I pause to scribble a note to my housekeeper to take care of my orchids before picking up my purse. My heart is pounding. I need to *go*.

In minutes we are in his car, flying down the empty streets. The sky is just beginning to glow with the first light of dawn. I normally hate to see the sun come up. It's always felt incredibly lonely to me. It still does. But there is also a sense of absolute safety, here in the car with Joshua.

He has a Hummer, one of the new smaller ones, but still ridiculously enormous. All black, sleek, masculine. Totally decadent. I love it immediately. It feels like him. Beautiful and luxurious but still a little bad boy.

He holds my hand the entire time, but we don't talk. I am exhausted, half out of my head. But so damn grateful to be here with him. His profile is almost too beautiful to look at, with the slowly rising sun lighting him up just a little in purple and gold that fades to gray as we get closer to the beach.

How is it that I've never been to his place? I don't even know where we're going until we hit Washington Boulevard and I can smell the ocean through the closed windows of the Hummer. A few more blocks and we're on Pacific Avenue, that funky end of Marina del Rey where there are a handful of restaurants and cafés on a winding road leading to the beach. As we move away from the big hotel strip, it feels more like one of those small beach towns that dot the southern coast of California: Huntington Beach, Sunset Beach, Laguna.

He takes a right, pulling into one of the back alleys all of these beachfront houses have. He hits a button on the remote built into the dash and the garage door on a two-story Spanish-style goes up.

Joshua insists on helping me from the car, which I secretly love. Taking my hand, he leads me into the house.

His house.

It smells like him. That's the first thing I notice. The second thing I notice is that it feels like home.

"I'll show it all to you later. Let's get you into bed."

I follow him silently, through the shadows of his house. Down a wide hallway and into his bedroom.

There's an enormous window with an incredible ocean view. The sun is a dim red glow, forcing its way through the fog. And in that pale light I can see a big bed, a wooden four-poster with all white bedding. Simple. Beautiful.

He undresses me quickly, tenderly. Then he tucks me beneath the covers, under the crisp white sheets and a heavy down quilt, before he moves around the room, sliding the drapes closed, hanging my dress in the closet. He gets undressed, and I watch him through sleepy eyes: the smooth expanse of his broad chest, the tattoo on his biceps, his muscular thighs.

A lovely surge of heat between my thighs, but I am so tired suddenly. He slips in beside me, holds me close, stroking my hair, kissing my temple, my eyes. He's whispering to me, but I don't know what he's saying. His voice is soft in my ears as I drift toward sleep.

Safe at last.

Chapter Eleven

I WAKE UP, BUT I don't want to open my eyes. I've been having this lovely dream about Joshua, about lying in his arms, in his bed. About surrendering to that sense of being absolutely cared for, allowing myself to depend on it.

I squeeze my eyes tight, but no matter how much I don't want to leave the dream behind, I am awake.

I open my eyes. And smile.

He's not here in bed with me; I can sense it before I turn to see the divot in the pillow where his head rested. But I can hear him. He's whistling from some far-off room, which makes me smile more. The acrid scent of coffee is rich in the air.

This must be what normal feels like.

The sun is shining through the heavy curtains. I glance at the clock on the nightstand; it's almost two in the afternoon.

The bed is like some enormous womb, and I lie there for a while, luxuriating in the soft sheets, the weight of the comforter on my body.

My mind, sleepy and on autopilot, wants to think about

how I might fuck this up. But right now I'm simply too happy to allow myself to go there.

"Valentine, you up, baby?"

Ah, there he is. So damn sexy in his dark blue pajama bottoms and nothing else. I am crazy about his bare chest. I really am. The muscles there are heavy, thick, his skin a perfect shade of light gold. And I know what it feels like to have my cheek pressed against his heart.

"Hi."

"Hi, sleepyhead. I thought you were going to sleep all day."

"I'm sorry."

"Don't be." He moves across the room, sits down on the bed, leans in and kisses me with his coffee-scented mouth. "Mmm, don't move."

He slips off his pajama bottoms and gets under the covers, his body warm and strong next to mine as he pulls me into his arms. I rest my head on that curve of muscle that runs from the underside of his arm to his shoulder. Lovely. I want him. But I also revel in simply being with him, like this. I could stay here forever.

Tilting my head to look up at him, I touch the scar on his lip, as I often do, and he kisses my fingertip. He is idly running his fingers through my hair, his eyes half lidded, just a glow of green and gold peering out from beneath his thick lashes. "Tell me something, Valentine."

"What do you mean?"

"Something else about when you were a kid. No . . . tell me about the beginning of sex for you."

"You mean when I lost my virginity?"

He's quiet a moment, thinking. "Not necessarily. I mean that time in your life when you first became aware of sex." He's watching me in that penetrating way he has.

"I haven't really thought about it."

"Haven't you? That's such a turning point in anyone's life. It seems that way to me, anyway."

"Yes, I suppose it is."

"So tell me."

I close my eyes, letting my mind drift. How far back? It seems a lifetime ago. Maybe it is.

With my eyes still closed, I remember.

"I was eleven when Billy Carrow moved into our neighborhood. All the girls were in love with him instantly. He was maybe a year older than I was. But so pretty. Not that he looked like a girl, but he had the longest eyelashes I'd ever seen. And dark, hooded eyes. Sleepy. He was a bit exotic to me, because he really was so . . . beautiful. He exuded sex, even at twelve. And he was bad. He had that aura of danger about him, even at that age. He was always getting into trouble at school. Getting caught shoplifting, stealing from a neighbor's garage, crashing his bike and breaking his arm. I remember watching him step out of his house for the first time and feeling that tingle between my thighs. It was frightening and exciting. I didn't know how to feel about it.

"But I always watched him. In school, around the neighborhood. He used to hang out at this liquor store down the street with some older boys, and I was always hunting for change to buy candy. Not because I wanted candy, but because it gave me an excuse to go to the store. No one stopped me. No one really cared what I did."

I stop and think about that for a moment, about wandering the neighborhood, not having to report in at home like the other kids did. It was a little scary. And exhilarating. It made me feel grown up.

"I remember purposely putting on my shortest shorts, my

tightest tank tops, to go to the store. Using Vaseline on my lips before I was old enough to buy real lip gloss. And walking into the store, passing Billy and those older boys, that thrill going through me when one of them turned to watch me. I didn't understand until I was a lot older how sexual even that was for me."

"Did anything ever happen with him?"

I pause, looking at him, but his face is blank, innocent. He gets my silent question right away.

"Valentine. Come on, you were a kid. I just want to know you. I wish I knew you back then. I wish I'd seen you as a young girl." He reaches out, strokes my cheek, and I go soft and loose all over, as I always do with him. He murmurs, "I bet that Billy kid was in love with you."

"I don't know about that. But he was the first boy I ever kissed."

"Oh, this you have to tell me." He's grinning now.

I roll my eyes, trying not to grin back. But I tell him.

"It was the summer I turned thirteen. Billy had two older brothers, and one of them had a room off the garage. He took me in there. I mean, he just came up to me on the street one day and took my arm and said, 'Come with me.' It wasn't a question. I went. I remember the smell of the garage: dry and dusty with a little motor oil mixed in. I remember how warm his hand was on my arm as he led me through the garage and into his brother's dark room. I remember my heart pounding in my chest. I wasn't sure what would happen. But simply being alone with him in the half-dark room seemed forbidden. Exciting. And then he just pulled me to him and kissed me."

"And . . . ?"

"And I was wet instantly. I didn't know what it meant. It almost hurt. He pushed his tongue right into my mouth and

I was shocked and ridiculously turned on. And he was pressing up against me; I could feel his erection against my thigh. I was squirming. I didn't want him to stop. I don't know what would have happened if his mother's car hadn't pulled into the driveway right then. He pulled away from me and I was just . . . stupid. I couldn't speak. I could see him smiling at me in the dim light coming in through the curtains. Then he said, 'Come on, let's get out of here.'

"Nothing ever happened with him again. He moved away a few months later. But I thought about that one moment for years."

Joshua runs a finger over my lower lip, down my jaw, my neck. His voice is quiet. "Do you know how your voice lowered as you were telling me this? How your cheeks flushed?"

"Really?"

I smile at him, take his hand and slip it between my thighs. He goes instantly to where I need him most, his fingers sliding beneath the edge of my panties.

"Do you have any idea what that did to me? Hearing the desire in your voice . . ."

He pauses, his fingers slipping into my wet cleft, and I am as hot and wet as I ever was with Billy.

"Come on, Joshua." I arch my hips into his hand.

"Come on, what?"

"I need to feel you inside me."

I can't wait; I climb on top of him, reach down and wrap my hands around his already-erect cock. Nice. I lean over, grab a condom from the nightstand, sheath him with shaking hands.

He holds onto my hips, lowering me onto his shaft, sliding in, clean and smooth, driving into me. And it is better than anything I felt with Billy Carrow. Better than what I've felt with anyone else, ever. My memories fade, and all I am is this moment, *right now,* with him. Nothing else matters.

WE'RE STILL IN BED an hour later. Lazy. Lovely.

"Are you hungry, baby?" he asks me. "You must be starving. I swear I was going to bring you breakfast."

"This was better."

"It was. It is." He runs a hand over my side, down my thigh, and I shiver. "But we have to eat eventually. I didn't have anything here but crackers and beer, so I went down to this little café this morning. They make the best croissants. And I got apple juice, some fruit, a few other things. What can I get for you?"

"No, you don't have to do anything. I'll get up."

"I want to. Stay right here."

He disappears for a few minutes, comes back with a big red ceramic coffee mug in one hand and a plate in the other. He sets them both on the night table, a large, dark piece, like everything else in the room. Imported furniture, like my own.

The coffee smells wonderful. I pick it up, sip it, let him feed me bites of pastry and fruit while he tells me what he's seen on the news that morning, how the stock market is doing.

I'm hardly paying attention. I am in some dreamlike space, and I want to hold on to it. It's too precious to me to let go.

"Do you want a shower?" he asks me. "We should go down to the beach. It's not too cold. I actually love it when it's like this, gray and cool. And there aren't too many people there on a weekday."

"I'll shower later. I can be dressed in five minutes."

Suddenly I want to see his beach, if only because he wants me to.

I get up, slip on my linen pants and a tank top. He gives me one of his hooded sweat jackets with some hockey team logo on it, and I slide into my sandals, then we're out the door.

The sun is still fighting the fog, but I'm warm enough. And his hand is warm in mine. I feel good. Better than I have in a long time. Lighter, somehow.

We walk the one block to the beach, and soon we're on the sand. I take my sandals off and carry them as we move closer to the water. There are only a few other people there. I'm glad it's quiet, uncrowded. It helps me to maintain this fantasy bubble I've constructed around us.

At the edge of a shallow dune, we stop, and Joshua pulls me down to sit on the sand beside him.

"It's beautiful, isn't it?" he asks me.

I look out at the Pacific Ocean, thundering against the shore, the blues, greens, and grays out beyond the swells, where water meets sky in a rippling line.

"It is. It's a little sad on a day like this. Maybe other people need it to be clear and sunny to think this is beautiful. But I like it just like this."

He squeezes my hand. "You see? Everything doesn't have to be someone else's idea of perfect to be beautiful, Valentine."

I look up at him and he's watching me in that way he has.

"Yes. I suppose so."

"You don't really believe it yet, though, do you? Even after I told you what I'd done, about my own glaring flaws?"

I shake my head, look away, digging my toes into the sand. It's cold beneath the surface. Calming, somehow.

"Joshua . . . I don't quite know how to believe. I'm trying.

But I need . . . I need practice. My whole life has been one thirty-year lesson in how *not* to trust anything. It's going to take some time."

"And meanwhile?"

"Meanwhile I guess I'm living on faith. Which is pretty damn hard for me since I don't have much of that, either." I look back at him. His eyes are still on me. Beautiful in the pale sunlight, like everything else about him. "Except for my faith in you."

He leans in, kisses me. And I curl my hand around the back of his neck. His skin is so warm beneath my palm. He pulls back.

"I meant what I said, you know."

His hazel eyes are on me, searching for something. I don't know what he's getting at.

"You meant what?"

"That you don't need perfection for something to be good enough."

I nod my head. I want to understand.

"Let me tell you something, Valentine. About my family."

"Okay. I want to hear whatever you want to tell me."

He pulls his knees to his chest, settles in, holding on to my hand. "I told you how crazy my parents were about each other. I grew up with the understanding that this was possible. But their relationship wasn't always easy. They worked hard for what they had. And they had a rough start.

"My mother was one of those debutante girls from a rich Connecticut family. Maybe that doesn't mean much anymore, but in her day it was everything. My father was from that same set of people, East Coast society. Their families knew each other. And my parents were friends growing up, although Dad told me later he'd been in love with her since he was fourteen years old. When my mom turned up pregnant at nineteen, unwilling to name the father of the baby, her family was ready to disown her.

"The father was someone who had passed through town, one of the summer people. A fling. This was unacceptable in that culture. My dad stepped in and married her, knowing he wasn't the father. But he loved her. He went against everything their social circle believed in, and he took her away from there so they could have a life together. So her child wouldn't have to grow up with that stigma."

"That baby was you?"

He nods. "I'm grateful to them for that. Growing up, I spent time with my grandparents, my aunts, uncles, cousins. And there was always this tension. There still is. The elephant in the room that is the circumstance of my birth, but they're all too polite to mention. I don't see them much anymore. It's such bullshit. But I didn't know any of this until later. Not until my dad died. Until then, I had no idea why we lived in California, so far away from the rest of the family. I had no idea why we were always treated as outsiders."

"That must have come as a shock."

"No. I don't know. Maybe a little, at first. I couldn't think of my dad as anyone other than my dad. But I was only twenty, and it was more the idea of my mother having had sex with someone other than my father. I couldn't care less now, but at the time, well, you don't think of your parents having sex, do you?"

I look away. "That was inescapable in my family. I was locked in my room for hours with that soundtrack playing in the background."

"Shit. I'm sorry, Valentine."

I just shake my head, turn back to him. "Forget it. Go on."

"So. Mom and Dad got married and it wasn't all happily ever after. Mom was so relieved to be saved from a life of shame and rejection, she was grateful. But she wasn't in love with my father. He knew that. But then I was born, and my dad stepped in, really stepped up to being a father, and it all came together for her. That's when she fell in love with him. She was able to forgive herself because he was able to forgive her. That was a first step for her. And *my* life was good because Dad was able to forgive her. Once I knew the truth, I couldn't help but understand that."

"And the guy? Your biological father? Did you know him?"

"No. I still have no idea who he is. I don't care. I don't need him for anything. I wanted to know for about five minutes, and then . . . I realized very quickly that he wasn't important. My father, the man who raised me, was my dad. This other guy who had disappeared wasn't a real person to me."

I nod again, feeling a bit the same way about my own father, other than a lingering resentment. But it all seems vague now. He seems vague to me now, ghostlike.

"But my point is," he goes on, "even after I was older and Dad was gone, even after I found out that their life together hadn't been without its problems, I understood people can still love each other completely. That love exists despite our flaws. Despite my own flaws. Despite yours."

He takes my chin in his hand, forcing my gaze to meet his. My heart is fluttering at a thousand miles an hour.

"This is why I'm here with you, Valentine. Regardless of what you've done in your life, how hard it is for me to process it all. And believe me, just because I'm not hammering you over the head with it doesn't mean I'm not thinking about it, that it doesn't hurt."

"God, Joshua . . ."

"No. It's okay. It is. I'm still here, aren't I? I'm trying to tell you it's because I believe." He reaches up, tucks a windblown strand of hair behind my ear. "And because I'm falling in love with you."

My heart tumbles in my chest, a long fall into a warm darkness. "Joshua . . ."

He's looking into my eyes, his gaze so intense I can hardly stand it. But I can't look away. I don't want to.

"Do you love me, Valentine?" he asks quietly.

"Yes. I do. I love you."

My heart is going to burst, it is pounding so hard. He kisses me again, then. And all of the world's imperfections melt away beneath the soft press of his lips.

My heart is still thundering; I'm so damn scared. But it feels good, too. Incredible.

He keeps kissing me and kissing me, until my body is flooded with heat and desire.

Finally, he pulls away, says gruffly, "I need to get you back to the house. I need to be alone with you."

He pulls me to my feet and we make the walk back to his place as quickly as we can. His arm is around me, and I can feel the heat of his big body through my clothes, feel it in the pit of my stomach. Between my thighs.

I can smell the desire on him. Or maybe it's my own?

He jams his key in the front door, pulls me inside. I still haven't had a chance to really look at his house, I realize vaguely as he pulls his shirt off, then mine. Then he slides my pants down my legs, pulls his own off, and I am unable to think anymore. We are naked together, which is what I want at this moment more than anything. To be naked with him, to touch him, to have him touch me. And as he fills his hands with my breasts, as he kisses me until I am breathless, the only thing I can hear are the words he said to me. The words no one has ever said.

I'm falling in love with you.

My heart throbs; my body throbs. It is all one sensation as he touches me, loves me. And I need to feel him inside me, as much a part of me as he can possibly be.

He is pushing me down hard on the wide brown leather sofa in that way I love. But I put my hands on his shoulders.

"In the bedroom, Joshua. Please. In your bed."

He freezes, tenses a little all over. The current of our desire is dampened suddenly, even with his body pressed against mine, flesh to flesh. Even with his rigid cock lying on my belly.

He says, very quietly, "You cannot clean me up, Valentine. Sex with me is not always going to be soft and pretty."

"That's not what I'm trying to do."

"Isn't it? The shower, the bed."

I'm silent. I don't know what argument I can make.

His voice lowers even more. "Sometimes, Valentine, all I want is to throw you up against the wall, pin you there, and fuck you so hard you scream. Fuck you so hard I hurt you. I want to do everything to you. With you. I want to tie you up. I want it to be dirty, raw. And not because of what you've been. Not because of some twisted idea of it being a novelty with you. But because you are so damn beautiful, and I want you so badly I can barely control myself."

I'm shaking all over. With the fear of being so open to him. But even more with need. I am melting inside. Hungry for exactly those things he's talking about.

"Joshua . . . you're right." My voice is trembling. "God, you're right. I want . . . I want it all, too. I want it with you. Only with you."

He picks me up then, shifting me in his strong arms, pushing me against the wall beside the big window overlooking the ocean. I can hear it, smell it, the thundering waves, the salty air. I can smell him again, or still, his scent stronger than ever as he pushes his tongue into my mouth. Soft, sweet, yet his hands on me are rougher than ever, gripping my hips as he lifts me, spreads my thighs, and I wrap my legs around him. Then he spreads my pussy lips with one hand, plunging two fingers into my wet heat. Desire, molten hot, shafts deep into my body, and I gasp, writhe against his hand.

"I'm going to fuck you, Valentine."

"Yes!"

He pulls his fingers from me, brings them to my lips, watches my face intently as he presses them into my mouth, and I can taste my own juices, salty sweet, before he lowers his hand. He grasps my hips, lifting me.

"Now, Valentine," he growls before impaling me on his hard cock.

He slides right in, up to the hilt. Pain and pleasure all at once. Too good, this sense of being commanded by him.

Possessed.

That's becoming my favorite word.

His hips begin to piston, and he drives into me, pleasure knifing into my body. Pleasure and a sense of belonging I can hardly describe, even to myself.

"Just need to fuck you, baby," he says between teeth clenched in pleasure; I can see it on his face. "Just fucking you."

He slams into me, and the wall is hard and cold against my back, and he's fucking me so damn hard. Desire builds inside me, hot and shimmering, my sex filling, swelling. My nipples hard against his chest.

"Joshua . . . more!"

He drives deeper, and it really does hurt now. The wall is digging into my spine, his cock is digging deep inside my body. But he feels so good. Better than anything I've ever felt before.

"Joshua . . . Joshua . . . God . . ."

"Tell me you love me, Valentine," he demands, his voice rough.

"I love you. I love you . . ."

His hands tighten their grip, his nails biting into my skin. And I hold on to his shoulders, gouging his flesh as he thrusts into me, over and over, driving my pleasure higher and higher.

"I'm going to come," he tells me, "into you, baby. Love you, baby . . ."

"Yes . . ."

I am right there with him, my sex clenching, clasping him, pleasure like a hammer, shattering me inside. And as he cries out, my body convulses, a long, shuddering wave. I am coming so hard; coming itself is that same pain and pleasure, intensified, overwhelming.

It goes on and on, our shivering bodies sealed together by sweat, by heat, by our unwillingness to separate. I don't know how I know this, love being such an unfamiliar concept to me, but I do.

We are both panting. But his grip on my body, holding me up, is as strong as ever. He carries me back to the big sofa, lays me down, settles in beside me, an arm around me, our legs entwined. Lovely. I breathe a sigh of . . . I'm not sure what it is. Gratitude? Relief?

I have never felt so happy before. This is bliss to me.

The sun is dipping low in the sky, filtering in through the wide expanse of glass that is the front of his house. No drapes in here, just wooden shutters, folded back now to let the view inside. There is enough light still that I can see the room. So oddly like my own house: the imported furniture, all dark, heavy pieces, some of them carved, inlaid, and painted in the way Indian and Balinese and Moroccan furniture often is.

There are enormous pieces of gorgeously carved teak on the walls, from Indonesia, I know, because I have two of them myself. A small collection of baskets that are clearly African sit on a hand-painted Indian chest. Beautiful. And again, amazingly similar to the things I have in my own house.

I smile to myself, feeling a new surge of familiar comfort.

Don't get too used to it.

I really have to shut down those old tapes in my head. I'm going to have to find a way if we are to have anything together. Because I am damn well going to get used to it. I am going to get over all the shit that is my life so I can find some sort of life with him. I have to learn not to believe those voices.

It's going to be hard. Because the fact is, I still do. Everything I'm doing right now is pretend to me, on some level. Deep down, I'm still afraid the idea that this is going to last is nothing more than illusion.

Don't think about it.

No, just be here with him, with this man who says he loves me. With this man I love. Keep pretending as hard as I can.

I had no idea love would be so overwhelmingly wonderful. I had no idea love could hurt this much, simply at the idea of losing it.

WE MADE LOVE ALL weekend, ate, walked on the beach, got coffee at the funny little café down the street from Joshua's house. Then made love again, letting it turn into raw, lovely fucking, in his big bed, on the floor, in the backseat of his car on the way home from dinner.

I hate Monday mornings. I always have. I remember as a kid, that sinking feeling of waking up on Monday morning, time for school. I never wanted to let the weekend go.

I feel like that now.

Joshua had to go to work. He's asked me to stay at his house, which I'll do for a day or two. But eventually I'll have to get back to my house, check on my orchids. Deal with the lingering ashes of my life.

I need to go talk to Lydia. Joshua has offered me the use of his other car: a black Lexus sedan. An incognito car. I like that idea. I don't want to be myself today.

He's left already. The scent of coffee and toast lingers in the kitchen, and as I clean up the breakfast dishes I have this odd flash of myself doing this very thing forever.

Don't be stupid.

No, it's Monday, reality time. Hasn't that always been what Monday is for?

I shower, dress in a pair of jeans and my cashmere sweater. Then I call Lydia. She can see me in an hour. I'm not sure if this is fate intervening, but it feels like it. It feels almost ridiculously important that I see her now.

I get into the car and pull out of the garage, a knot of dread in my stomach at leaving the womblike safety of Joshua's house. But I swallow it down as I hit Pacific Avenue and head north toward Santa Monica.

At Lydia's office, she greets me with a warm smile, as always. Why is my pulse racing?

I sit in my spot on her sofa and she settles in opposite me.

"Tell me what's happened, Valentine."

"How do you know anything has?"

"You called and asked for a same-day appointment, which I assume is somewhat urgent as I know you're no longer working and don't have a full calendar. And even if that were not the case, you're pale as a sheet."

"You don't beat around the bush, do you?"

"Would it be at all helpful to you if I did?"

"No." I have to smile a little.

"So . . . ?"

"A lot has happened. A lot." I pause, catch my breath. "I told him. Everything. About what I do. What I've done. I told him how it happened, how I ended up here. That I've quit. I told him that I love him."

"Ah. And what does he have to say about it?"

"He's been incredible. So accepting. I mean, it's been hard for him. He asked me some pretty tough questions. He wanted details. And I really did not want to tell him that stuff, but I felt I had to. He said I owed him that, and he's right. So I told him. How I got into the business, the kinds of things I've done with my clients, with the other girls. But he still wants me, still wants to try. And I still only half believe it." I stop, run my hands through my hair, take a breath. "I'm afraid to . . . I'm afraid to let myself depend on that. But he says he loves me. I don't know why."

"Why not?"

"Come on, I'd think that would be obvious."

"Valentine, you don't have to sell yourself short because you earned your living in the sex trade. You don't have to punish yourself that way, you know."

"No, I don't know that! I don't know that at all." I'm angry. But none of this is her fault. "I'm sorry. I don't mean to be sharp with you."

"You don't have to apologize to me. Part of what we do in this room is to help you face your feelings, and some of those feelings are going to be anger."

"Yes. I have a lot of anger. I know that."

"What is the main source of that anger, Valentine? Because once you identify it, you can really begin to deal with it, to process it and move forward. Do you know where the anger begins?"

"Of course I know. That's something I've never been in denial about. It begins and ends with my mother."

"And how have you dealt with it? With her, with those emotions?"

"I haven't seen my mother for years. I put her behind me."

"Did you?"

"What are you saying?"

"Refusing to see her doesn't mean you've put her behind you. It may mean that you've done nothing more than ignore her, and all of those feelings of anger and sadness that are attached to her."

"I never said I was sad."

"You don't have to."

"No, you're wrong there. I'm not sad. Not about her."

"Okay." Lydia nods, smiles. She's being patronizing. And I'm getting angrier.

"So, what do you suggest I do, Lydia? That I go and see her and look for some sort of closure? Well, it won't work. That woman will never change. She's still exactly the same, I'm sure. Just a stinking, rotting alcoholic. She'll never change."

"But you have."

"Not that much!"

"But you want to."

Fuck. I hate it when she makes sense that I don't want to hear.

I'm quiet, absorbing.

"So . . . you really are saying I need to go see her. Is that it?"

"I am suggesting you think about it, yes. But you have to go in with an open mind, or it won't accomplish anything. Are you ready to do that?"

"Yes!" I stop, tug on the ends of my hair. Am I really going to do this? It's been so long. "I don't know. I'd like to think I am. To think I'm ready for anything. I know my life has to transform completely, that I have to. I know you're right about dealing with my mother. But it's not like she's going to welcome me with open arms. It's not as though she'll apologize for anything."

"No, she probably won't. This isn't about what she does. It's about adjusting your own perspective. And perhaps seeing her through adult eyes, eyes that have been opened a bit, will color your worldview a little differently."

I nod my head. "I understand what you're saying." And I do. It's almost habit that's keeping me from going. But look where habit has gotten me. "I know you're right. I know I need to do this. I need to face her. To stop running from her." How did Lydia manage to turn this around so it seems like my idea? "Okay, I'll go. Maybe I'll even do it today. I might as well get it over with."

"It's entirely up to you."

I nod, knowing damn well it's not. I would never have thought of this if it weren't for Lydia.

"Okay. Okay. I'm going to do it."

We talk a little more, but it feels like filler. I can't forget that I am going to see my mother this afternoon. That I have to face her, and everything her presence in my life has meant for me.

I do not want to do this. An evil necessity.

When my appointment is over I get in the car and head into the Valley. If I don't do this now, I may never do it at all.

The trip goes quickly. And as soon as I come up over the rise of the 405, the San Fernando Valley spread out before me, my stomach lurches. But I make myself do it, following the 405 to the 101, taking the too-familiar exit.

The houses become more run-down with each passing block as I get closer to my old neighborhood. Pale. Miserable. The neighborhood has changed, fallen apart over the years. Maybe she doesn't even live there anymore. Maybe she's dead. Anything could have happened. It's been at least eight years since I drove down this sad street.

It looks a lot like it did when I was growing up, but dingier, more depressing than before. Houses and apartment buildings with faded paint, weeds in the yards. And I know the moment I pull up in front of her house that she is there, inside it.

I park the car and have to breathe, pulling air deep into my lungs, fighting the nausea.

Just do it. Get it over with.

It would be easier if even a small part of me was convinced it would do any good. If I believed it would make creating a new life for myself, being with Joshua, any more possible. But I have to try, don't I? I have to practice believing.

I get out of the car, holding my purse tightly in my hand, as though it's some sort of talisman. The house is in bad shape. The paint is absolutely peeling off the walls. The weeds are knee-high, and the hardy rosebushes that once bloomed against the front windows are dead and dried. A victim of neglect. I can relate.

Heart hammering in my chest, I reach out and ring the bell.

Chapter Twelve

NOTHING FROM INSIDE, NO sound at all. But I have this odd feeling she's in there. I know it down in my bones. I ring the bell again. And again, nothing.

Maybe this was a mistake. If it were meant to happen, she'd answer the door.

I have this sudden, horrible flash of her lying dead in the living room, a glass clutched in her cold hand, a little vodka pooled in the bottom of it. Too fucking awful. Even worse that I feel a wave of sadness.

I shake my head, turn to go, and the door swings open behind me.

"Who's there?"

God, her voice, the same under the unfamiliar creak of a woman who is old now. But she couldn't be more than fifty, fifty-two maybe. Far from old. She sounds like she is a hundred.

I turn, but the house is dark and dingy inside, and all I can see is the dim outline of a person. Not even recognizable as female. Not recognizable to me at all. She steps closer, opens the torn screen door, and I see her.

She's a mess. Hair cut short yet still askew, wearing torn sweatpants and an old pink sweater. Her face is lined, radiating a sadness I can't even begin to fathom. And unexpectedly, my heart breaks a little.

"Mom?"

"What?"

I realize she has no idea who I am.

"It's me. Valentine."

"Valentine?" Shock in her voice, and booze, despite the early hour. Did I really expect anything else? Some of the anger comes back, but it's diffused now.

"It's me, Mom. Can I come in?"

She takes a moment to answer. Maybe she'll say no. I suppose I wouldn't blame her if she did. Finally, she says gruffly, "I guess so," and holds the door, letting me pass into the house.

Stench of sour alcohol and old cigarettes. It's overpowering, nauseating. Or maybe that's just the fear kicking in again; I can't tell at this point.

The living room is lit only by a small crack in the faded and crooked curtains and the flickering, silvery-blue wash from the TV.

She goes to sit on the sagging sofa. It's the same terrible floral print that was here the last time I was in this house. She doesn't invite me to sit down, and there are no other chairs in the living room. I look around, go to the adjoining kitchen, and pull a wooden chair into the room, across from her, but not too close.

She picks up a crushed pack of cigarettes, lights one with an unsteady hand, rasps out, "So, what do you want?"

"I just . . . I want to talk to you."

"So talk."

I study her for a moment. Beneath the sagging skin, the dark circles under her eyes that are exactly the same shade of green as my own, the puffiness from too much drinking, I can see the old beauty in her face. My one gift from her. I can be grateful for that, at least. I would be nowhere without it. A sad truth.

"How have you been, Mom?"

"How have I been?" She laughs, a sharp, snorting sound. "If you really cared you wouldn't have disappeared for . . . how many years?"

"I know," I say quietly. "I should have come to see you. I shouldn't have turned my back. I just . . . I didn't know what else to do. I was too angry. Too resentful. And then it just became . . . habit."

She takes a deep drag on her cigarette, the ash on the end growing long, perilous, but she ignores it. "I didn't miss you that much anyway."

Such an ugly thing to say. And I can see from the tears brimming in her eyes that it's not true.

My chest is absolutely aching.

"I don't blame you for that, Mom. I really don't. But do you understand why I had to go?"

She throws back a good finger of vodka, doesn't say anything for a moment, her eyes on the bottom of the glass.

"I gave you what I had, girl."

I know she doesn't mean money. I understand her exactly. And there is nothing more to say about it, is there? I'm not here to torture her about how she raised me.

"How's Dad?"

"He's dead, that's how he is. Bastard finally left me for good, and it killed him. Heart attack. And I'm better off."

"I'm sorry."

Am I going to hell because I'm not? I can't find it within myself to feel bad for him. To feel anything. But I can see she's paid for it, that loss. And suddenly I *am* sorry, for her. For the hell her life has been, even if she chose much of it herself.

"Mom, I really am sorry."

A tear spills over her cheek and she wipes it on her sleeve. "I need a drink."

She gets up, goes into the kitchen, and pours herself a double shot of vodka, not even bothering with ice.

It is eleven o'clock in the morning.

She comes back, grunts as she sits down again. "So, what have you done with your life, Valentine? You and your fancy clothes? That fancy car you drove up in? I can see you're doing pretty well, huh?"

I shake my head. "No. I haven't done well at all. Oh, I have nice clothes, a nice car. I've made some money. But I've had nothing else."

"What else do you want?"

An excellent question. One I need to find a way to answer for myself. That's part of why I'm here.

I can't remember now exactly why else I came. Did I think she would welcome me with open arms? Did I think she would have cleaned up her life, stopped the drinking, the resentment that has eaten her up inside for as long as I can remember? Did I think my parents would suddenly be living here together, happily surrounded by a white picket fence?

I have to admit, some small part of me was hoping for exactly that. As though that would redeem me, somehow. Or them, at least.

You're a fool.

She leans forward, the drink cupped between her hands, the cigarette hanging at an angle from between her fingers. "I could really use some cash, Valentine." She's not looking at me.

"What? Oh, of course. Is . . . is a check okay?" I fumble for my purse, pull out my designer leather checkbook, a pen. Why do I feel so fucking guilty? So incredibly sad and as though this is all my fault somehow?

I write out a check for five thousand dollars. It won't help to assuage the guilt entirely, but it's something. I hand it to her and she looks at it, her watery eyes going wide.

"Jesus Christ, Valentine." She stops, looks up at me, pauses to drag off her cigarette. She blows the smoke out in a harsh blue stream. "You could come by more often."

I nod my head. But I have no intention of coming back here.

The anger has been slowly draining from my body since I arrived. How can I be angry at this woman? She has nothing, has done nothing with her life. And it's clear her life is pretty much over.

I still have a chance, don't I?

As Joshua said, it's all about re-creating yourself. About choosing. I need to choose what I want to be, who I want to be.

The idea is pretty overwhelming: re-creating my life at almost thirty.

I can't stand to be here any longer. I'm not going to get any closure from her. All I can do is accept who she is, and move on. Maybe that's all I need from this visit.

"I have to go, Mom. I'll send you more money, okay?"

She shrugs, as though it doesn't matter. "Wouldn't hurt."

I walk to the door. She sits on the couch, waves to me with the check in her hand. She's already absorbed in her glass of vodka again as I let myself out.

Outside, I take in deep gulps of air. I don't know if what I did was right: coming to see her after all these years, then staying only fifteen minutes. Giving her the money, which she will no doubt spend on booze. But what else can I do? Each of us has to choose our path, and she's chosen hers. I can't make her change. I have no desire to do that.

It's time for me to choose for myself now. And I know what I want. But I'm still having a hard time with the believing part. I don't know if that's ever going to change. I have no idea what I'm capable of.

Taking one last look around the drab neighborhood, I get back into the car, lock the doors, start the engine. When I glance back at my mother's house, she is standing at the window, the curtain held aside in one hand, her stubby cigarette in the other. I wave to her. She steps back, drops the curtain.

I am absolutely drained. By the time I drive back over the hill and into Marina del Rey, I am completely unable to think, to figure anything out.

Later. Think it all through later.

I let myself into Joshua's house with the key he gave me. It's cool inside, clean. Inhaling deeply, I breathe in the scent of safety. I head into the bedroom, take my clothes off, climb into bed, and fall asleep.

I WAKE UP TO the sound of Joshua's keys jangling. The sun is going down outside; I've slept all day. I seem to be good at this sort of escapism. At all kinds of escapism.

"Baby, are you here?" he calls out.

"I'm in here." My voice is thick, mumbling, as I sit up, leaning against the headboard.

He walks into the room with that muscled grace I find so beautiful in him, comes to sit on the bed, ruffles my hair.

"Have I been keeping you up at night? But you're the one who's insatiable. Or as insatiable as I am, anyway."

He's smiling at me, that lovely mouth of his, and I tremble with a sweeping surge of that absolute happiness I feel with him.

"Kiss me," I demand, and he does. A long, sweet kiss that turns into a trail of kisses down my neck. I hold his head in my hands, my fingers going into his short, thick hair.

"Tell me what you've been doing all day," he says, bringing his face back to mine, searching my eyes. "You didn't spend the day at the beach."

"I went to see my therapist, Lydia. Have I told you I have a therapist?"

"No. We haven't had a chance to tell each other everything yet. But we have plenty of time. And I'm glad to know you're doing therapy. I think you need it right now. How did it go?"

"I . . . It's hard to tell, sometimes."

He nods. "It's supposed to be a journey, right? A progression. I guess you don't always know how it'll turn out until you get to the other end."

I nod my head. "Well, today . . . today, talking with her made me realize a few things. Important things." I have to stop for a moment, to organize my thoughts. "I went to see my mother, and that was . . . intense. I felt so helpless, just as I did as a kid. Until I realized that I could get out of there. That I could really just walk away."

"When was the last time you saw her?"

"Years . . . eight years ago. A long time."

"Do you want to tell me what happened there?"

"Not much, really. She was the same, but older, every-thing more . . . exaggerated. So incredibly sad and bitter. I didn't stay long. I gave her some money. Nothing else hap-pened, other than what happened in my head, which was . . . a bit of a surprise."

"What do you mean?"

"I felt sorry for her. She's so pathetic, so completely bro-ken down. I had this glimpse of what her life must have been like all these years. And I was able to feel sympathy for her. Maybe . . . maybe I don't have to be so angry anymore."

"So, you feel better for having gone, seeing her?"

I have to pause, think about how to answer. "I feel dif-ferently about her than I did before. But I'm not sure yet how that translates into how I feel about myself."

"You need some time to absorb it. Then you can tell me more, if you want to."

I nod again. "I do want to tell you. But I'm not used to thinking things through like this. Not emotional issues." I stop, push my hair away from my face. I feel tight all over, ach-ing and dizzy. As though I've been out in the sun too long, or drank too much. "Joshua, I want to tell you something now. Something I've just figured out."

"You can tell me anything."

He takes my hand, and that makes it easier, somehow.

"The hard times for me were always when I wasn't work-ing. I had this warped idea that I was at my healthiest when I was working, that there was this sense of personal power in it. I felt . . . liberated. But I see now that it was escapism for me, every bit as much as my mother's drinking is for her, as much as sleeping the day away like I did today. I've spent most of my adult life trying to escape, whether it was being paid for sex or sleeping too much. And it's like an addiction, and that addiction is not really about the sex at all, even if that's sort of what I told myself. It was about approval. Needing to find that sense of personal power from outside myself. That's what I became addicted to."

He is simply listening to me, holding on to my hand.

"Today I saw a woman who lives in such an extreme state of escapism that she has excluded any sort of possibility of a life. I don't want to be that woman. I didn't even like who I was in her presence. I have to truly begin to take some responsibility for who I am."

"Yes. But you also have to stop blaming yourself for it all. Because until you do, you can't guarantee that you're over the addiction. No, I don't mean that. Shit." He pauses, runs a hand over the back of his neck. "I don't mean to sound like I know it all."

"No. It's okay. It's true. But I swear to you, Joshua, I am over the part where I act on it. I am working through this stuff. That's what today was about."

"I know. I'm sorry, baby."

"I think . . . I can't think any more today. Can we just stop here and talk about it later? Please?" I get up, swing my legs over the side of the bed, taking a throw blanket from the end of the bed and wrapping it around me.

He is immediately contrite. "Of course. I don't mean to pound this stuff into you. I really don't. I know what you did today was hard." He reaches out to me and I go to him. He wraps his arms around me, lays his head on my blanket-covered stomach. The heat of him envelops me, as strong as his arms, like a protective cloud. And I am so damn grateful that he's here with me.

"Joshua . . ." I drop the blanket, baring myself to him. "Fuck me, please."

He doesn't say a word. But his clothes are coming off, falling into small piles at his feet. He pauses to grab something from the nightstand drawer, tosses the box of condoms and something else—I don't care what at this point—onto the floor and pushes me down, onto the thick carpet.

He spreads my thighs with his hands. No preamble; he is giving me exactly what I asked for, what I need. He leans in, sucking my clit into his mouth. A kind of desperate pleasure shoots through me immediately. Deeper still when he spreads my pussy lips with his thumbs, shoves them inside me.

"Ah, yes, Joshua . . . just like that."

I am soaking, trembling already. And he is sucking, sucking, until my clitoris is sore and tender and I can hardly take any more.

He lifts his head. "Are you going to come, Valentine?"

"Yes. Yes . . ."

He turns me over suddenly, his hands rough on my body, and I love it, love being handled like this. I need it not to be romantic, not to be pretty, and he understands exactly.

Yes, he's fucking perfect, this man.

And he is about to fuck me.

He lifts my hips, positioning me on my knees. Spreading my ass cheeks, he presses his condom-sheathed cock at my opening. I surge back against him.

"Just do it, Joshua. I need you to. I need to . . . to lose myself. Please . . ."

"I know just how to do it, baby. I know what you need." There is a darkness in his voice that's all about sex, about taking me over.

He slides the tip of his cock inside me, and my body clenches.

"Oh, yes . . ."

Then his hand comes down between us, his finger slipping between my cheeks and stroking that tightest of holes. His finger is slick with lube, I realize, before he presses it in.

A shock of pure lust goes through me; being filled this way, pussy and ass, makes each sensation more intense.

He pumps into me, his cock driving deep, and with his finger he presses harder into my ass, moves it in a circular, twisting motion that has me writhing and panting.

"Please, Joshua."

"Please what, baby? What do you want? I'll give it to you, whatever it is. All I need to know is that you want it."

"I need you to . . . I need you inside me everywhere."

He pushes his finger in deeper, thrusts his cock inside me, and pleasure courses through me, hot and powerful. I am losing all sense of anything but his hands on me, his cock, his skin against mine, and the sharp scent of sex in the air.

"You want me to fuck you in the ass, is that it, Valentine? To really take over?"

"Yes. Please, Joshua."

I am nearly sobbing with need now, squirming against his finger, his thick cock.

"Anything for you, baby." Lust in his voice, adding an edge that reverberates through my body.

He pauses, and his finger slips out of me for a moment, comes back covered in lube. He pushes it into my ass, big gobs of it, and even that makes me shiver, makes my hard clit throb, pulse.

His finger slides out of me, then his cock, but in moments

I can feel it at the entrance to my ass, his fingers stroking, teasing. His other hand slides around my body, finds my clitoris, and begins to massage it.

"Oh, God, Joshua! I'll come too fast. And I need to feel this."

He slows down, his fingers still pressing onto my clit, but gently now. With his other hand he guides his cock into my ass, just the tip. There is that familiar burning sensation, but it is gone in moments as I breathe into it, let him past that ring of tight muscle. I am shaking all over. And I realize that despite how many times I've had anal sex before, this time it's as much about trust as anything else. I press back against him, taking him deeper.

"Ah, you do need it, don't you, Valentine? You need me to love you everywhere. I do, baby. I do."

He presses deeper, an inch at a time. I breathe into it, relax my muscles, rocking a little with him. And with every inch the pleasure shafts deeper into my body: my sex, my belly.

When he shoves two fingers into my pussy I gasp, pleasure like a shock to my system. I am filled completely. Possessed. And it is flawless.

He thrusts his hips, not too hard, but enough that I really feel it. And when he moves his hand so that he can thumb my clit while his fingers move inside me, I gasp for air. Pleasure runs hot in my body, electric, exquisite. And as he whispers into the back of my neck, his breath warm and lovely against my skin, I come, my climax crashing down on me like the weight of the earth. I can hardly breathe as I cry out his name, over and over.

He is still pumping into me from every direction, milking my orgasm for all my body has. I am coming and coming, shivering, tears rolling down my cheeks.

When he tenses, a long shudder rippling through his body so that I can feel it inside my own, my sight dims, and I am momentarily blinded, breathless. Pure bliss, his climax and my own, and this moment of giving myself over to it all. To him.

He slips out of me, fingers and cock, rolls onto his side, pulls me up against him, my back to his chest. We are damp with sweat, panting. Beautiful.

The thought goes through my mind that this is all I'll ever need.

I know even now that's not true. But at this moment, it's enough. More than I ever dared to dream of.

TUESDAY MORNING AND JOSHUA decided to go into work late so he can take me to breakfast. We got up early and drove to Lily's, this funky place on Abbot Kinney in Venice Beach. It's packed, even at eight a.m. on a weekday. The usual eclectic mix of beach people: writers with their laptops, teenage kids with their skateboards, the local soccer moms in their jogging suits, babies in designer strollers.

The place is tiny, the tables almost on top of each other. But the coffee is superb and it smells like heaven: fresh pastries and bacon and a little patchouli from the bohemian crowd.

I've ordered French toast, a childhood favorite. The waitress brings it to the table and I smile at Joshua as I pour too much maple syrup on and dig in.

He fits right in here. His hair is a little mussed, spiky. It usually is, even when he's in a suit. But I like him even better like this, in his cargo pants and a T-shirt. Casual. Comfortable.

"You look happy this morning," he says, forking a bite of eggs into his mouth.

"I am. Happier than I've been in a long time."

He lowers his voice, leans forward, a glint in his hazel eyes. "I should fuck you in the ass more often."

I laugh. "Maybe you should. But that's not it. Well, that's certainly part of it. God, I don't know. I just feel . . . different. In a good way. It's as though things are shifting around inside me, and it's an almost physical sensation."

He nods his head. "I felt that way when I came back from Europe. Stronger. Even though what happened there, and before, was hard."

"Yes, that's it exactly." I take a bite of my French toast, savor the sugary syrup on my tongue. "I realized something when I woke up this morning."

"What was that?"

"That there are three different sides to me." I sip my coffee, enjoying the heat of it. "No, four. The old me, who I was growing up in that house, with my parents. I saw a glimpse of that yesterday, and I didn't like it. It was . . . frightening, to feel like that again, even that small hint of it. It was sad."

"What about the other sides?"

"There's the working me I created when I left home. That person is someone I made, pulling bits and pieces out of thin air. A design I furthered by going to college, taking classes. A doppelgänger, almost. And I lived like that all these years, in ghost form. Does that make sense?"

He nods his head. "Sure it does. But it wasn't all bad. You speak how many languages?"

"No, it's not all bad. I managed to get an education of sorts, even if it wasn't very specific. And that's more than anyone from my background could have expected, I suppose."

He nods, and I'm glad he's not arguing the point with me.

I go on. "There's the person I am when I'm in Lydia's office. And that person is so damn honest it scares the hell out of me sometimes. That person is angry and raw. But also thinking, exploring, trying to figure it all out. My life. But that me spends a little too much time intellectualizing everything. I know that. I'm sure Lydia knows it, too. And then there's who I am with you. And that me is also working, trying to figure everything out. Working really hard." My throat is closing up, and I have to swallow a few breaths to make it open up again.

He reaches across the table, covers my hand in his. "I know that, baby. I can see it."

I nod, continue. "That's when I'm the most vulnerable, when I'm with you. I don't always want to be, but it just happens. It's happening right now. But as wide open as I am with you, I still don't feel like that's my true self. Not yet. I haven't discovered yet exactly who that is." I pause, wrap my hands around my coffee mug, sip the hot, sweet liquid.

He says, "Maybe you have to find a way to integrate all of those selves before you find out who you really are."

"Yes, that's what I've been thinking. I wish I could just do it, that grasping the concept would make it happen."

"It'll happen. I know you can do it, Valentine."

"I hope so."

He picks up my hand, brushes a kiss across the knuckles.

I have never wanted anything more in my life than I want him. And not just sexually, although that's there, too, a sharp current always running beneath the surface. I want *him*.

What I want is a real life. And I'm so afraid I'm going to blow it.

"Baby, you need to stop worrying so much."

"I don't understand how you can be so calm."

He's quiet, watching me, his golden-green gaze on mine.

Shadows pass across his eyes as he's thinking. "I'm not always calm about it. You know I'm not. But I understand that if I dwell on the obstacles, I'll miss all the good stuff that's happening every day with you. I wish you could see it that way, too. I think it's a lot harder for you. I wish it wasn't so hard, baby. I wish I could make it easier for you."

His gaze is warm on mine. He squeezes my hand hard.

"I love you, Joshua."

He is still looking at me. His eyes are so beautiful, his long lashes lit by the easy morning sun.

"I love you, too. If you can't believe in anything else yet, believe in that."

I nod, smile. Deliriously happy and so damn scared all at the same time. Have I ever really believed in anything? I don't think I've had the chance to.

I think I'm afraid to. And I'm afraid that fear is what's going to blow this, to blow everything apart.

Don't fuck this up, Valentine. Do not fuck it up.

Please.

Chapter Thirteen

How many people ever get to know on a true, deep level what the word "idyllic" means?

I remember learning that word as a kid, reading it somewhere, looking it up. I imagined people who had perfect lives, but I thought of their lives as artificial constructs. I thought of the Brady Bunch as plastic. I was so jaded, even then. I think I was the only kid who didn't just swallow it.

I've had a taste of it now. And it's beautiful and terrifying and *real*.

I've spent all week playing housewife. Not that I've done any actual housework, other than washing a few dishes, making Joshua's coffee every morning before he goes to work. And sometimes I cook for him, which I love in a completely sentimental and ridiculous way. I feel so proud when I serve a meal to him. It's pretty wonderful simply indulging myself, doing something I love. But so much better doing it for him. I feel like I should be wearing an apron and a God damn string of pearls sometimes, some twisted version of June Cleaver.

Twisted far beyond any sort of amusing irony. But I still love it, even then.

We haven't talked about what I'm doing here, exactly, or when I'm going home.

During the day I walk through town, go down to the beach, and sit on the sand. Sometimes I bring a book with me. I've been reading a volume of Walt Whitman that I found tucked in a bookshelf in Joshua's house, but in a lazy sort of way. It's so luxuriously sentimental; I can only take a few pages at a time.

Sometimes I think ahead to what I might want to do with my life. I'm thinking a lot about those young girls I read about in the magazine. I wonder if there's any way I can help. I don't know where to begin, who to talk to. Maybe Lydia can point me in the right direction, when I'm ready.

Mostly, though, I just watch the water and the sky, the colors shifting with the time of day: blue, green, gray. The beach is so peaceful; I could spend hours there, and I do.

I've already made a habit of getting an iced mocha latte and a brownie in the afternoons at the little café closest to the house. The girl behind the counter with the facial piercings and purple hair knows my name already, knows what I always order. The ritual is comforting to me. And I realize I am creating these new rituals in an almost conscious way.

It's Friday morning, and as I get up, shower, dress, I realize I'll have him all to myself tomorrow. Lovely. I don't know what I'll do today. Probably what I've done all week. Or maybe I'll take the Lexus out and do some shopping. I've been wearing the same few pieces of clothing all week long.

I don't want to go back to my house yet.

But maybe I can check my messages, make sure there's nothing important from my housekeeper, my accountant.

Hardly anyone else has my home number, just those few impersonal people—hired staff—and even fewer friends.

I dial and enter my PIN. I have four messages. One from my housekeeper, letting me know my orchids are fine. Sweet of her. And three messages from Regan, each one more frantic than the last.

Shit.

I should call her. I know I should.

It makes me nervous, to even come close to my old life. But that's ridiculous. That was my life for over nine years. And Regan is my friend. An unusual friendship, but one of the few I actually have.

I take a breath, dial her number. She picks up on the first ring.

"Val! Where are you? Are you okay?"

"Yes, I'm fine. I just got your messages."

"Have you been out of town? You didn't say anything. God, never mind. I just want to know what's going on. Zayed wants us to go to Miami tomorrow, but The Broker says you're not going. She's sending Bella instead. You're not sick, are you?"

"No, not sick." I take the phone and sit on the end of the bed. Joshua's bed. It's solid beneath me, a safe haven. "Regan, I . . . Look, I've quit."

"What do you mean?"

"I've quit the business."

"Are you kidding me, Val?"

"No, I'm not." I tug on my hair, twist a strand around my finger. "Regan, I'm sorry I didn't tell you. I should have. But I've been . . . I have a lot to work out. Do you remember that guy I told you about? Joshua?"

"Jesus, Val. Don't tell me you're still seeing him."

"It's not like that. I mean it is, but it's . . . more. I'm *with* him. And he knows about my life. I've told him what I am. What I was, because I've stopped. I'm never going back."

"Jesus," she says again. She's quiet a moment. "This is a lot to take in."

"Yeah. For me, too."

"I just have to ask, Val . . . Are you sure about this?"

"I'm not sure about anything right now, except how I feel about him. And that I've given up the business. For good."

My heart is pounding. But it feels good, too, to say it out loud, to know the truth of it deep down.

"I can't believe you told him. Wow." She's quiet for several long moments. I can hear her breathing. Then, "I'm going to miss you, Val."

"We'll still see each other. Don't worry about that."

"Will we? And how will you introduce me to your new boyfriend?"

That point hits home, like a small knife in my chest.

Regan lets out a long, sighing breath over the phone. "I'm sorry. I am. God, I don't mean to be a bitch. I'm just . . . trying to figure out how this is going to work out for you."

"Yeah, me, too."

My fingers clench on the phone. My skin feels too tight, suddenly.

"Regan, I mean it. I want to see you and Rosalyn. I just have to figure this out . . . my life. This relationship. I need to come to some conclusions before I can do anything else. I just don't want you to take it personally that I've been out of touch. That I might be for a little longer while I get my head on straight."

"I won't. But I'm worried about you. I'm worried about how you're going to feel about yourself, putting yourself into this situation where someone who's important to you might be comparing you to some standard that doesn't even apply to people like us. I don't want you to do that to yourself. Can you tell me you're not doing that already?"

She's twisting the knife, and it hurts. But I have to consider what she's saying, because there's some truth in there.

"No. I can't tell you that's not happening. I don't mean him, I mean me."

"It's all too easy for girls like us to lose our confidence, what self-esteem we're able to pull together from our weird lives. From nothing more than being wanted."

She's getting emotional now; I can hear it in her voice. And this is something I've never really heard Regan do. It's affecting me; I can't help it.

"Just protect yourself, Val," she tells me.

"I will. I'm trying. I understand the validity of what you're saying. But I have to do this."

She's quiet again. "Val, call me any time, okay? If you want to talk . . . whatever. Okay?"

"Yes, sure."

But I know I won't call any time soon. It's too much, talking to her, hearing these truths from her. Too much to face right now.

"I have to go, Val. I have to get packed for this trip. I wish you were coming with us."

"I know."

What else can I say? That I wish I were, too? That would be a lie. I can't stand the idea.

"Go, Regan. Have a good trip. Tell Rosalyn you spoke to me. Tell her I'll call her soon."

"Okay. Take care of yourself. I mean that."

"I will."

We hang up and my gut is all twisted inside.

Did I think talking with her now would be easy? I don't know what I thought. My brain is full, overflowing. And everything in there is obscured by some sludgelike pool of murky water that I can't see through no matter how hard I try.

Except for one thing. The one thing I can see clearly is that I love this man.

I wish that were enough. But there is so much more, I don't even know where to begin.

—

I HEAR JOSHUA COME in the door and I pull him inside, start tearing his clothes off, and my own. I know I'm frantic. I don't care. I've had too many hours in which to think—to overthink, I know damn well—and now I just need to feel something good. To feel *him*.

"Hey, baby," he says with a smile, that beautiful, devastating smile, before I kiss him hard, still trying to get his pants off.

He's cooperative, kicking off his shoes, helping me with my bra before I sink to my knees before him, slide his boxerbriefs down over his muscular thighs.

His cock is hardening, beautiful, the shaft thick, the head glistening with one pearly drop of pre-come. I dart my tongue out, lick it off. He groans, his hands going into my hair.

"Ah, Valentine. Love that, baby. Love your mouth on me. Come on, take it in."

I do, wrapping my lips around his flesh, sucking him deep into my throat. Oh, yes, that's a trick I learned long ago. But I don't want to think about that now. I don't want to think at all. No, just focus on the flavor of his skin, the scent of desire coming off his body, the way every muscle clenches when I stroke his balls with my hand.

His hips are pumping now, an easy thrusting rhythm, his cock moving deeper into my throat. I want all of him, want to please him, want to give him the best head of his life. I want him to love me.

Somewhere in the back of my mind I know this is not why he will love me. Or why he won't. But this is all I have right now. This is what I know. I am vaguely aware of how desperate I'm feeling.

Still, his cock feels so good in my mouth. I've always loved giving head. I really do. I suck him harder, and he's groaning now. So damn sexy. My own body is already hot for him, wet. But I can wait for my own pleasure.

"I'm going to come," he says, gasping.

I grasp his buttocks, pull his hips in, swallow him, right down to the base of his cock, sucking, sucking. There is nothing else for me at this moment but his cock in my mouth, *his* flesh. And my need to make him happy.

"Jesus, Valentine! Jesus, Jesus . . . Ah . . ."

He comes, bucking, his seed sweet and salty going down my throat. I swallow it all, wanting that from him, like some sort of gift. I need it. His hands are tight in my hair, possessive. His grip loosens as his body calms, but I hold his cock in my mouth, loath to let go even as he softens.

"Come on, baby. Come here."

Pulling me to my feet, he holds me against him for a moment. I can feel him shivering the tiniest bit, just beneath his skin. He half-lifts me, lays me back on the sofa, kneels on the floor, and slips my panties off. His face is soft, his features loose with the aftermath of his orgasm, his mouth lush and full. I reach up, trace my fingers over his lips, over that small scar which only makes him more beautifully masculine. Grabbing my hand, he holds it as he pulls my fingers into his mouth and begins to suck.

Oh, this is lovely, this warm, wet sensation. And his gaze intent on mine. Fucking amazing. My sex is swelling, needing him. I push my fingers a little deeper into his mouth, and he takes them, his tongue swirling against my fingertips. I'm squirming, barely able to hold still.

"Joshua, that's so good. I need more . . ."

He takes my fingers from his mouth. "Shh, baby. I'll take care of you."

He pulls them in once more, soft and hot. And I almost feel like his mouth is on my hungry sex. But I wait.

Excruciating.

Lovely.

While I watch, and with his green-and-gold eyes on mine, he slips my fingers from his mouth, uses one hand to part my thighs, and takes my hand, my own slippery fingers, and guides them between my legs.

A shock of lust goes through me. Even better when he presses my damp fingers to my aching cleft, uses his free hand to spread my pussy lips, guides my fingers so that they are on either side of my swollen clit. Then he moves my hand with his, rubbing, rubbing. Pleasure, like a hot current, moves through my body. And the whole time, his gaze on mine, so intense I can barely stand to look at him. But I can't look away.

"Do you want to be fucked, Valentine?" he asks, his voice quiet. His eyes are hot with desire again. Burning.

"Oh, yes."

He picks up my hand, slides it into his mouth once more,

leaving my fingers wetter than ever. Then he does the same with his own fingers. I am nearly dying from anticipation.

He moves my hand between my thighs once more, finding my clitoris, holds my hand and begins to rub, circling, pressing. It feels so damn good, better than my own hand should. And then he slides his fingers inside me, into that wet, needy hole, and begins to pump. And God, I am ready to come almost instantly. His fingers moving inside me, my own sliding across my hard little clit, and most of all, his gaze on mine, as though he can see inside me.

I moan, pant, and watch his dark pupils expand. His gaze bores into me, burrows deep, as deeply as his hand in my body, pumping, pulling pleasure from me in long, lovely strands.

"God, Joshua . . . Yes, fuck me, baby, please . . ."

He moves deeper, faster. And I no longer know if I am moving my fingers over my clit or if it's him. And everything is so slippery, so burning hot. And I am poised on that keen edge, waiting to fall.

"I love you, baby. Love you, love you," he whispers.

And I tumble over, stars behind my eyes, exploding in my head, like a million points of diamond-bright light, expanding into an entire universe in which nothing exists but he and I.

It's much later when I wake up from a deep sleep. He is lying next to me on the sofa, his long body stretched out against my side, one arm thrown over my waist.

It's dark outside, the dim moonlight coming through the windows, but filtered by the fog, as it often is here at the beach. It's peaceful. So quiet that I can hear the faint sound of the ocean, that soothing white noise I have come to love these past days.

I have come to love everything about this place. But mostly that it's his.

I want to be here. I don't even want to go home. And that scares the hell out of me.

A hard thump in my chest.

This place is not yours.

No. I have been pretending. I'm good at that. This is not news.

How can I be so happy and so bitter at the same time?

He stirs a little, his hand wandering over my side, caressing my breast. I look at his face and I see his eyes are open, two dark orbs in the pale light of the moon.

"Hi, baby," he says, kissing the top of my head. "Are you hungry? We didn't have dinner. Again."

"No. I'm not. What about you?"

"It can wait. I don't want to get up yet. This is too good."

I run my fingers through his hair, touch his cheek, needing to know he's real. He is as solid beneath my hand as anything has been in my life.

"It is," I tell him. "Too good. That's it exactly."

I really did not mean to say that out loud.

He raises his head. "Valentine? You okay?"

"Yes. Sure." But I have to look away. I can't look him in the eye and lie.

He takes my chin, forcing me to face him. "No. Tell me."

I shake my head. Why can't I keep my mouth shut? I don't want to ruin the evening. But it's too late. He sees right through me.

"Come on. Talk to me."

He pushes himself up on the pillows, taking me with him. I'm shivering a little in the night air; he pulls a throw blanket from the back of the couch and drapes it over both of us. It would be a warm, sweet cocoon if we didn't have to talk right now. But we do.

"Joshua . . . I'm sorry. I've been thinking a lot today. Well, I've been thinking a lot in general."

"And?"

I can hear the tension in his voice. I don't blame him.

"There's a lot going on in my head. A lot of . . . thoughts, ideas. A lot of . . . doubts."

"About me?"

"Mostly about me."

"Mostly. But not all."

I'm quiet for a moment, tugging on a bit of fringe on the edge of the blanket, twisting it between my fingers. "I have to wonder, Joshua . . . I can't help but think about how things are going to go between us. I don't claim to know much about relationships, but I do know they're never easy. And we have this extra thing to deal with. My past. You can't deny it's a huge issue. I don't know how you'll handle it long term. I don't even know how I'll handle it. It's just so damn hard."

His jaw is clenched. I've made him angry. And that makes me want to cry. But I don't.

"Do you think this is easy for me? That I fell in love with a woman with your history? I don't mean to hurt you, Valentine, I really don't. But we have to be honest with each other. And the truth is, loving you scares the hell out of me. But I love you. There's no getting around that, so I deal with it. And it's not denial, if that's what you're worried about. It's a process, but one that's happening on the inside. I feel like it has to, or I'd be punishing you for the way you've lived your life, and I can't do that to you, to what we have together."

He stops, rubs a hand over his face. I can see beard stubble shadowing his chin. He looks so human to me right now, so vulnerable, the tension around his eyes, his mouth. I hate that I do this to him.

He goes on. "I need you to know that I don't think there's something bad, evil, in what you did. I didn't think it of those girls I paid for sex in Amsterdam all those years ago. But I understand there are reasons why you ended up in that life. I know you're working on it now. And I'm sticking while you do that. I think you can do it, overcome your past.

"But I'd also be a liar if I said I can be one hundred percent certain everything will be okay. I understand I have very little control over how it all goes with us, and that makes me fucking crazy. But I love you. What else can I do but wait and hope you get it worked out in your head? There's not one more God damn thing I can do."

I want to cry, the tears fighting to come out. I bite my lip, hold them back. "Alright. I get all that. I really do. But . . . Joshua, I need to know if . . . if you forgive me."

He looks taken aback. "Forgive you? Of course. No, that's not it. Because I don't think there's anything to forgive. I couldn't be with you otherwise."

"I guess I don't understand how you *can* be with me."

He's quiet again, but his jaw is loosening a bit. I'm still shivering, but it's not the cool night air.

He's quiet a few moments, gathering his thoughts.

"I told you how in love my parents were. They were really happy for a long time," Joshua goes on. "And then they went through a rough period after my sister was born. Lanie was a difficult baby, didn't sleep for two years. She was sick a lot. It took a toll on them both. And Dad cheated."

"What?"

I don't know why I feel so shocked. It happens all the time. But the relationship between these people sounded so solid. So sweet.

"Yeah. I didn't know about any of this until Dad died.

The day of the funeral, Mom was sitting out on the back porch, alone, while there were probably a hundred people in the house. I found her out there and it all came pouring out."

"God, Joshua. You were so young to hear all that. To handle it."

"It was part of the reason why I took off for Europe. Knowing too much damaged the way I thought of my dad for a while. It hurt. I'd always had him up on a pedestal, and when people die, we tend to deify them, anyway. So it really blew my mind. But eventually I realized that we are all human. We all fuck things up. And the fact is, my mother took him back, forgave him. And together they got over the hurt. She made a point of telling me that. They did it because they loved each other that much. Because that's what real love is. That's how powerful it is. I believe that. That's what helped me work through my own shit. Knowing that is helping me work through this with you. It showed me what a force love can be, defined it even further than just knowing how much my parents loved each other. It showed me that people who love each other can get through anything. Anything."

"I understand it works that way for you, Joshua. I understand that your experiences, your parents' experiences, led you there."

"But . . . ?"

"But I'm not there yet." I'm trembling, but I need to be honest with him. "I love you. But I don't have that kind of faith."

He blows out a long breath. Runs a hand through my hair, his fingers catching in a tangle. "Fuck, Valentine."

The tears are stinging my eyes again. I blink, hard, shake my head mutely.

"Fuck," he says again before he pulls me into his arms,

holding me so tightly I can barely breathe. "As long as you love me. As long as we can work on this."

I'm nodding into his shoulder. "I do love you."

"Okay. Okay."

He strokes my hair with his hand, and I swallow my tears, warm and weak all over with relief.

I'm going to try to believe that love is enough, that it will get us through this. That we can survive not only the reality of what I've done, but my own shame.

I wish I could make the heavy pit sitting in my stomach go away. That pit still holding on tight to the belief that things will be over, sooner or later. That I am not worthy of his love.

You do not deserve him.

Oh, yes, that is the thought running through my mind like a broken record. Even now. No matter how much I've thought things through, faced the issues of my past. How much stronger I've been feeling lately, how determined.

I don't know how I will ever make it stop.

Chapter Fourteen

WE HAVE BEEN TOGETHER for just over a month. I've gone home a few times, brought my car, some clothes and personal items back to his place. I can't stand to be in my house, the house I once loved so much. I'm not even as concerned about my orchids. I pay my housekeeper well to go by twice a week and care for them. But if they all died I wouldn't be crushed, as I might have been once.

I am still floating in some odd state, still spending much of my time at the beach, reading, or sitting at the little café drinking coffee. I've brought my laptop with me from home, and I take it there and cruise the Internet, looking for books: art, poetry, cookbooks. I've looked at some resource websites for troubled teens.

I've been back to see Lydia a few times. Probably not as often as I should. But I've run out of things to say. At this point I feel I have to work a lot of things out on the inside, in my head, before I can really move on to the next level in therapy.

When I was a kid there was a small playground by our house. Maybe it's still there; I don't know. I used to go there and swing on the swings. I'd go as high as I could, pumping my legs until they ached, just for the dizzying thrill of the height. I was an escapist even then. That excitement would take me right out of my head, and in those moments, nothing else existed. Nothing else mattered. I've spent my life searching for that same sensation. And I found it, didn't I?

When I'd gone as high as I could, I would jump off, flying through the air. It scared me. But I still did it every time. Those brief moments when I was sailing through the air, waiting to hit the ground, were truly terrifying.

I sort of feel that way now. Terrified, but choosing to jump anyway.

I don't know why I'm thinking of this now. Maybe because Joshua got up early this morning, too early for me; I was feeling lazy, and he went to the Farmers' Market they have in Santa Monica every Sunday. I've been tense ever since he left the house, missing him, wishing I'd gone with him. Too much time alone to think. I do enough of that during the week, when he's working and I'm alone. The house is too quiet for me, but I don't want to leave; I don't know when he'll be back.

I get out of bed, go into the kitchen, and put the kettle on for tea, decide to check my messages at home.

One from my accountant with a question I can deal with on Monday. I make myself a note on a pad of paper next to the kitchen phone, wait for the next message.

The Broker.

"Hello, Val. I hadn't heard from you. I hope you're well. I think we should talk. Come to my apartment. I'll be here on the weekend, then I'll be in London for a week. Best if you see me now."

The royal command. I don't want to go. But she's right, we do need some sort of closure. Maybe it'll be good for me?

I take a quick shower, get dressed, leave Joshua a message on his cell phone when he doesn't pick up, letting him know I'm meeting an old friend for lunch.

The Broker could hardly be called my friend. But I don't want to say those words to him: "my madam."

I'm in my car, heading for Deirdre's place before I realize I haven't called her to tell her I'm coming. But she'll be there.

It's a short drive up the 405 to Wilshire, then east on Wilshire Boulevard into Beverly Hills. Deirdre inhabits one of those ridiculously expense penthouse apartments on condo row, right at the mouth of Beverly Hills. It's one of those towering, pseudo-old Hollywood buildings, so picture perfect, as though no one actually lives there. This entire section of Wilshire looks this way to me. Too pristine. It's all beautiful but sterile. Just like Deirdre herself.

I check in with the doorman and he calls up. In moments he's holding the door aside for me. I walk inside, and the temperature drops, all icy marble floors, bright lighting in flawless golden fixtures. Everything so perfect. Do they know one of Beverly Hills' most successful madams lives here? Maybe not so perfect after all. Maybe Joshua is right—nothing is.

I get into the opulent, mirrored elevator and the attendant, dressed as though he's a liveryman from another era, holds the door for me, pushes the button for the penthouse, politely inquires how my day is going.

The door slides open with a heavy whisper and I step into the penthouse foyer, another cool space filled with marble and an enormous urn ovflowing with what I know must be hundreds of dollars in fresh Casablanca lilies, trailing ferns, smaller accent flowers. Very European. Very Deirdre.

Everything stunning, speaking of staggering amounts of money. Which I now know is not everything I once thought it was.

Deirdre's maid opens the door leading into the apartment, and I nod at her, try to smile. I don't know her name. I've only been here a handful of times; The Broker doesn't encourage much personal contact with her girls.

She leads me down a long hallway. The floors are done in pink, gray, and white marble laid in a harlequin pattern. There are gilt-framed mirrors on the walls, more tall vases full of flowers. The scent of lilies is a bit overwhelming, a bit too sweet. My head is pounding by the time we reach the living room.

The view is incredible: all of Beverly Hills laid out below. But the woman standing in front of the floor-to-ceiling windows commands even more attention than the view.

Deirdre must be in her fifties, but her figure is better than most twenty-year-olds. She is dressed in a black pencil skirt, a white silk blouse. Her skin is luminous, her fine bone structure flawless, her face perfectly made up in an understated way. That icy elegance. Except there's a certain flatness in Deirdre's large brown eyes that reminds me of a shark.

"Val, you've come." That familiar, crisp British accent. I've always wondered if she's really as upper crust as she appears. Are any of us what we appear to be?

"Yes. You asked me to."

"You didn't return my call, however."

She arches an elegant brow. She does love to scold people for the smallest infraction. I used to bow down to it, I realize. But I'm not bowing now. No, now I'm a little annoyed.

"I knew you'd be here," I say. "You told me so in your message. And you did ask to see me, for me to come here."

"Yes."

She seems unsure for one moment, but it's fleeting. The Broker isn't a woman anyone can unsettle easily.

"Come, Val, sit down."

She gestures to a delicate gold and cream settee. She has a good eye for French and English antiques, and the apartment is full of these pieces.

I sit, and she takes a large chair on the opposite side of the table; not too close. The chair appears thronelike with her elegant figure seated in it. Something she's thought out, staged, I'm sure. Deirdre is nothing if not incredibly clever. That's how she's come as far as she has.

The maid is at her elbow, and Deirdre speaks softly to her. I can't hear what she's saying. The maid hurries off.

"I've ordered tea. I hope that's alright with you." She doesn't wait for my answer. "Tell me what you've been up to, Val. You've seen Lydia?"

"Yes, a number of times. Thank you for referring me to her. She's been very helpful."

I have to give her that. It's true.

"I'm quite happy to hear it. And have you moved beyond this burnout stage, do you think?"

She is so fucking condescending.

"Deirdre, this isn't a burnout stage. That's not what it's about for me."

"What are you saying, Val?"

I hate when she calls me that. Not that I really want her to call me anything else. But it grates on me. It reminds me of what I am to her.

The maid returns with a tea tray, and we spend several minutes going through the polite ritual, with Deirdre pouring, dropping a cube of sugar into a translucent china cup, handing it out to me on a saucer.

"So," she says. "Please continue."

"Deirdre, I'm not coming back to work."

"Oh?" She is trying to appear calm, but the tight line of her lips betrays her. She's surprised to hear it.

"I can't do this anymore. I'm done. I'm sorry I didn't tell you sooner." It feels good to say it to her. It feels fucking wonderful. But my pulse is racing, thready.

She sips from her cup, sets it carefully on a side table, taking her time. Finally she says, "You think you're done, Val?"

"I know I'm done."

She's really pissing me off now.

"Let me tell you a story. It's not one I share often." She pauses. A bit dramatically. I imagine I'm supposed to be impressed. "Do you know how I came to be in this business? How I came to be in this position?"

"I didn't think anyone knew."

"Few do. But these are special circumstances."

Another dramatic pause, and I want to roll my eyes. But I don't do it.

She goes on. "When I was twenty-one I came here from England. I had hopes of becoming an actress, as many young girls do. I'm not proud to say how naive I was. But I was quite young. One of those casting couches we all hear about, which we all know exist, led me to this business.

"There was a woman who had a house set up here in Beverly Hills. And I became one of her girls for a time. Does that surprise you? Yes, I can see that it does. It surprised me, too, at the time. I never became used to it. Luckily, one of my clients, a very well-to-do older man, was quite entranced with me. He asked me over and over to become his private mistress, but I refused. There was no security in such a position, after all. Once he realized I was serious about my refusal, he proposed marriage."

"I never knew you were married."

"Again, this sort of personal information is not something I often divulge to my girls. It's not necessary, is it?"

"Why do you feel it's necessary now?"

"You'll understand once I finish my story." She sips from her tea, holds the cup in its saucer on her lap. "My husband, as you can imagine, was not faithful to me. I didn't love him; it never bothered me on that level. But after a time it became too well known and it was humiliating, which I refused to put up with. I divorced him. But he hadn't handled his finances well and there wasn't as much money as I would have liked. So I went into business for myself. And of course, this is the only business I knew."

Yet another heavy pause in which her flat, dark gaze meets mine. "So you see, Val, there is never truly any getting out of this business. It is always a part of us. It becomes so deeply ingrained, it is a part of our very nature. If you think you're simply going to walk away, well, I assure you, it does not work that way."

She looks so self-satisfied with this little speech, I want to slap her. But of course, I would never do anything like that.

My hands itch. I clench them, the nails biting into my palms.

"Deirdre, I'm sure everything you've said is true. For you."

"Don't be so arrogant as to think you're any different, Val. A woman in your position cannot afford such foolishness. You've become used to a certain lifestyle. And you've become used to a certain kind of sex. Don't think I don't know everything about you, Val. I make it my business to know."

I'm fucking furious now.

"You don't own me, Deirdre. What do you think this is, the Mafia?"

"Of course not. And I take no credit for what is in your blood."

"No. That's bullshit."

She flinches at my language. I don't care.

"Be very careful about the bridges you burn, Valentine."

"Don't call me that."

She stares at me, her gaze hard on mine. Her beautiful face is tight. She is waiting for me to back down. I'm not going to do it.

"Very well. You've had your say. I do wish things had ended on a better note. But that was your choice."

I nod my head. I'm not going to deny it. I'm not going to defend my actions. I am certainly not going to apologize.

She stands, cool and elegant once more. Restrained. Regal. "I believe we're done here."

I stand, watching her. And I see for the first time how this cold, hard armor she wears is just that. And I feel the slightest bit sad for her.

I extend my hand to her and surprise flashes across her features for one brief moment before she takes it. Hers is cool and dry and perfectly smooth. It hardly feels like flesh to me.

"I wish you well, Deirdre. But I won't be back."

She nods her head, lets go of my hand. Her maid appears at her side as if magically summoned.

"Lucia will see you out."

Back in my car and heading toward the freeway, I feel a strange combination of things. I didn't expect to feel sad, but I do. Sad for her. Sad for myself. For all of us call girls. Hookers. Whores.

I play again in my head what she said to me about how we can never free ourselves entirely of what we've been. But I refuse to believe I am permanently tainted. I'd rather believe in what Joshua has told me. And seeing Deirdre has only made me more clear about what I want for myself and what I absolutely don't. I am more done with my old life than ever.

My new cell phone rings and I see Joshua's number on the screen, smile as I answer.

"Hey, baby." His voice makes me melt a little, as always. "I just got a call and I have to be at a job site in San Diego later today, see an anxious client for dinner, but I want to take you to lunch first. Where are you? How are you?"

"I'm good. I have something to celebrate." I am still flying from my conversation with Deirdre. I feel victorious.

"What?"

"I went to see Deirdre today. My . . . madam."

He pauses, and I hurry to explain. "I had to tell her in person that I'm done. Not that I was any less done before I saw her, but seeing her was . . . different. More final."

"I think I get it. How did she react?"

"She was coldly furious. Trying to tell me I can never escape that life. It felt pretty damn good to tell her she was wrong. It felt like . . . the end. Do you know what I mean?"

"I think so. Sometimes we have to face our demons head-on."

"Oh, she's an old demon, alright."

"How do you feel now?"

"Good. Stronger."

"Yes, let's celebrate. I'll order a bottle of champagne."

"That's perfect. Where should I meet you?"

Twenty minutes later we're at The Lobster in Santa Monica. The place is right on the pier and is all soaring glass with a stunning ocean view. The waves, shades of green, gray, and blue, sparkling in the sun, thunder on the sand below us. And the sun is lighting up Joshua's hazel eyes as he sits across from me, smiling as we drink our champagne, waiting for our food.

Lunch is lovely, relaxed. Gorgeous seafood and this gorgeous man across from me, holding my hand between bites. Impossible that he loves me, but he does. I can feel it in every look, every gesture.

I have never been so happy in my life. I have never even imagined this.

After our meal we have dessert, a nice chocolate mousse, which he feeds me with his spoon. We drink more of the sparkling wine, talking about inconsequential things. Like normal people, after all.

I just want to get him home, to strip our clothes off, to lie beside him, to touch his naked skin. It makes me smile that I will, eventually, later tonight when he's done working. That I can actually have what I want.

We get up to leave, and Joshua comes around and wraps my sweater over my shoulders in an old-fashioned gesture I love.

The place is really filling up now with the late-lunch crowd. We're making our way through the throngs of people toward the front door, Joshua leading me by the hand, when he stops.

"Greg, hi." He turns to me. "Valentine, this is Greg Stockton. We worked together on the Seal Beach restoration project."

"Nice to meet you," I get out, offering my hand, before I realize who this man is.

My client.

Elegant in his gray suit that matches his hair, with his shiny arm-candy wife beside him.

The champagne bubbles in my stomach like a witch's cauldron.

Somehow, I manage not to let my smile falter, to shake his wife's hand, to shake *his* hand, which makes my skin crawl. His flesh is cool to the touch, too dry, like a reptile's. He is uncomfortable, but hiding it fairly well. If only he'd stop looking at me like that. Like I'm a piece of meat.

That's what you are to him.

I hang on to Joshua's hand tighter, and he turns to look at me, a question in his eyes.

I feel dirty standing next to him, with this man, this client, in front of me. With him eyeing me this way, probably remembering fucking me on the dining room table in his weekend house in Playa del Rey a few months ago, handing me a pile of hundred-dollar bills.

"I'm sorry. I'm not feeling well. I have to go."

I let go of Joshua's hand, leaving mine cold and empty, and walk outside, take a gasping breath of the sea air. Joshua is right behind me, catching up to me in the parking lot.

"What just happened in there?"

I can barely breathe. I can barely stand to look at him.

"That man . . ."

"What?"

"He's . . . an old client of mine."

"Shit."

He takes a step back, recoiling.

Somewhere down deep, I always knew this would happen. That at some point, the reality of what I've done will hit him full force. I guess I just didn't expect it to affect me this way.

I can't even say anything to him. All I can do is stand there helplessly, watching his face shut down.

Finally, he reaches out for me, pulls me into him hard, wrapping his arms around me.

"Valentine. Shit. Okay. It's going to be okay."

"Will it?"

I just don't know anymore.

"That was . . . bad. Hard. But it doesn't change anything."

"I don't know if that's true. For you or for me."

"It doesn't have to, Valentine."

I burrow into his chest, hiding my face, rubbing my cheek into the comfort of his fresh, crisp shirt. I take in a breath, breathe in the scent of him. So precious to me.

"Damn it. I have to go, get on the road. I can't be late. Valentine, just go home, to my place. Wait for me."

I nod my head. He tucks his fingers beneath my chin, lifting my face to his, forcing me to look at him. His eyes are blazing. "We'll talk. Okay? As soon as I get home."

"Yes. Alright."

But I am already going dead inside. All but my heart, hammering out my panic at a thousand miles an hour.

He kisses my forehead, then my mouth. Is he really as distant as he feels, or is it just me? My fear?

"I love you," he whispers before he lets me go, helps me into my car. "Go straight home, alright?"

"Yes. I will."

The beach is fogged in when I get back to Joshua's house, after a quick stop at a convenience store to buy a bag of gummi bears. Silly, I know. But I plan to crawl into bed, to make my escape, and this is part of the old ritual. I just need a break, some time to breathe.

I let myself into the house—*his* house—undress quickly,

and crawl into bed in my underwear, the small plastic bag in my hand. Curling up beneath the sheets, the heavy weight of the comforter, I tear the bag open, spill a few of the candies into my palm, put them in my mouth.

That familiar sweet sensation, so sweet it almost hurts. I am trying hard not to think about what just happened. I don't need anything right now but to make my mind go blank, this small shock of sugar on my tongue, and then, blissful sleep.

But I smell his scent all over the pillows, almost as though he is there with me.

Joshua.

I am too much in love with him.

Each day I feel closer and closer to him. Even our little argument drew us nearer to each other. And yet there is this part of me, locked away inside, that's like a hard lump of granite, and even I don't know what's in there. But I know it's ugly.

I am afraid to let it out. I know I can't do it in front of Joshua. And I know I won't be able to really heal and move on until I take that dark place apart, expose it to the light, and deal with it.

Yeah, I know, I sound like some self-help guru. I sound like Lydia. That doesn't make it any less true.

Running into a client today made me realize just how much I am going to have to deal with. Maybe I knew it before, on some level, but having it shoved in my face like this . . . It does change things, regardless of what Joshua says.

Too much. Don't think about it now.

I close my eyes, let the candy melt in my mouth, the bag clutched to my chest. Pulling the covers over my head, shutting out the misty mid-day light, I drift off.

I don't know how long it is before the telephone wakes me up. I'm afraid to answer it at first. Reaching over to the extension on the nightstand, I see that it's Joshua, and I am more afraid than ever. He'll know something is wrong and I can't explain this to him. Not now. But I answer anyway.

"Hello?"

"Hey, baby."

It almost hurts to hear his voice.

"Hi."

"You sound sleepy."

"I was . . . napping. Sorry."

"You don't have to be sorry. Do whatever you want. Whatever makes you happy. I'm sorry I woke you."

"No. No, it's fine."

"I was calling to tell you I'll be home late. I probably won't get there until after ten."

"Oh. Alright."

"Valentine? You okay?"

"What? Yes. Fine. I'm fine. Just . . . I'm not quite awake yet. I'll be fine. Go finish your meeting. I'll see you when you get home."

"Okay. I'll get there as soon as I can. And we can talk. Or not. We can wait until tomorrow, when we're not tired. We can talk whenever you're ready. This place makes a great tiramisu; I'll bring you some dessert."

"Yes, I'd like that."

We hang up, and I immediately curl back into the bed.

I have been playing house here with him for weeks. But it's not right. I have no right. He is too good. But I cannot figure it out right now. My head is fuzzy, heavy.

Settling into the pillows, I bite back the tears and pop another gummi bear into my mouth before I fall back into a dreamless sleep.

I SENSE HIM IN the room even before he says my name.

"Valentine. Wake up, baby."

Then he's there next to me on the bed. I reach for him in the dark and find he's undressed already. Ah, the smooth texture of his skin beneath my searching hands, the fine, strong muscles of his shoulder, his chest. His nipples stiffening when I brush my fingertips over them.

He leans in and kisses me and my hands go into his hair, pulling him down into me. He kisses me hard, sensing my need. And his hands are everywhere, hot, skimming over my skin, lighting me up all over.

I am wet for him; I always am. All it takes is a single touch, a look. Oh, yes, the way he looks at me, really *looks* at me, as no one has ever done before. And I don't have to think right now, not with him this close to me.

He is climbing in with me now, pushing back the covers, slipping my panties off, and laying his body over mine. I love this, the sweet weight of him on me. So sentimental, but I can't help myself.

His cock is a hard length resting at the apex of my thighs, and I open for him, arch up against him. Reaching down between our bodies, he strokes me with his hand, and I sigh into his mouth. I am trembling already, suffused with pleasure. And my chest is tight with emotion. But it is all sweetness and tenderness: his caressing fingers on my cleft, his lovely mouth on mine.

"Joshua, come on," I whisper against his lips. "I don't want to wait."

He reaches into the nightstand and finds a condom,

sheaths his beautiful cock. And in moments he is poised at the entrance to my body, while I lay trembling with need, sharp and bright, beneath him.

"Ah, Valentine." His voice is a low murmur in my ear, his cheek resting against mine.

And when he slides inside, it is like silk against velvet: that smooth, that fine. My body clenches around him, my legs wrapping around his waist. Reaching up, I take his face in my hands, holding it above me, needing to feel his gaze on me. I need to see that small glimmer of his eyes in the dark, with only the fog-veiled stars and moon to show him to me.

He begins to move, a lovely, stroking rhythm, and pleasure builds inside my body. I pull him closer, until my breasts are crushed against his chest.

"More, Joshua."

He thrusts deeper, but slowly, his body grinding against mine. And with each thrust he burrows farther inside me, pleasure swarming me in a warm current.

My arms tighten around his neck. "Come on, Joshua. Deeper. Please . . ."

He pushes into me, and still, I can't seem to get enough. He cannot go deep enough.

I am shivering, with desire, with yearning. I have never yearned this way for anything, anyone. He reaches down between us once more, his fingers stroking my clitoris. I don't want it to be over so soon, but I am lost in pleasure, my body filling, bursting in a flood of blinding heat. My mind goes blank, and I am only these sensations, his big body against mine, inside me, his scent in my head.

He calls my name, thrusting, thrusting. And then he tenses, his lips coming down to crush mine, his sweet tongue in my mouth as he comes into me. And it is almost as if we are, for those brief moments, one being.

Except that we are too separate, he and I. I can't quite believe that we are meant to be.

Even in this moment, that fear is in my heart, which shatters into a thousand jagged pieces.

I MUST HAVE SLEPT. Through the window I can see the pale orange glow of sunrise. I hate this time of day. I always have. It is the most lonely time, too dark, too empty.

Joshua sleeps beside me, his breathing regular and shallow. He is lying on his stomach, as he often does, and I can see the outline of his body, so damn beautiful. Fucking glorious in the cool, silent dawn.

Why do I feel lonelier than I ever have in my life?

No matter how much I sleep, no matter how many times he makes love to me, I cannot get the truth out of my head. The truth that Deirdre spoke to me, that Regan tried to. That slammed into me like a brick wall running into Greg Stockton yesterday.

I should never have let this happen.

I have to stop before ... before what? It's too late already, far too late. It's not fair to Joshua. How can I do this— condemn him to a life with a woman like me—to someone I claim to love? Do I even know what that means?

I shake my head, sit up in bed. He is so peaceful. He has no idea what I am about to do to him. What I have already done to myself.

My throat is closing up on me, but I cannot cry. Not here. Not now.

I slip out from under the covers, the warmth of his body leaving my skin immediately. It's painful.

Finding my clothes from yesterday, I get dressed quickly, silently. In the living room, I find my purse, and slip out the door and into the still-dark morning.

My mind is absolutely numb as I drive north, then east, heading away from the rising sun. If I drive fast enough, maybe I can escape the new day.

I head into Beverly Hills, drive the familiar streets until I am in front of Louis's place. It's beautiful, imposing behind the tall iron gates. I stop, letting the motor run, just watching the house for a while.

How many times have I been with him over the years? How many more times would I have been if I hadn't ever met Joshua? And how would it have ended, as it inevitably would have?

I'm done with hookers, thank you very much, here's a thousand dollars for your trouble.

I know I soothed Louis, made him feel good. But I was never anything else to him. I couldn't be.

I rev the engine, shift and pull onto the palm tree–lined street. A sharp pang as I drive by the Beverly Wilshire Hotel, where I always see Enzo. But I can't face this place, not today. I have no idea what I'll say to him. I know The Broker has called him, told him I'm no longer available. But Enzo brought me to her. Our connection predates her, has nothing to do with her. I need to talk to him myself, eventually.

He hasn't called me. I know he's respecting my need for silence. But suddenly I *need* to talk with him. Maybe more than anyone right now. Enzo is where this all started for me. He is so much a part of what I am. He saved me from that sad, terrible life I'd found myself in at twenty years old, helped me find something better. Maybe I need him to help me make this new transition? It sounds all wrong, but still . . . maybe . . .

I let the hotel pass with one glance into my rearview mirror as it disappears, lost in the pink and red glow of the rising sun behind me.

Yes, go home and call him. Maybe go see him. Go to Rome.

I keep driving, though. I'm not certain of where I'm going until I'm in Hollywood already, pulling onto Sunset, then following some of the side streets until I find it: that faded hotel where I met Colin a few weeks ago.

On the corner in front of the building are a pair of working girls in their short, candy-colored skirts, their long legs and platform shoes. They look cold, tired. Miserable. It must have been a long night, and it's too cold now to be out there in their skimpy clothes.

That could have been you. It could have been worse. So much worse. Be glad for what you have.

But I am still grieving for what I can't have. Fuck it. I haven't even begun to grieve yet, have I? Things are going to get much harder.

I'm starting to cry as I head home. But it doesn't feel like home. I know even before I get there that it is no longer the safe haven it used to be. It may never be again.

When I walk into my house it feels like a mausoleum: that cold, that empty. As though no one has lived there for years, rather than weeks. My footsteps echo on the hardwood floor as I drop my purse on the console table in the entryway, walk into the kitchen. I don't know what to do, where to settle.

I pull a glass from the cupboard and pour a shot of gin, not even bothering with ice or tonic water, take it, and stare out the window. The sun is up now, but the day is gray still. The light is fighting its way through, touching the tips of the leaves on the big eucalyptus trees. The rest is still in shadow.

I am in shadow.

I take a slug of the gin and it burns going down.

I do not want to think. But I know my usual escapes will be denied me now. I have gone too far for such easy relief.

Lifting my glass, I swallow again. The gin warms me a bit, but it is a shallow warmth and dissolves quickly. And it only makes me hate myself, this stupid drinking. I set the glass down and don't touch it again. This is not what I need. It never has been.

I walk into the living room. My orchids are there, lovely and graceful on their spindly stems. They have been doing fine without me. Pacing the living room, I feel as though my body is filled with adrenaline, but I have no place to go. I feel fucking trapped. Here, in my house. In my head, which will not stop spinning. No matter how I try to shut my brain down, those ugly voices fill it, practically shouting at me:

You will never change. You will never be good enough.

And Deirdre's voice, that spiteful bitch. But I can't fight the truth, no matter how much I don't want to hear it. That's why I had to leave him. That's why I have to get the hell out of here now.

I pick up the phone and dial the airline, make my plans. Then I call Lydia. It's early, but she picks up the phone. I tell her I'm leaving for a while. She's kind to me, calm, tells me to do what I need to do and to call her when I get back. When I'm done, I sit down, and wait.

It's only an hour later when he arrives at my house, pounding on the front door.

"Valentine! God damn it, open up!"

Oh, he's furious. I knew he'd be hurt, but his anger surprises me.

Moving like a zombie, I open the door. Even with him standing there before me, his face full of pain and fury, I am half numb. I step back and he brushes past me.

"What the hell is going on?" he demands.

"I had to go, Joshua. I had to." I shake my head. I am hanging on to my sanity by such a narrow thread, I'm not able to explain any further.

"That's not good enough. Try again."

"I'm sorry."

He grabs my arms, and it hurts. I won't fight him. I couldn't even if I tried. I am too full of my own pain.

"Valentine, you explain to me right now what the hell is going on in your head. Tell me why you left in the middle of the night. Just because we ran into one of your clients . . . Shit, it was bound to happen. We have to deal with this."

I can't look at him. My gaze lands on a spot just beyond his shoulder, my vision blurred by a thin sheen of tears. "Joshua . . . I've just realized that I have to do this on my own."

"No you don't. That's what I'm here for. That's what love is for!"

"No. Not for people like me. I'm too . . . damaged."

"You can choose not to believe that, Valentine."

"That's what I've been trying to do, but it's all a sham." I look at him then, into his green-and-gold eyes. His pupils are huge. "Don't you see? You were the catalyst that led me to all of this self-exploration, but I can't get everything I need from you. In the end, I have to do this myself. And I have no idea where I'll end up when it's over, or how long it'll take. I can't drag you along with me. It's not fair. And let's be honest, Joshua. Okay? Let's be perfectly honest, all of this love stuff aside. All of these lovely fairy-tale scenarios. I am a hooker. A hooker!"

"Don't make it any more harsh than it has to be," he says through clenched teeth, his fingers digging into my flesh.

"The situation *is* harsh. It's real. Wishing it away isn't going to work. You can't tell me that it will. And you can't tell me you've ever dealt with something like this before."

"No. But neither have you."

"I've been a call girl for almost ten years, Joshua."

God, I hate saying it to him. Rubbing his face in it. But we both have to face it. It's time.

"That's not what I'm talking about. I'm talking about love. Don't you think that has any value? Any power?"

"You are not going to convince me that love will get us through this."

"Actually, that's exactly what I'm trying to tell you. Christ, Valentine." His grip on my arms tightens even more. His eyes are absolutely blazing. "It's a God damn good place to start. Can you think of anything else that would even come close?"

I can't stand to see him this way, to feel the tension in his hands, to feel them on my skin.

"Maybe not. But any relationship between us is . . . a house of cards, Joshua. It's too fragile, because I'm just learning how to do this. The obstacles are fucking enormous. You can't tell me they're not. It's too much for me to go through on blind faith alone. Faith I'm not even sure I have. I've said it before. It's still true, more true than ever, maybe."

He drops his hands, takes a step away from me. His voice still holds some anger, but mostly what I hear is defeat. "You have to believe in something, Valentine. Why can't you believe this? That I love you. That you love me. That it's enough."

I just shake my head, trying not to stumble while my whole

world crashes down around me. I am too overwhelmed with fear and pain and longing to really let any of it surface. If I do, it will swallow me up. The pain sits in my chest like a cold, hard stone, weighing me down. I don't know how long I'll be able to stay on my feet.

"Joshua, please understand. It's not that I don't love you . . ." My breath hitches hard in my chest. "But I have to do this on my own. I have to figure this out, why I can't even trust how I feel about you. It's not something anyone can help me with. It's up to me. Can't you see that?"

"No, I can't." He pauses, his voice lowering. "But I can't make you stay with me. I can't force you to let me help you."

I'm quiet, staring at the floor. I don't know what else to say. I only know what I have to do.

"What happens now, Valentine? We just go our separate ways?"

I nod. "I'm going away."

"What? Where are you going?"

"To Europe. I need to . . . I need some distance to figure things out."

"And you expect me to wait for you?"

Some anger there, still. Not that I blame him.

"Oh, no. I don't expect that. How can I, when I don't even know what will happen to me while I'm away? I have no idea what conclusions I'll come to. But I need to find out."

God, it hurts, saying these things to him.

"Fuck, Valentine. Fuck!"

He turns away, paces the floor, a hand going into his hair. I know the silk of his hair beneath my fingertips . . .

Don't go there.

Tears sting my eyes. I really cannot take much more.

"Please just go. Joshua. Please. Let me do this. I have

to . . . I can't simply decide to turn my back on what my life has been and pretend it never happened. I have to resolve my past, who I am now, who I'm going to be. I understand that . . . you might not be here when I get back."

Fucking awful.

Even worse, the hurt on his face.

He shakes his head, his eyes full of shadows.

"Alright. I'll leave. You go to Europe, figure your life out."

So much pain in his voice, defeat. And no promises. But what can I expect after what I'm doing to him?

I nod, stare at the floor once more, and when I look up, he's gone, leaving the door open behind him.

I am in hell. But I put myself there. Every choice I've made has led to this moment. I hate myself more than ever.

Chapter Fifteen

SHE IS PULLING ME *through the heavy door, and the moment
we are in the bar I am assailed by the sharp stench of stale booze
and cigarette smoke, and, very faintly, the hard, female scents of
lipstick and cheap perfume.*

*We've been here before. I like it and I don't like it. It's excit-
ing and scary. But this time something is different. Because I am
here, inside this little girl who is me.*

*I want to scream at my mother to take me home. But I can't.
All I can do is watch, exist in the moment.*

I am trapped.

Inside this little girl. Inside myself.

*She's pulling really hard on my arm, and my shoulder aches.
I reach up with my free hand to rub it as she yanks me along.*

*There they are: the pretty women. They wear the shortest
skirts I've ever seen, and high-heeled shoes. One woman has red
shoes on, and I wish they were mine. Maybe someday I'll have
shiny red shoes, just like hers. But when I look up her face is*

hard and mean behind a blue cloud of cigarette smoke, and I'm scared again.

I will never be that mean.

Mom is still pulling on my arm, almost dragging me, and muttering. I know what she's saying, but I don't want to hear it. I don't like those bad names. I don't like it when she's angry. I don't like being here.

But I can't stop looking at the women.

There's loud music, talking, laughing. Everyone looks like they're having fun, except that somewhere inside I know they're not.

There are men talking to the pretty women. They aren't nice men, but they are being nice to the women. Smiling. Leaning in close to talk to them. The men love them.

She finds him, the man who is my father, but who I hardly know. He's mad. Mom is mad. This is not going to be good.

Shouting then, and she lets go of my arm and I back away. But there's nowhere to go here.

I am trapped.

Inside this moment. Inside myself.

Dad grabs Mom by the arm and drags her out, and I follow them into the living room, which smells a little like the bar. They're laughing now, quietly, and I know what's coming next.

Mom takes my arm again and pulls me into my room. I'm hungry, but I know that doesn't matter to either of them. I'm lonely, but I know that matters even less. I climb into bed and pull the covers over my head, hearing her turn the lock on my door.

I listen for a while, waiting until their laughter drifts away, then I reach out, find the cigar box I keep in my nightstand drawer, and pull out my bag of gummi bears. I take a red one, my favorite, and slip it into my mouth. So sweet on my tongue. I can always lose myself in the sugar. For a little while, anyway.

But they're making so much noise now. Laughing and moaning and the furniture is bumping around and it feels like there's an earthquake. It scares me.

It scares me even more that they've left me alone again. Maybe someday Mom will lock me in here and never come back. I'll be trapped forever.

My skin feels too tight for my body and I want to scream. I open my mouth but nothing comes out but a little red sugar from the gummi bear.

Only it's not red sugar. It's blood.

I try to be good, I really do, but it doesn't matter. I'm never good enough. So they lock me in here when they're together, keeping me separate. Keeping me out. And it's all my fault.

It's all my fault.

It's all my fault.

I try to scream again, and this time there is a long, loud wail, and it is my voice, screaming for them to love me.

I wake with a start, and remember that I am in Rome even before my heart stops pounding. I breathe in the unfamiliar night air, pulling it deeply into my lungs, commanding myself to calm down. But there is a lump in my throat that won't go away.

I can still see the dream in my head, as though that's where I was all night. Maybe I was. I can almost smell the rancid booze, the waxy lipstick scent. I can taste the gummi bear and the blood in my mouth. I can taste the fear and the disappointment. I can taste my shame, sharp and bitter.

I know, logically, that my parents' behavior wasn't my fault. But I also realize that on some deep, emotional level I don't like to look at, I am still that scared little girl. I just don't know what the hell to do with her.

Maybe I don't want to let her go. Maybe that's too new, too

frightening a prospect. The familiar is comforting, even when it's not necessarily good. At least I know what to expect. And suddenly my entire life is one big, unknown factor. No wonder I'm such a fucking mess.

I am shivering all over, simply contemplating all of this.

I lie back in the plush, canopied bed, pull a pillow to my chest, curling my fingers into the softness while I force my mind to go blank, and wait for the dawn.

It comes slowly, revealing my surroundings in misty, gray-veiled shades of amber light. The room itself is beautiful, everything done in heavy damask, in rich hues that match the rising sun: pale gold, red, yellow. It is unbelievably pretty, every piece of furniture, the small crystal chandelier that hangs in the center of the room, the paintings on the walls. And the view is one of the most spectacular in Italy.

The InterContinental Hotel De La Ville sits at the top of the Spanish Steps, the entire city spread out below. From my window I can see Saint Peter's Dome and the Pantheon, which looks like some mythical otherrealm beneath the low-hanging clouds.

I have been here for three days. I haven't left the hotel, haven't done any sightseeing. I've just been holing up in my room, eating my meals here, taking long baths in the deep, luxurious marble tub, staring at the view. I've watched some Italian television. It doesn't seem to matter that I barely understand anything the people on the screen say. I'm too much in my own head to pay much attention.

The weather here is dreary, which is fine with me. Sunshine would seem too optimistically cheerful to me right now. I don't think I could take it.

It's raining, and I can hear the quiet patter through the glass doors leading to the small mosaic-tiled terrace outside my suite. After the dry desert air of L.A., the damp feels heavy to me here, almost as though it is holding me down. Holding my emotions in check.

I have not cried once. I am surprised and yet not surprised. In the worst of times I have always sought outer forms of comfort, rather than dealing with whatever the issue is head-on. Burying what I feel is habit for me. Lydia has been trying to tell me that.

Joshua was trying to tell me that.

Was it a mistake, leaving him, coming here?

I still don't know. All I know is that he was too close to me in L.A. I have no objectivity in his presence. How can I figure out what I'm doing for the rest of my life with him so close to me?

How am I ever going to figure it all out?

Three days of utter solitude hasn't helped. Maybe nothing will. I feel stuck.

Trapped.

Maybe that's what the dream was all about, rather than containing some profound message. Simply a manifestation of my current emotional state. But I don't quite believe that. I think there's more to it. And it's almost beginning to gel, but not quite. It's as though the answer is at the tip of my tongue—the tip of my mind—but I can't get to it. It's possible I never will.

As I've often said before, I am nothing if not a realist. And we humans are such a fallible lot. Me, more than most.

Finally, I get up, take a shower. The bath feels too self-indulgent to me today. Today is a day for action, finally. I don't know how I know this; nothing apparent has changed since I arrived. Maybe it's just time.

I get dressed in a pair of brown wool slacks, a black

turtleneck sweater, a scarf I bought in Paris a few years ago. I can't seem to get warm, even though the temperature is no lower than the sixties.

I order room service: a cappuccino, some pastry, fruit. But I can't eat. I drink the coffee quickly, letting it scald my tongue a little. Stupid of me; the caffeine immediately makes me feel more jittery. Still, I ignore my nerves, pick up the phone, and dial Enzo's number.

It rings and rings, and I am suddenly overcome by doubt: he's away, out of the country. Maybe even filming in some remote corner of the world. Maybe gone for months.

Or, even worse, he sees my cell number on his caller ID and has no desire to talk to me.

And then, miraculously, his voice on the other end.

"Valentine!"

"Enzo?"

I want to cry. But I don't.

"Where are you? What have you been doing? Are you well?" That familiar Italian-accented voice. One of the few things that feels even remotely familiar lately.

"Yes, I'm okay. Well . . . no, I'm not. God, I'm sorry. I'm not making sense, even to myself. Are you here, Enzo? In Rome?"

"I am in Florence. Where are you?"

"I'm in Rome, Enzo. I'm at the InterContinental Hotel De La Ville. And I'm—"

But my throat just closes up and suddenly I'm choking.

"Valentine? What is it? Tell me what is going on. What are you doing in Rome? No, never mind. I heard from Deirdre. I have some idea. I didn't want to call you. I knew you would contact me when you were ready."

It's another full minute before I can force the enormous

lump in my throat away and breathe again. "I'm sorry, Enzo. I should have gotten ahold of you myself."

"We have known each other too long to worry over details. I will return to Rome immediately. Stay there. Will you do that?"

"Yes. I'll wait for you."

"Tomorrow. I will call you as soon as I return."

I nod into the phone. "Yes. Alright."

"And, Valentine?"

"Yes?"

"This was the right thing, to come to me. I don't want you to doubt that. I will see you as soon as I can."

"Yes. Okay."

We hang up, and I'm not sure if I feel any better, although I do feel in some strange way that I'm one step closer to . . . I'm not sure what. A way to move beyond my past? A way to live my new life?

I put the phone down on the night table, look around the room. But it feels so small to me suddenly; I can't stand to be there any longer. I pick up my purse from the floor where I discarded it three days ago. I have only touched it to look for tip money for room service. Slipping it onto my shoulder, I head out the door.

It's a short ride in the elevator, then I'm walking through the elegant lobby I barely noticed when I arrived. It's all marble and crystal and gold accents. Beautiful. But I don't want to linger.

Pushing through the revolving door and outside, into the damp, gray air, I make my way to the famous Spanish Steps, pause at the top to look at the city. It's a bit gloomy this time of year, but still heartbreakingly lovely. Such a waste that I haven't spent any time seeing it. But what would I absorb right now, anyway? And I'm not here on vacation. I'm here on a mission, aren't I?

I start making my way down the endless, ancient staircase, my boot heels clicking on the stone. The morning rain has changed everything: the scent in the air of old, wet stone, as though the history of the city is that much nearer to the surface. And the streets gleam wetly, making them appear cleaner than they really are.

As I descend I can smell garlic in the air, and baking bread. And as I reach the square, the inevitable smell of garbage, urine. The scent of humanity that is present in some form or another in every large city, except that here there is also the musty scent of the Italian waterways that run everywhere through Rome. And suddenly I am desperate to get to the street, to walk. To think.

Yes, I need to think. I need to stop running every time my brain kicks into gear.

This late in the fall is the off-season, and the streets are mostly empty; just a few hard-core tourists, students in their torn jeans and backpacks from every corner of the world, the locals on their bicycles and Vespas.

I wander, simply walking the streets. Slowly I make my way down the Via dei Condotti, pass the designer shops, the cafés tucked in between them. But I don't want to shop, no matter how beautiful the items in the brightly lit windows. I need to keep moving, need to think. My mind is full of one idea and image after another: The Broker's face when she was telling me how I can never escape my life, being at the hotel in New York with Zayed, Regan, and Rosalyn, my pathetic mother sitting on the sagging sofa with a cigarette hanging from her mouth. And I'm angry. In a rage.

And then there's Joshua.

His face, his hands. If I close my eyes I think I could almost draw his scent into my lungs, hold it there as though it's something precious. It is to me. But I don't let myself do it. It's too hard, still, with him so far away.

I keep walking, taking one turn after another. I can feel the timelessness of this place, like a weight holding me to the earth, and I think it was right for me to come to Rome.

The walking is beginning to calm me, finally, the movement over the old cobblestone streets working some of the fury out of me. I'm able to take in some of what I see around me now, the old, beautiful architecture, unlike anything to be found in the United States. Some of these structures look as though they've been here forever, and something in their solid presence comforts me.

My feet are beginning to hurt and I want to stop, to rest. I find myself in front of one of the ancient basilicas: San Lorenzo in Lucina. I pause in front of the colonnaded building, gaze for a moment at the stucco façade, which is a sort of pink and gold in the late morning light, like everything else in this city. It's imposing, formal looking, a mixture of ancient Rome and Greece, as a number of buildings in this city are.

It appears to be open to the public, and I slip through the ornate gates and go inside.

I don't know what I'm doing here; I'm not at all religious. But something about the serenity of the place draws me.

This structure is spectacular, unexpectedly colorful and grand, every corner, column, and archway painted in great detail, everything highlighted in gold, and the intricate, coffered ceiling vaulting overhead. I move a few feet in, over the patterned gray and white marble floor, and sit in the first pew I come to. The wood is hard beneath me. The place smells like incense and incalculable centuries.

At the other end of the endlessly long aisle is an enormous painting of Christ over the gold and marble altar, as bloody as these images often are. Grotesque, in a way. But so horribly sad.

But it's really just my own sadness. It's everything I've been through, everything I want. Everything I've convinced myself I can't have.

I think once more about what Joshua has said to me, about change, about being able to choose. If only it were as easy as making a choice. I don't know; maybe it is. Maybe I have to choose to get over it all, to really leave all the garbage in my life behind me. Choose to be with him.

If he'll even still have me, after what I've put him through. If I can ever give him what he deserves to have.

Fuck.

The gruesome image of Christ seems to stare down at me from the altar, and I feel the sadness in the figure like a lump of solid lead in my chest. It weighs on me, as though the sadness itself will push me down, into the pew, right through the floor to the earth below. The sensation grows heavier and heavier, until it's hard to breathe.

My gaze darts around in a panic, over the bleeding Christ, the golden altar, the painted columns, but I don't know what I'm looking for. It's too quiet here. There is no sound to distract me from the voices in my head, the ones that want to talk about everything that has happened to me in my life. About what is happening now. It's too much. But maybe I need this. Maybe I came here for a reason.

I don't know what it is about this church. If it's the history of the place, the hushed air making it feel sacred, even to those of us who are sinners. Or maybe this is simply where I happen to be at this moment. I don't understand any of it.

All I know is the wrenching sensation in my chest, and

I pull in a long, deep breath. And as I let it go, I let myself begin to think about my life. How long am I going to blame everyone for what happened, including myself? How is blaming in any way constructive? I take responsibility for what I've done, the choices I've made. What more can I do? What more is necessary?

It's time to let that go.

This is what Lydia has been trying to tell me. And as I think this through, I feel some of the weight lifting from my body, a physical sensation of becoming lighter.

It hurts, this letting go, as much as hanging on to the old shit does. But what did I expect? This stuff that Lydia calls "archaic issues" has been with me my entire life, building and building as the experiences of my childhood stacked up, as I added to it by selling my body for sex. No matter how I convinced myself I was being of service to my clients. No matter how sympathetic I felt toward those like my blind Louis, like Zayed and his emasculating erection problems. It made me feel accomplished, somehow. But it was all bullshit. All a veil behind which I hid myself, like the glamour a witch puts on. Except that I've been seducing myself with that glamour as much as I have anyone else. I've needed to believe in it as much as they have.

Now I need to believe in something a lot more real. Why is that so damn difficult for me? But I have to figure it out.

The tears come then. Just a few, but I am horrified. I look around the church to see if anyone is watching. I don't know why I care; I don't know these people, this handful of tourists, an old Italian woman in a black head scarf praying in the front pew. They don't know me. But suddenly everything feels so damn important!

Sacred.

My blurred gaze goes back once more to the altar, to the woman in the front pew, her eyes on the bloody figure of Christ. She's passing a rosary through her hands, whispering, praying. I don't understand it. I've never had one moment of belief in God, in any sort of religion. I wish I had it, that faith. That kind of comfort.

I watch as she raises her face, kisses the cross on her rosary. Even in profile I can see the glow of hope there, the small smile on her lips. Beautiful.

A shiver runs through me.

Is it possible for me to feel that kind of hope, hope driven by nothing more than pure faith? I don't believe in God; I think that's asking too much from someone like me. But love? Can't I believe in love? How can I have a future without hope?

I think again, as I have so often lately, about those girls in the article. The woman who was helping them did more than give them shelter, clothing, teach them how to get through a job interview. She gave them hope.

Maybe I need to start by giving myself hope. And maybe I can do that by believing in love, by having at least that much faith in something.

I am filling up inside. It's scary and lovely all at once, sweet and painful. It is a physical sensation, and I am about to burst with it. It's too unfamiliar; I have to swallow it down. But it's there.

Faith. Love.

I don't know what to do now. If this small epiphany will make any difference after this moment. It feels almost too easy, as though it doesn't hurt enough.

But I've been hurting myself all these years, haven't I? And it's time to stop. Stop punishing myself. Stop punishing

Joshua, who does not deserve it. The man loves me. *Loves me!* And I love him more than I ever thought possible. Maybe it really is that simple. Maybe the rest doesn't matter nearly as much as I thought it did.

I am dizzy with this idea. Breathless. Afraid.

I want to talk to Joshua, to tell him about all of these thoughts going through my head. To let him comfort me through this. But it's too soon.

I can't even contemplate how much I miss him.

The damn tears are clouding my eyes, until the colors of the church blend together, gold, white, and red, like a water-color painting of itself. Stubbornly, I blink them away. I have no patience for tears. I don't care how healthy it might be for me at this point. This is as much crying as I can stand.

Wiping my face on my sleeve gracelessly, I stand up and walk from the church, back onto the street. But I can't stop crying. Small, noiseless tears as I make my way down the street. I'm not even certain what I'm crying for. I don't feel so sad anymore, exactly. I feel . . . as though I'm flying without a net. That familiar comfort of knowing what my life is about. Even being free from some of my old baggage scares the hell out of me. The freedom itself is making me cry, maybe. Or maybe I'm just detoxing.

I walk for a long time, and the tears stop eventually. The afternoon sun breaks through the gray clouds, and I'm hot, hiding my swollen eyes behind my sunglasses, which isn't working very well, wiping my nose with a crumpled Kleenex I find in my purse.

Exhausted, I make it back to my hotel, stumble through the lobby, dig my key out of my purse, let myself into my room.

It feels stuffy after the outside air. Heavy. My body feels

heavy, as though I am weighed down all over: my arms and legs, my stomach, my head.

I drop my purse on the floor, pull my clothes off, and sit on the side of the bed in my underwear with my cell phone in my hand.

God, I want to call him. Need to hear his voice.

Joshua.

But I'm not ready yet. I'm not done with what I came here for.

I shake my head, set the phone on the night table and get under the covers, curl up, and wish I'd thought to bring my gummi bears with me. But I don't really need them, do I? It's habit. I'm fine. I really am. For once.

I'm just tired, so tired. My hand smooths over the damask bedcover, my fingers stroking the satin edging. I feel . . . grateful. Dizzy with these new thoughts in my head, but in a good way. Soon, the emotional exhaustion of the day creeps over me, and I sleep.

IT'S LATE MORNING NOW and I am still red-eyed, my head full with too much sleep. I slept like the dead all night. Must have been twelve, thirteen hours. I am still jubilant, fearful, my pulse racing every time I think about yesterday, about faith, about love. I have just this one more thing to do.

I'm on my way to see Enzo. He called me an hour ago, told me where to meet him, at some small café on the Via de Fiore, a few blocks from the hotel.

He never suggested coming to my hotel room. He understands on some instinctive level why I can't do that.

I pass stranger after stranger, hidden behind my sunglasses, even though the sun is barely peeking through the clouds. It rained again early this morning and the streets are wet, shining in the diffused sunlight. It makes everything seem surreal. And I feel this momentary sense of total disconnection from everyone around me, as though I am not quite a part of the human race.

I realize how often I've felt like that. And just as suddenly, the feeling disappears as I understand how ridiculous it is. How self-indulgent of me. I am just as human as the rest of the people on this planet. Just as fallible.

Forgivable.

Another element to absorb. But later. After I've seen Enzo, spoken with him, heard his advice. I have been too much alone in my own head. I don't know any longer what to do with all of these new ideas, how to organize it all.

I see the green awning of the café from a distance, with the name in white lettering: La Dolce Vita. How perfect, when I am about to really begin my life.

And there he is, Enzo Alighieri. He is so elegant, with his thick silver hair and his neatly trimmed mustache, the way he dresses, the way he holds himself. Utterly Italian as he sits at the picturesque sidewalk café, leaning back in his chair in a perfectly relaxed pose, as though he knows he belongs there. He is confident, solid.

My heart lurches in my chest. I don't want to have this conversation with him. But I must. I owe him every good thing there's been in my life for the last ten years. And I need him. Need some sort of answer from him.

He smiles when he sees me, waves me over, stands to kiss me chastely on the cheek, holds a chair out for me and orders a coffee in rapid Italian.

We sit at the small, round, marble-topped table and simply stare at each other for a minute or two. Then he asks, "How are you, Valentine?"

"I'm good. Better than I've been for a very long time. Better than I've ever been, maybe. So much is happening to me."

He nods, as though he understands what I mean without my having to explain.

The coffee comes, a small cappuccino, and I hold the cup in my hands, warming them. Enzo is quiet, waiting for me to speak.

"You're probably wondering what I'm doing here . . ."

"I have some idea, as I said yesterday. I know you've stopped working. And knowing you as I do, I understand something important must have happened to you."

"I'm sorry to take you away from your vacation, Enzo."

"No, no, it's fine. I was bored with all the socializing. The four-hour dinners and the wine we are expected to drink. I am getting too old for this sort of thing."

"Never, Enzo." I smile at him. "You know, you're one of the few people I've ever really trusted," I tell him.

He nods his head. "This has been the nature of your life."

I nod my head.

"But that is changing, is it not?"

I nod again, still smiling despite the fear of what might lie ahead.

He reaches out, covers my hand with his. That old buzz is still there. I am still attracted to this seventy-year-old man. He has been my mentor. My lover. My friend.

"Valentine, life is changeable. It is supposed to be this way."

"My life was the same for ten years. And I liked that. I thought I did, anyway. But now . . . now everything is shifting and I'm not certain how to handle it. But at the same time, it's absolutely necessary." I pause, look into his dark eyes. "I've met someone."

Enzo is smiling at me, as though he is truly pleased for me. He nods for me to continue, and I do.

"This man . . . Joshua has come into my life at the right time. No matter what happens, this experience has changed me. And I needed to change. But now . . . I don't know what happens now."

"What would you like to happen?"

"Do you mean in my little fantasy world in my head? Or in terms of what is actually possible?"

"Perhaps a little of both."

I stop to bring the cappuccino to my lips, sip it, buying time to think, focusing for a few moments on the people passing by on the street. There is a young boy on a blue bicycle, a woman holding the hands of two small children. A couple with their arms twined around each other. They are absorbed in each other, rapt.

"I want . . . some small sense of normalcy. I want to believe it can happen. I want to do something real with my life. Something to do with art. Or maybe . . . maybe to be of some help to other girls going through this stuff. I have some ideas about that. Maybe I can find a way to blend the two. But that's still a way off. What I really want is . . . love. Just that."

"Ah, yes. This is the crux of it, isn't it? Of life."

"Yes. I realized that just yesterday. I mean, I really came to understand it. To believe it. But I still have some doubts. Questions. It's hard because I never had any sort of good example. What I saw of it as a kid was almost a farce. My mother's desperation. That wasn't love, even if she thought it was. I knew that even then. And so many of my clients all these years have been married . . . including you, Enzo. What does that say about love?" I look up to find his dark, intense gaze on me. I can't tell what he's thinking. "I'm sorry. I don't mean that as any kind of judgment. I'm the last person who would judge you. Who would judge anyone."

"Valentine, there is something you must understand about me. Something I assumed you already knew. I believe very much in love. I am Italian, after all; I am a man of great passion. Great love. My wife, my mistress. You."

"Enzo . . ." But I can't finish. My eyes fill with tears that won't quite come out.

He waves a hand. "My darling Valentine, do you think I would have spent all these years with you, taken you under my wing, if I didn't love you? In my own way, perhaps, yes. But love is love, regardless of the form it takes. And yes, I know, I am not excusing my own behavior. I am simply telling you how I feel. Love is as imperfect as we are. I have abused it, perhaps. Yet love itself remains as beautiful, as essential, as ever."

"Enzo . . . How could you have . . . loved me? *Me?* How could you love someone who does what I do? Who you hire for sex?"

"Would I have had you any other way? Would you have paid attention to an old man if it weren't for the money?"

"God, you make it sound so shallow. Fuck. It was shallow."

I really do want to cry now. But there have been enough tears. I need to stop the self-pity and pay attention.

"No, *cara,* it was never shallow. You always meant something to me. But we both know what the money was about for you. It wasn't the money itself that was important to you. It was what it symbolized. It was the sense of control it gave you.

And you cannot blame yourself for that, or judge yourself. You are a good person, Valentine. And that is how I loved you, why I will always love you. That is why this man loves you. Why he *should*. Don't be so afraid of love that you turn away from it, Valentine. Don't be afraid that it cannot exist because of anything you might have done."

I nod. It's becoming clearer to me. I don't know why I need Enzo to validate these things for me; I just do. Maybe because he has been the only person I've truly trusted for the last ten years. The only one in my whole life. Until now. Until Joshua.

"What do you need from me now, Valentine?" he asks quietly.

"You've already given me more than I expected. Everything you've done for me over the years. Talking with me today. Loving me." I stop, smile at him. "I love him, Enzo," I say, my voice so soft I can barely hear myself.

He nods, smiles a little, is quiet for several long moments while he sips his cappuccino. "I won't see you after this, Valentine," he says.

I look at him, at his handsome, lined face. The sincerity and sadness in his dark eyes.

"No." I smile at him once more, even as new tears fill my eyes.

He grasps my hand again, holds on, his fingers warming mine.

"Remember that I loved you, Valentine, if you remember nothing else."

"I'll remember everything, Enzo, all you've done for me."

"No. There is no need. I do what I want. I am a self-indulgent man; I know this. And all of that, it is not important. I think you understand now what is." He pauses once more, sets his cup down on the saucer with a small *clink*. "Go to your young man, Valentine. Have a life. Have love."

He stands, and I can hardly bear to see him go. Yet I can't wait another moment to call Joshua.

Enzo takes my hand, lifts it to his lips, and kisses it carefully, his lips warm and dry. Sweet. My heart is breaking, and so full at the same time!

"Be well, my Valentine."

"Enzo. I'll miss you!"

He smiles, a real smile this time, even if the sadness lingers at the corners of his eyes. "No. No, you won't."

I watch him walk away, two women turning to admire his elegant form as he strolls down the street as if he doesn't have a care in the world.

I pull my cell phone out of my purse with shaking hands. *Joshua.*

I dial, wait the endless moments for the phone to make the international connection. My pulse is a hammer in my veins, threatening to break me.

Please answer . . .

"Joshua Spencer."

My heart lurches at the sound of his voice, and it takes me a moment to find mine.

"Hello?"

"Joshua."

"Valentine?"

"Joshua!"

And then I'm crying, so hard I can't speak. He'll be angry with me, I'm certain, and I can't blame him. Oh, God, what if he doesn't want me, after all I've put him through? After what I've finally discovered?

"Valentine, calm down. What is it? Where are you? Are you okay? Talk to me."

"Joshua . . . I have so much to tell you."

"Then tell me."

I can picture his face, his hazel eyes, his dark lashes. I can imagine the intensity of his beautiful features. I can't stand it that he's so far away.

"I'm so sorry, Joshua. That I had to go away. That I was so confused. I didn't mean to be melodramatic. But . . . I think . . . I think I understand now."

"What do you understand, Valentine?" His voice is soft, uncertain.

"That I love you. I love you. That it's all that really matters." The tears are coming so hard now, I can't see. It doesn't matter. All that matters is how I feel, Joshua's voice on the other end of the line. "God, I love you."

"Valentine. God damn it." I hear his voice break. "I need to be with you. I need to hold you."

"Yes, I need all of that. I need you. I finally get it. I get that I need you, and that it's okay. I'm not so scared anymore. Because I finally believe it, Joshua. I believe in love. I believe I can have it, that it's real. That it means something. That it carries its own power. But, Joshua . . . what if I don't do it right?"

"There is no right way. That's one of the ideas you have to let go. There is no perfect relationship. There are no perfect people. We all just flounder around and hope everything turns out okay. I don't expect you to be perfect. I just expect you to be you, to be true to your feelings."

"I think I finally can be. I think I've finally figured out a way to integrate all of those parts of myself we talked about.

I know where to begin, anyway. I need to begin by trusting myself. Trusting how I feel about you. Trusting that love *can* get me through. Can get *us* through."

"It was so damn hard to let you go, Valentine, but I knew I had to. That you really did have to figure some of this stuff out for yourself. Tell me what's happened. I need to know."

I wipe the tears from my cheeks, take a deep breath. "I found . . . faith. In some ways, it's as simple as that. There's more, but that's the most crucial part. We can talk about the rest when I see you. I can't wait to see you. I want to love you, Joshua. I want to accept that you love me. And I do. I believe it."

"Valentine . . ." His voice is gruff with emotion. I've hurt him so much.

"It's still hard. The old stuff hasn't entirely gone away. You've helped me so much, even though it's taken a while for me to absorb it all, and I know I'm not done yet. But I want to be with you while I do it. Is that . . ." I have to stop. I can hardly stand to ask him, to hear his answer. "Is it okay with you? Can we . . . Joshua . . ."

"Valentine, I love you. Come to me. We'll do this together. That's what I've been trying to tell you. Just come to me."

"God, Joshua. I love you."

"I love you, baby."

How is it possible that I have this? That somehow I've come full circle, only to end in a better place than I started? But this is my new reality. Impossible. And yet, here it is. Love. The one intangible thing in my life. The one thing I've always yearned for, even if I never knew it.

He loves me. And I love him in a way that is so powerful, it makes anything possible.

"Joshua, I love you so much. And I need you. Not just anyone, not just an escape. But *you*."

I know what I have to do. And I know what I want. And for the first time, these things are one and the same. I'm finally able to let the past go. To move beyond it. And to truly live. To truly love. To find myself, on my own and with this amazing man. His love for me, my love for him, redeems me as nothing else could.

For the first time in my life, I am no longer flying without a net.

"Come to me, Valentine. I can't wait."

"I'm coming. I'm coming home."

Epilogue

THE SUN IS SETTING in a blaze of fall glory outside the windows of our home. It used to be Joshua's home, but over the last year it has become mine, ours.

I can't believe it's been a year. I can't believe what I've learned in that year with him. How happy we've been together. Not that every moment has been easy. But it's all been beautiful, even the hard parts.

I am a different person now, yet essentially the same, which is what Joshua was trying to tell me from the start, what Lydia reminds me of all the time, what Enzo told me in Rome: that who I *am* is good enough.

"Valentine," Joshua calls from the bathroom, "you almost ready to go?"

"Almost."

"Roy called. He and Carrie are meeting us there a few minutes early."

"Okay, good."

So nice to have friends in my life. Unbelievable still, sometimes. Carrie and Roy are good people; supportive, kind. Normal people. They've heard my story, the one I will tell in front of two hundred people tonight. And they're still my friends.

I pull my gaze from the window back to the mirror over the dresser. I look very much the same as I always have. Just happier. And my eyes are alive with excitement, with nerves.

I pick up the lovely, square-cut emerald Joshua gave me when I came home from Rome from a shallow bowl on the dresser, struggle to get the long, gold chain hooked. Joshua comes up behind me, takes the necklace from my fumbling fingers, and fastens the clasp, turns me around in his arms. I can smell the soap on him; his hair is still damp from the shower. I want to take him to bed right now. I always want him, but I love it when he's clean like this, with a fresh shave, making his face look innocent, sweet, except for that small scar, the wicked gleam in his hazel eyes.

"Do I look alright?" I ask him.

"Beautiful as always, baby."

"But am I . . . presentable?"

"Don't worry so much. You'll be fine. You'll be wonderful." He strokes my cheek with one fingertip, making me shiver. He always has that effect on me. No matter what else is on my mind, a lovely, momentary distraction.

"I've never spoken in front of a group before. And this is so important."

"I know it is. But you'll be fine *because* it's so important to you."

"This" is the first big fundraiser for my foundation, Lost Girls. We plan to open by next summer. A halfway house, a job training program. I've already made connections with two of the local drug treatment programs, been shameless in hitting up people I know in the film industry for donations, using my old connections, as odd as that seems. But it's been a way for me to turn the shit that was my old life into something positive. I even asked Deirdre. The witch surprised me by sending a check for twenty thousand dollars.

Joshua's invited everyone he knows, people he works with, people I've come to know. He's proud of me. *I'm* proud of me.

I lean into Joshua, breathe him in, feel the solid strength of his body beneath my cheek.

"I couldn't do this without you," I tell him.

"Sure you could. You've always had the strength, Valentine. You just had to learn to see it."

"I really want to make a difference."

"You will. You're the right person to do this, after what you've been through. You're a survivor. That's part of your gift to them."

"I feel like I'm finally doing something worthwhile with my life. I have purpose. And I have you."

He squeezes my hand, warming me up inside. "Yeah, you do. You always have me. Always."

He lifts my hand to his lips, kisses the back of my fingers, turns my hand over to kiss my palm, making me shiver.

He's watching me in that way he has that turns my entire body to liquid. His beautiful eyes are gleaming metallic in the amber light: malachite, gold, silver. He leans in, my hand still in his.

He says, his voice low, steady, "Marry me, Valentine."

I am too stunned to speak. No one has ever said these words to me. I would never have expected them. Not from anyone else. But from Joshua, they sound exactly right. They sound perfect. My pulse is racing, my body lit with a pure, clean pleasure.

My throat is so tight with emotion, it's hard to speak. "I love you, Joshua. So much."

"You know how much I love you, baby. Say yes."

"Yes!"

We smile at each other, hugely, foolishly, and it is as though time has stopped and nothing else exists but the two of us in this moment. Together. The rest of the world, my worries about the evening ahead, fades away as he pulls me to him and kisses my smiling mouth. Sweet, lovely kisses. I can never get enough.

My world is perfect, somehow, despite my imperfections. That's what he's been teaching me. That love itself is perfect if we allow it to just *be,* despite how human we are, how flawed. That love can still flourish. And it does.

Hungry for more?

Read on for a sneak peek of Eden Bradley's
scintillating new novel

The Darker Side of Pleasure

Coming soon from Black Lace

**BLACK
LACE**

CHAPTER ONE

BONDAGE. THE WORD REVERBERATED THROUGH Jillian's head, through her body, making her muscles tense and quiver.

Her stomach clenched as she pulled her sporty BMW into the driveway after a long day at work. She peered up at the sleek, modern expanse of redwood and glass her husband had designed for them six years ago, right after they'd married and moved to Seattle.

She took a deep breath and forced her hands to stop gripping the steering wheel. Tonight was the night. The night she and Cameron were going to start trying to put their marriage back together.

She yanked a little too hard on the parking brake, then grabbed her purse and the pretty pink shopping bag that held the new lingerie she'd bought for the occasion. Cameron was right. It had been ages since she'd dressed up for him. Hell, she'd been sleeping in the guest room for months. Not that that was his fault. It was her. She knew that. She just couldn't stand to be so close to him, with so much distance between them. It hurt too much.

Her nerves jangled as much as her keys did when she opened the front door. "Cam? You home?"

No answer. She exhaled on a sigh of relief. She needed some time to make herself ready. Not just physically, but emotionally, too—even though they'd talked about this almost a week ago. Maybe she'd had too much time to think about it. She did have a tendency to overanalyze things. She let her purse fall to the hardwood floor, gripped the lingerie bag, and headed down the hall.

Stripping off her clothes in the half-dark bedroom felt like a ritual, somehow. The house was quiet. The soft glow of twilight filtered through the Japanese paper shades that covered the ceiling-high bedroom windows. There was the faint scent of him in the air, that sense of intimacy in the room where they'd slept up until she'd moved into the guest room a few months ago. But they hadn't made love for too long before that. And on those rare occasions when they had, she felt as though she weren't entirely present in her own body, as if she were watching it from the outside. But tonight was supposed to help change that. The idea made her stomach clench up again.

She stepped into the slate-tiled bathroom and blasted the hot water, wanting the sheer force and heat of it to wash her nerves away. This was her own husband, after all. She closed her eyes as she moved beneath the spray and let the water sluice over her, trying to steer her mind down a more positive path.

Cameron. He'd been so young when they'd first met,

only twenty-one. She was an old lady of twenty-five at the time. But he was so mature for his age, so somber and responsible. And there was always something of the darkness about him that made him seem older than he was. Perhaps it was the tattoo that circled his right biceps, a sinuous circle in a dark tribal design. Maori, he'd told her. She loved it. She'd loved his tall, lean, yet muscular body. God, he had the greatest abs she'd ever seen on a human being. And she loved the way his straight, coal black hair fell into his eyes, even the dark-framed glasses he wore for reading.

That's how Jillian had first seen him, in her English Lit class in college. He was bent over a book, and he glanced up as she passed a printed handout to him. And those smoky gray eyes peered up at her—eyes fringed in thick, sooty lashes any woman would envy. Those startling eyes and that serious expression on his angular features, yet his mouth was lush and sensual, a stark contrast.

He still wore those glasses. And even after all they'd been through, a small shiver of excitement would course through her whenever he put them on. If only he had come to bed early enough to read, while she was still awake, while she'd still been sleeping in their bed.

But no, she shouldn't think about that. Tonight was for new beginnings, not old pain.

She shut off the water, stepped out onto the cool tiles, and began to rub scented lotion into her skin. It was Cameron's favorite vanilla scent, the one he used to say made him want to run his tongue all over her body. Her sex gave a quick, involuntary squeeze, surprising her.

Drawing her pale green silk summer robe around her

shoulders, she went to pull her purchases out of the bag. The bra was black and lacy, with demi-cups that barely covered her breasts. The matching thong was a whisper of lace. It made her feel sexy, she had to admit, admiring her reflection in the big full-length mirror in her walk-in closet. Despite her breasts and thighs, which weren't as firm at the age of thirty-three as they'd been when she and Cam had met eight years ago.

No, don't think about that now.

She pulled her long honey blond hair up with her hands, considering, then decided to leave it down. Cam liked it better that way.

When she drew the first black lace stocking over one leg, she began to get a real sense of ritual, of formal preparation. For some reason she didn't understand it sent a small thrill through her, raising gooseflesh on the back of her neck. And when she slid her feet into the impossibly high black pumps Cam had insisted she buy, the feeling was complete. She understood suddenly that she was doing this for him, but that it also fulfilled some need in her. To please in order to feel whole.

This was a new concept for her. She'd been inside her own head for so long, immersed in her grief, that she'd forgotten to look outside. To look at her husband.

When Cam had first suggested they try to find their way back to each other through sex, she'd balked. In fact, that was putting it lightly. She'd flat out refused, thought he was being selfish and ridiculous. But then he'd reminded her that sex was intimacy, and that bondage was the purest form of mutual trust. It took her a while to absorb that, but she eventually came to realize he had a valid point. And they needed to try something, anything, before the gap between them grew any wider. Tonight was to be a true test.

She drew the stockings up her legs, her hand brushing the honey-colored curls at the apex of her thighs. Blood rushed to the area so fast, she had to cup her mound with her hand and press there. Strange! Why was she so hypersensitive, when she'd been completely shut down for almost a year?

The loud rumbling of her husband's prized Harley pulling into the driveway brought her head and her hand up fast. Cam!

She took one last, desperate look in the mirror, added a little lip gloss with a shaking hand. She was ready for him.

She thought she was. She shivered in fear and anticipation as his steps drew nearer. The door opened with a graceful swing, and there he was. Her husband. He looked so damn good standing there, she had to smile.

He smiled back. "Almost like the old Jillian. I love it when you smile like that. Like you mean it."

"I do." She dropped her head, suddenly shy.

He crossed the room, slid his hands around her waist, ran them up her sides, traced the curve of her breasts. "God, you're beautiful."

His words warmed her, but it was still hard for her to look at him. He tipped her chin up with his fingers. She thought he'd want to talk more, but he just leaned in and kissed her. That lush, kissable mouth of his covered hers, and when he parted his lips she could taste mint, and underneath it the faint sweetness of Scotch. So he'd been nervous, too. She suddenly wanted to cry. This was why she'd been avoiding him, why she hadn't been able to sleep in the bed next to his big, warm body.

He pulled away and said simply, "Are you ready?"

Her stomach grabbed again, but she nodded. "Yes. But what are you . . . I mean, how is this all going to happen?"

"We talked about it, remember? If this is going to work, you have to trust me enough to turn yourself over to me. That's what tonight is all about. We have to learn to trust each other again. Do you remember your safe words?"

"Yes. Yellow for slow down, red for stop."

"Good."

He stepped back and his eyes roamed over her. She knew she looked better than usual in this outfit, so she didn't mind. And she could see his eyes glittering as he looked at her, his pupils widening with lust. He placed his hands on his hips, licked his lips. He gestured toward the bed with his chin.

"Sit down."

She just looked at him for a moment. She wasn't used to this simple, commanding tone from him. He didn't sound mean, but it was clear she shouldn't try to argue with him. A chill of pleasure ran up her spine.

"Now."

Another command; this time his tone was low and demanding. Her sex exploded with heat. She sat.

Cam paced the room slowly, looking at her from all angles, before he said, "Get rid of the bra."

She unhooked it immediately, her full breasts springing from the lacy confines. They felt plump and tender and wanted to be touched, something she hadn't felt in a long time. The fact that she could have this sort of reaction to nothing more than a certain tone of voice was almost shocking. She was trying hard not to analyze it.

Cam walked up to her and touched her breasts with his fingertips, just lazily brushed them over the curved underside, traced them around the edge of the areolas. Her nipples sprang up, hard and ready. But he didn't touch them.

When she looked up at his face he was smiling, just one corner of his mouth quirked up. Rakish, sexy.

He stepped back again and unbuttoned his shirt. She had always loved him without a shirt. He had one of those long, lean, cut torsos, with just the right amount of silky black hair in a line down the center of his well-defined abs. He was built like a pro basketball player: well over six feet tall, with broad shoulders and those lanky, beautifully defined muscles. His black work slacks hung low on his narrow hips and she could see that he was hard already, the outline of his large erection shadowed against the fine wool.

She squirmed on the edge of the bed, her lace thong growing damp.

"I'm going to ask you to do things for me tonight you've never done before. Are you ready to do that, Jillian?"

She swallowed, hard. Was she? Her natural mental response was to fight against the whole idea. She was normally someone who was strong, in control. But her body was rebelling already. Still, how could it be this simple? She knew that Cam's angle had been that bondage was all about trust, that there had to be complete trust in order to make it work. He saw it as a way to get back to each other. It made a sort of weird sense, but she still had her doubts.

Cam repeated, "Are you ready?"

His voice seemed so different tonight; his whole persona was different. Confident. Commanding. But it was still Cam. She could do this. She would do it for him. For them. And, judging from the unexpected way her body was responding already, for herself.

"Yes. I'm ready."

He turned then and moved to the tall dresser, pulled a CD from the top drawer and popped it into the CD player. She recognized the trancelike tones of Enigma immediately. She watched him as he lit a pair of tall pillar candles. The scent of amber wafted into the air, and the warm candlelight was soft and sultry, aided by the glow of sunset outside the windows.

He bent and opened a bottom drawer and took out a long coiled length of black rope. She hadn't known it was in there, didn't know where he'd found it. She didn't really care right now. All she could think of was that he was going to use it on her. Nerves and pleasure washed through her in an exciting, confusing tide.

Cam came to stand before her while the music played, and he rested his hands on her shoulders. After a moment, he swept them up her neck in gentle strokes, then back down, over her arms to her wrists. Gently, he gathered them into one of his big hands and pulled her arms up over her head. She shivered again, feeling unsure, vulnerable.

"Cam?"

"It's okay."

His soft voice was reassuring, but he didn't release her wrists. With his free hand he began to stroke her breasts again, and despite her hammering pulse her body responded to his touch. Her breasts filled, her nipples aching as he teased her skin with the lightest touch. When he finally brushed one hard nipple with his fingertip her whole body arched toward him.

"Patience, Jillian." He sounded amused.

She moaned softly. He rewarded her by tweaking one nipple, rather hard, but she liked it. Somehow it was just what she needed. Her sex began to pound and she squeezed her legs together.

"Lie back on the bed," Cam said.

"Why? What are you going to—"

"Shh. No questions. You're mine tonight. Turn yourself over to me, Jillian."

Yes. She wanted this. And not just because she was following the plan. Now that they'd started she knew she was going to like it, even if it scared her a little. Or maybe the fear was part of what drew her?

She lay down on the bed.

When Cam came to stand over her with the ropes in his hands, her body gave a convulsive shudder. Of need. Of lust. She had never felt anything like it. Gazing up at his tall silhouette in the dim light, she suddenly knew she'd never wanted anything so much in her life. To give herself over. To let herself go. This was exactly what she needed. Yet at the same time, she struggled with the notion. How could this be what she needed? Wasn't it proof of her own weakness?

Cam bent over her and kissed her gently on the lips, then took her lower lip between his strong, white teeth and bit down. It hurt a little.

"You're mine, Jillian. Say it."

The chill that ran through her was part lust, part awe. And she knew that after tonight, she would never be the same again.

"Yes, Cam. I'm yours."

He smiled at her. "Very good. I want you to lie perfectly still now. I'm going to play with you a bit before I tie you up."

Tie you up. Oh, my. He really was going to tie her up. A thrill ran through her, bringing goose bumps to her skin once more, but this time they ran the entire length of her body.

But she didn't have long to think about it. Cam's hands were on her, stroking her stomach, running up her thighs. They seemed to be everywhere at once. She watched him, a look of intense concentration on his face. Finally his hands came back to her breasts, covering both of them, massaging, kneading. Her nipples were hard, hot nubs against his palms.

He looked up at her face, his gray eyes watching her as he took both nipples between his fingers and thumbs and began to roll them. Fire shot from her nipples straight to her already aching sex. She tried hard not to squirm. But when he pinched, hard, she shot up off the bed.

"No, Jillian." He pressed her back down onto the mattress. "Lie still."

She tried. She drew in a deep, shuddering breath, and then he began again, pulling at her nipples, twisting, pinching. They were so hard and engorged she thought they would burst. And her sex was full and throbbing. She wanted his hands there. But she knew she had to wait. To trust him.

Cam kept working her nipples, and she wondered for the first time in her life if it was possible to come just from that. She didn't know how long it went on, an impossibly long period of time in which she was finally able to shut her brain down, to stop thinking, analyzing. Her nipples were sore, but she didn't care. She bit down on her lip to keep from crying out, to keep from moving, but her thighs spread open of their own accord. God, she needed him to touch her there. To use his hands, his mouth. She didn't care. But she didn't want him to stop torturing her breasts.

Finally, he bent his head and flicked his hot, wet tongue at one rigid tip. She groaned. He moved his head and flicked at the other one. Then, using both hands, he pushed the full mounds of her breasts together and moved his head back and forth, his tongue a damp spike of heat as it flickered over her stiffened nipples. His hands felt so good on her, so firm on her flesh, and his tongue was driving her crazy. She almost begged him to take her into his mouth. And then, as if reading her mind, he did.

He drew one nipple in and sucked. He was almost too gentle. She could hardly stand it. She gathered and bunched the bedspread in her hands, trying to hold still, to keep from crying out, from begging him to suck harder. Her sex was absolutely drenched by now. Her whole body quivered.

And suddenly, he pulled back.

"Cam?" Her own voice sounded loud and breathless in her ears.

He straightened up, half turned away from her, and ran a hand through his dark hair.

"Cam, what is it?"

She heard his long, slow exhalation. Waited for him to turn back around, to talk to her. Her thighs clenched around the damp, swollen folds of flesh between them.

"Maybe we need to talk about this some more."

"What?" A startled laugh escaped her lips. "Now? When I'm just beginning to . . ." She couldn't finish the sentence, couldn't say out loud that her body was responding in a way it hadn't for months. Couldn't tell him how desperately she craved his touch. Why couldn't she say it?

When his eyes met hers she saw the confusion there, saw that his breath was coming in short, sharp pants.

"This is . . . already more intense than I expected."

"Yes." It was all she could manage to get out.

He came and sat on the bed next to her. His warm hand fell on her shoulder. "I need to know this is what you want. Not just with your body, but in your head. What is this making you think? Making you feel?"

How could she explain? "Like . . . like maybe I can let go, finally. But it's a little scary at the same time. And physically, it's . . . almost a shock. Do you know what I mean?"

He nodded, his gaze on hers. "It's like you're coming alive under my hands." He reached out and stroked a finger across her hot cheek. "But when you shiver, I don't know if it's because you like it, or because I'm making you afraid."

"Maybe a little of both."

His eyes swept her face. They were filled with concern and burning lust at the same time. "Jillian. Honey. I don't ever want to scare you."

She shook her head, her hair sweeping across her cheek. "It's not you that's scaring me. It's me."

"I'm right here with you. Okay?"

"Yes."

"This is for us. And if it doesn't work, we'll try something else. But I want to do this. And the more I touch you, the more I want this."

"Yes. Me, too. Maybe that's what scares me the most."

Cam leaned in and brushed his lips over hers. Again came that hint of mint and liquor. His hand curled around the back of her head, firm, possessive, as he parted her lips with his hot, wet tongue. Her mouth opened beneath his, letting him in. Her tongue met his, curled and tasted. Her shoulders relaxed as the heat of his mouth flowed through her and came to rest somewhere deep in her belly.

Then he was pushing her down onto the bed, holding her there. She had a quick moment of panic when she realized how firmly he held her, but she was too turned on to let the panic take hold.

Don't think, Jillian.

Again he grasped her wrists and drew her arms over her head, making her feel vulnerable, exposed. Her eyes fluttered open so she could see his face above her. And again she saw that expression of concentrated lust in his gray eyes. He was so focused, so intense. And still his mouth was that lush slash of deep pink that made her want to kiss him.

"Stay right there." His voice was low, a little rough around the edges.

It was hard to hold still all by herself, without him holding her there, while he moved about the room. She tried to concentrate on the music still playing in the background while he knelt beside the bed and wrapped some rope around the bed frame. She could sense what he was doing more than she could see it, but the idea sent a ripple of hot anticipation through her.

Cam moved to the other side of the bed, securing the ropes. If she turned her head a bit, she could see the muscles of his back and shoulders move beneath his golden skin as he worked. He was so beautiful.

He stood, towering over her. When he bent to part her legs with his big hands she tensed. But then he stroked the tender skin on the insides of her thighs, warming her flesh, making her sex fill with a quick rush of lustful heat again, and she opened for him.

He took her right hand in his, stroked her palm open with his fingertips, and leaned in to lay a kiss there, sending a shiver of heat up her arm. Her nipples immediately went hard once more.

Cam moved his mouth over her hand, kissing her fingers, her wrist. It took her a moment to realize that he followed the trail of kisses with a length of soft, darkly colored rope, winding a loop of it around her wrist. Her eyes flew to his face, and a small, reassuring smile played at the corners of his mouth.

"Breathe, Jillian."

Yes. She took in a lungful of the amber-scented air, let it calm her racing pulse. When he pulled the rope so that it had a firm hold, he dropped one last kiss on her hand, then moved to the end of the bed and took hold of her right foot. He massaged it for a moment, stroking with his fingers, then laid a soft kiss on her instep.

She couldn't remember him ever paying much attention to her feet. She couldn't remember ever thinking about it. But somehow that one brief kiss set her body on fire, a trail of flame burning its way up her calf, over her thigh, and straight to her sex, which was hot and needy already. She was soaking wet in an instant.

Cam glanced up, as though he sensed her reaction. He smiled, then kissed her foot once more. Again her sex throbbed with a sudden lance of need. She moaned softly.

"Amazing what we can learn after all this time together." His voice was barely above a whisper.

She couldn't respond. He was already wrapping the rope around her ankle, pulling it tight. Then he moved to her other foot, pulling it to the side, so that her sex was wide open and exposed, except for the scrap of damp lace that still covered it.

He ran his hand up the inside of her leg, brushing the top of her thigh. Her sex clenched in anticipation. But he moved away, back to her foot, stroking the skin of her arch, the undersides of her toes. When he bent his head and began a slow stroking with his lips, she thought she'd go mad with need. Her hips arched up off the bed. He held her ankle more firmly in his hands.

"Hold still, Jillian."

She loved the commanding tone of his voice every bit as much as she loved his mouth on her skin. But in a moment the rope was there again, wrapping firmly around her ankle. She pulled against it once, and found she couldn't move more than a millimeter.

Cam bent over her left side, taking her free hand in his. Once more the blazing trail of kisses, hot on her flesh.

Her whole body was on fire, her sex aching and wet. But when Cam pulled the rope around her wrist, she froze.

"Cam, wait!"

He paused, looked into her face. His was calm, but his eyes sparkled darkly. "Breathe, honey."

She tried, but the air seemed to catch in her throat. Somehow this last rope meant that she would be truly bound, unable to move. Completely under his command. As exciting as it was, it was also frightening on some deep level. She wanted to let go, wanted to trust him, but how could she when she didn't even trust herself?

"Jillian." His tone was low but firm. "I want you to listen very carefully. I am going to bind your wrist and you will not be able to move. You need to give yourself over to me. You need to let it all go. You will be in my hands. *My* hands. I love you, Jillian; you know that. This is your last chance to turn back before we really begin. Tell me yes or no."

She couldn't seem to think. Her body strained against the ropes already binding her feet and her other hand. Was this what she truly wanted? Could she do this?

Her mind was a whirl of chaos edged in panic. She took a deep breath, trying to calm down.

Cam put a hand on her chest, warming her skin. She closed her eyes, let the firm reassurance of his palm absorb the pounding of her heart. Her breasts tingled, her nipples came to peak, and she focused on the scorching heat funneling through her system. Despite her confusion, her body screamed one word at her. And finally she was able to let that word escape her lips.

"Yes!"